Shenandoah Crossings

D1606626

Winds of Change

* * *

Shenandoah Nights
BOOK ONE

Shenandoah Crossings
BOOK TWO

Shenandoah Dreams
BOOK THREE

WINDS OF CHANGE

2

SHENANDOAH CROSSINGS

LISA BELCASTRO

OAKTARA
www.oaktara.com

Shenandoah Crossings

Published in the U.S. by:
OakTara Publishers
www.oaktara.com

Cover design by Yvonne Parks at www.pearcreative.ca
Cover image © Alison Shaw at www.alisonshaw.com
Author photo © 2013 by Heidi Wild Photography

ISBN-13: 978-1-60290-379-1
ISBN-10: 1-60290-379-4

Printed in the U.S.A.

* * *

TO BRANT

You were my best friend, partner, better half, and the man who showed me what love is. Because of you and with you, I experienced a great love. And because of you, I am able to love another. You left us much too soon, yet I know you're smiling that beautiful smile every minute of every day in Heaven, free of pain and disease, filled with laughter, love, and light.

1

"DROP IT, TESS. This isn't the time or the place. By this time tomorrow it will be over."

Tess Roberts glared at her brother as she lifted the cans out of the shopping cart and banged them down onto the conveyor belt. She hated when he stated the obvious. The cashier raised an eyebrow after Tess slammed the third can of organic black beans in front of her. Tess smiled apologetically before placing the last of their groceries on the moving belt to be rung up.

She couldn't stop thinking about the ship. She knew Andy was right, knew it was the logical thing to do, knew it was the safe thing to do, but everything inside her cringed at the idea.

"Don't try to debate this, Tess. The cabin should have been dismantled a month ago. *Shenandoah* is finished for the season, and it's time. Nothing you can say to Dad will change his mind."

"I know, okay." Tess felt the sting of tears and shook them off before Andy or anyone else noticed. "But what if, Andy? What if?"

"Zip it, Tess." Andy cut her off, then glanced at the clerk.

Tess knew she couldn't talk about Rebecca O'Neill outside of their home or office. Still, not a day had passed during the last month when she hadn't wondered if her best friend really had traveled back in time to 1775.

She thought about Rebecca while he paid for the groceries. Her story had been too fantastical. Coming from anyone else, Tess would never have believed a person could spend a hot August night on a boat in the Vineyard Haven harbor and then wake up in 1775 Boston.

But Tess had known Rebecca her whole life. No one was more levelheaded. If Tess had said she'd gone back in time while sleeping in Cabin 8, everyone would have laughed at yet another Tess stunt. Rebecca, however, was calm, decisive, sincere, practical, and so unlike Tess that even her father, the venerable Captain Roberts, had immediately believed her, as had Tess.

When Rebecca had sat with her on the captain's bunk last month and told her about Benjamin Reed and traveling to Colonial Boston, Tess had been captivated and convinced. And, of course, there was the incident with Melissa Smith. No one in town would ever forget when Melissa disappeared off the *Shenandoah* without a trace. The Coast Guard had declared it an accidental drowning, assuming she'd gone night swimming and been caught in the current and pulled under. Now, five years later, the Roberts family finally knew the truth.

Tess glanced sideways at Andy. How he could stand there calmly handing the clerk his credit card while Rebecca might someday need to come home? Didn't he realize he was about to dismantle her only way back? What was wrong with him?

When Rebecca had told them she wanted to return permanently to 1775 to marry Captain Benjamin Reed, no one had stopped her. Tess had been eager to help her. But—a very big *but*—there was a huge difference between helping Rebecca leave and preventing her from ever coming back.

Tess knew that tomorrow her father and brother were going to remodel *Shenandoah's* only cabin that was still completely intact as it was over two hundred years ago. In Cabin 8, all the boards were in the exact same location as when the ship was built. The cabin had carried Rebecca to Ben and Melissa to Isaiah. And if they took it apart, moved one board, what would happen if Rebecca wanted to come back? Needed to come back?

A tap on her shoulder brought Tess back to the present as she turned to find Tom Wilson smiling at her and reaching around her to shake hands with Andy. "How's life, Drew? You folks done for the season?"

"*Shenandoah* is done. We're going to start breaking her down tomorrow. *Katherine* still has three weekends of sunset sails. How's the Decker house coming along?" Andy, or Drew as most Islanders called him, asked after a remodel Tom was doing on Daggett Avenue.

"I've got a few good weeks here. Lots of guys still on the island looking for work now that the summer people have left and the fishing derby hasn't kicked into high gear. We might make some headway before October."

Tom and Andy both laughed. Life on Martha's Vineyard revolved around two things for many of the laborers: summer residents and the Bass and Bluefish Derby, which started in mid-September. Tess liked to fish, had even entered the Derby a few times, but she'd never caught Derby Fever. For many, though, it was the ultimate event of the year.

As their laughter faded, Tom stepped around Tess and elbowed Andy, then pointed past the display case of candy bars and magazines and over at Jim Hensley, a tall, rather overweight man fairly hard to miss. "Have you heard the latest?" Tom asked, winking at Tess. "Let me ask him if the rumors are true."

"So, Jim," Tom called across the register, "what's this I see on your Facebook page? Did you really get married a few weeks ago?"

All eyes turned to Jim and his daughter, Megan. Jim, momentarily caught off guard, mumbled under his breath before replying, "Yup, I did."

If Megan hadn't been standing there, Tess would have made a few comments to Hensley. Everyone in town knew he was faking his marriage. Tess hadn't liked the man years ago when she babysat Megan and her twin brother, Brody, and she liked him even less today.

From some previous comments Tom had made, Tess knew he disliked Hensley even more than she did, so she didn't give him an easy way out. "Well, congratulations, then. So, when do we get to meet her?"

Jim avoided Tom's eyes. "She lives off island, not here very often."

A devilish grin appeared on Tom's face. "When are you moving in with her? Are the kids going to transfer schools? You're going to be a busy man if you're gonna commute every day."

Megan cast her eyes to the floor and shook her head. Tess wanted to walk over and hug the sporty teen she'd once taught to play Crazy Eights. She'd heard the rumors and suspected Jim's fake marriage was some sick revenge on his ex-girlfriend after she'd caught him cheating—a behavior he was well known for. His kids always ended up all too aware of their father's deceptions. Now poor Megan was trapped in another of his contemptible lies.

Jim didn't even seem to notice his daughter's embarrassment. He looked around at the dozen or so people listening to the conversation. "Well, she…"

Megan lifted her head, her face flushed red, and raised her voice. "He's not really married, Mr. Wilson. He's lying. It's just a sham he and Deidre are playing on Facebook."

The checkout area grew uncomfortably quiet. Tess felt certain every man and woman standing there was torn between comforting Megan and cracking up laughing at the fool Jim Hensley had publicly become yet again.

Tom broke the ice. "Okay, then, guess the best wishes can wait for another time." He picked up his black reusable cloth bag. "Good luck in your soccer game next week, Megan."

"Thanks." The five-foot-eight, fourteen-year-old freshman appeared to have shrunk six inches.

Tess wanted to scream. Andy must have read her mind. He shifted all the grocery bags to his left hand, grabbed Tess by the arm, and pulled her toward the exit.

Tess turned back, proud of Megan for speaking up and telling the truth. "Hey, Megan, well done, girl!"

Tess received a weak smile in return.

Andy placed the groceries in the back seat.

Tess slammed her truck door shut. "What was God thinking?"

"Take it easy, Tess. Everyone knows Jim's a liar with wandering body parts. Are you really surprised he would fake a marriage?"

"Yeah, Andy, I am. It's sick and wrong and—and what about his daughter? Did you see her face?"

For a minute, Andy said nothing, but his expression shifted. At thirty, he'd shown little desire to settle down, but he was a family man through and through. "Guy's a jerk. Reason number 6,743 why some people should not have children."

Tess shook her fist, barely containing her desire to smack someone or something. "How many more jerks are there like him walking around? And you wonder why I don't want to date! Creeps—way too many of them! Can you imagine how hollow Megan must feel, telling someone her dad is lying while her father is standing there actually lying to the guy! If he's the example of single men on the island, *Shenandoah*, take me away!"

"And what about Hawk? You've had a crush on him for the last two years. Don't bother denying it."

Tess snapped her head to the right, ignored her know-it-all brother, and stared out the passenger-side window. The coffee shop was closed, and the gym looked empty through the big glass windows. Only a few cars moved at a snail's pace down Main Street, and the yellow and orange mums in front of the bank were in full bloom. She thought about Hawk, his wavy blond hair, his gorgeous blue eyes, the way he smiled when the sails were being raised, and the sound of his laughter as he joked around with the crew or her father. And then she pictured every single moment she'd wished he had talked with her or smiled at her, but all he'd done was look away and ignore her.

Tess kept her eyes on the passing scenery and spoke softly, only the slight tremble in her voice giving away her feigned disinterest. "What about him? He barely gives me the time of day. Only nice guy around for miles and two years later he still can barely speak to me, never mind ask me out. Rebecca had the right idea. Maybe Ben has a friend."

Andy glanced in the rearview mirror, then slammed on the brakes. "Don't even joke about it, Tess. If Dad didn't kill you, I would. The boards are getting changed tomorrow, and that will be the end of any and all time travel from the *Shenandoah*. Got it?"

Tess didn't reply. She simply turned up the radio before slouching in her seat. Arms crossed, heart saddened, Tess closed her eyes. She thought about Rebecca and considered that maybe Captain Benjamin Reed, in his Colonial Boston sailor's suit, was a knight in shining armor. Maybe all the knights lived sometime prior to 1800.

Rebecca had been gone a month. Surely she'd have come home if she was unhappy.

Tess exhaled a long sigh. *She's probably married by now and blissfully happy. She did mention Ben had a younger brother. Wonder if she'd like a visitor?*

2

TESS WALKED AROUND THE YARD, trying to shake off her bad mood before dinner. If she had her mother's disposition, she'd be weeding while she fumed. But she wasn't much like her mother. The great Lady Katherine, as she was known to everyone who loved her, was a strong, beautiful woman with deep faith and more patience than anyone Tess knew. When she'd told her mother what had happened in the grocery store, her mother's quiet answer had been, "God is working on all of us, Tess, and Jim Hensley is no exception."

Tess had hated her response. She'd stormed off, slammed the mudroom door on her way out, and was still, an hour later, fuming in the backyard. She couldn't count the number of times she'd been told to control her temper. At twenty-five, she'd probably heard it twenty-five million times, but at least today she'd put her negative energy to good use.

She had stomped back to the woodpile, lifted the axe overhead, and brought it down dead center on an oak log. Forty-eight logs later, the split was perfect. She swung the axe into the chopping block and began to collect the firewood she'd made during the last sixty minutes while venting her frustrations.

It wasn't that she got angry with people, per se, at least not in the yelling sense. Well, sometimes maybe, but not always. It was just that life was unfair, and many situations were difficult or unjust, and Tess found herself furious on many occasions throughout the day. Where was God in this world? Everything was such a mess. People were cruel, life was harsh, and "a good man was hard to find."

To make everything worse, the annual end-of-the-summer beach bash was next Friday. Andy was going; the only question was with whom. For the third year in a row, Tess didn't have a date. Hawk was still here, but he'd told her flat out that he had other plans, just as he had the previous two years. She could get a date, if that's all she wanted. But she wanted more than a guy looking for a one-night stand. And she was tired of waiting. *Maybe I won't go.*

"Who needs a date with a gorgeous blue-eyed blond with a smile that could melt an iceberg?" Tess looked down at the logs she'd split and grimaced. "You're not going to talk to me, Hawk doesn't talk to me, and I'm standing in the yard talking to myself. God, I need a change!"

Two years ago when she'd first met Hawk at the start of the summer season, Tess had fallen hard. She remembered climbing up *Shenandoah's* ladder and losing herself in deep pools of blue. She'd barely heard him when he'd offered her a hand.

"Need a hand?" he'd asked simply enough.

"Ah, um, no," Tess had stuttered, never shifting her gaze.

He had grinned and her fate was sealed. "Can I help you?"

Tess had wanted to say, "I'm sure you can," but she'd played it straight. "I'm looking for the captain."

"He's below with the cook and galley boy. If you have a delivery, you can leave it with me," Hawk had said, pointing at the bag Tess held in her left hand.

Clutching the sack to her chest with dramatic flair, Tess flirted. "And who might you be? How do I know you won't eat his lunch?"

Hawk had extended his right hand, took her hand in his, smiled that amazing smile yet again, and slyly eyed the brown bag. "I'm sure there's something good in that bag, but hardly worth my job. If you happen to bring lunch again, you could bring one for the captain and another for the first mate. Name's Hawk. And you are?"

"Tess." His hand had felt perfect. Silly, really, to notice how nicely their hands fit together, yet Tess had become aware of the fit the instant their hands connected. And so had Hawk. Tess was sure of it. He had held her hand longer than necessary, longer than it took Tess to straddle over the cap rail, longer than the handshake that followed, and longer than the moment when she'd planted both feet firmly on the deck.

"Do you live on the Island?" Hawk had asked, still holding her hand.

"Born and raised here." She'd been amazed then that the words had come out, that she'd thought of anything intelligent to say when all she could feel and think about was their hands.

"Then I guess you know all the hot spots."

Their fingers touched, through the handshake and into something more. She hadn't wanted to pull back. Even now, in the middle of the backyard, Tess felt her hand in his, the callouses on his palm from years of working the lines, the strength under the surface of his touch. And she had let him know right then and there that she was available.

"There's a party tonight on South Beach if you'd like to go. I can give you a lift if you need a ride." She'd pointed to the shore and her Jeep parked near the Tall Ship office. In a second she'd realized her hand missed the feel of his, and she'd wished she hadn't let go.

He grinned at her. "Can I trust you to drive?"

"Depends on where she's taking you." A deep voice intruded on their flirtation. Two heads turned to find Andy smirking at them. "She's fairly safe on the roads, but she's a terror on the beach. Ask her about the tow truck in May. Isn't that right, Sis?"

Hawk took one large step back and stared wide-eyed at Tess. "You're Andy's sister?"

"Unfortunately."

"Well, thanks for the invite, but I really need to settle in here and get unpacked." Tess felt as though she'd been slapped in the face. The flirting and smiles were gone in an instant, replaced with an empty, cool look. "Andy, I'll see you tomorrow morning."

And without so much as a good-bye, Hawk had practically sprinted toward the bow and left Tess standing there, holding her heart in her hands.

From that day forward, Hawk had treated her as the captain's daughter—completely and totally off limits. *Which is why it's time to give up and get a life.*

Tess picked up four logs and carried them over to the woodpile by the garden shed. Her mother's gardens were legend. The vegetable garden took up about a quarter of an acre on the left side of the yard. Flowers bloomed everywhere three seasons out of the year. She looked at the tall purple asters swaying softly in the breeze. Her mother had planted almost every flower and bulb in the yard. There were borders and beds and a twenty-by-twenty wildflower garden that was Tess's favorite. In the right back corner stood an old beech tree, a tire swing still hanging from its branches, a remembrance of the easy days of childhood.

After a wistful glance at the swing, Tess continued stacking the wood. Lost in thought, trying to think of an excuse for skipping the party, she didn't hear her brother approach.

"Oh, this is rich. You've chopped about a face cord of wood. When are you going to chill out, Tess? Not that I'm complaining, because you just saved me an aching back, but really, Squirt, is Jim Hensley worth an hour swinging the axe? Didn't you chop a cord a few weeks ago too?"

Tess threw a small piece of kindling at him, and Andy jumped to the left. "Ha. You missed. Want to try that again?"

Tess dropped the remaining stick from her left hand. "No. Sorry."

"What is it now? You're really not still mad about Hensley, are you?"

"I'm skipping the party next week. You go without me."

"What? You're not going to the party? Since when are you staying home on a Friday night?"

"I've stayed home plenty of Friday nights. You seem to be confusing my social life with yours. Let's review Island life, shall we: girls outnumber men something like three to one, and what men there are either have a commitment phobia, like my own dear, sweet brother, or they live with their mother, or they have issues too long and numerous to go into."

Andy walked over, slightly sweaty from his hour run, and put his arm around Tess. "What gives? You've never missed a beach party, date or no date. Normally, you have some crazy antic planned. How are you going to top last year's high-dive jump? That was a classic. I still don't know how you convinced Bobby Larsen to fasten that twelve-foot ladder to his boat so you could cannonball into space while the boat was moving. You're lucky Dad didn't find out about that one!"

She almost smiled. "I haven't planned anything for this year. I just don't feel like it. I'm tired of parties."

He squeezed her shoulder. "Is this about Hawk? Did you ask him to go?"

Tess shook off Andy's hand and started walking toward the house. "I asked. He's not going."

Andy hung the axe in the tool shed and jogged up beside her. "Want me to call him? He's heading south soon. One party with my sister couldn't hurt."

Tess dropped her chin to her chest. "No. He doesn't want to be with me. I've got to give it up. Maybe it's time to look for a job off-island. Get off The Rock and widen my horizons. I've been back three years now, and maybe I need to be elsewhere."

"I agree about Hawk, Tess, but could you please not bring up moving at dinner? We've got a lot to discuss about the boats and the end of the season, and Dad will freak if you start that conversation again. Okay?"

Tess merely nodded. She wasn't going to agree because if the opportunity arose, she was going to ask her father to help her find a job somewhere on the Cape, maybe even Boston. Her parents knew enough people that they would find someone with a cool job opportunity for her in a great location, hopefully in retail. She loved chatting up the tourists.

Tess followed Andy into the mudroom, slipped off her muckers, and washed her hands in the garden sink. She could smell the roast chicken even before she stepped into the kitchen. Rosemary, lemon, and garlic infused the room. Her stomach growled, and her mouth watered.

She walked to the breakfast table as her mom was pulling the bird out of the oven. "Need some help, Mom?"

Katherine turned and smiled at her daughter. "No, thank you, honey.

Looks like you're feeling better. Why don't you go on into the dining room and talk with your dad? I'll be in with dinner in five minutes."

Tess reached into the blue ceramic bowl under the heat lamps on the stove and pinched two Yukon Gold potatoes.

"Out with you now." Katherine smiled again and motioned with her hands for Tess to head down the hall.

Her mom's smiles always filled Tess with warmth. Whatever she did wrong, which seemed to be a lot lately, she knew her mom loved her. She actually liked living at home. Her parents encouraged her—in fact, her and all of her siblings—to stay as long as they wanted, but they had also offered to help whenever they were ready to leave. She knew they both wanted her, their only daughter and youngest to boot, to stay. So did she want to move, or was it just another crazy idea? She didn't know, but something had to change—and soon.

Andy and their father were already in the midst of conversation when Tess strolled in.

"What time are we starting tomorrow?" Andy asked.

"I told Hawk we'd row out at ten." Captain Roberts paused and waved Tess to the chair on his right. "Hello, beautiful. How was your day?"

Andy gave Tess a look that she knew meant *shut up and don't say a word about Rebecca or your idea that we shouldn't change the cabin.*

"The day was good," Tess replied. "We had a few early weekenders window-shopping. Nice couple from New Hampshire stayed and gabbed for a bit."

"Are you working tomorrow, or will you be helping us on the *Shenandoah?*"

Tess winced. Andy held her gaze. "I took the day off. I want to help you. But can I—"

Andy spoke over her. "Did the lumber arrive today? The truck hadn't been by before I left."

"Hawk called about forty-five minutes ago. Big Mike dropped the shipment."

Tess reached a hand over toward Captain Roberts. "Dad, can I say something?"

"No," Andy snapped.

Their dad looked from one to the other. "Okay, you two. What's going on?"

"Dad, I don't think we should change the boards. What if Rebecca ever needs to come home? What if she gets sick and needs medicine or surgery or

10

chemo or—"

Her father's hand covered hers. "Tess, love, I understand you're worried about Rebecca. We must believe she is safe, that her journey to 1775 was successful, and that she is happily married to Captain Reed."

"I do believe that, Dad. But I want her to have a way to come home, just in case. And what about Melissa?"

Captain Roberts patted Tess's hand affectionately. "I know Rebecca was—is—your friend. She chose to leave, honey, as did Melissa. Whatever force allowed them to travel back in time through Cabin 8, Rebecca and Melissa elected to remain in Colonial Boston with men they love. Whatever illnesses or misfortunes come into their lives, we must trust that the good Lord is watching over them and will care for them.

"It is understandable that you're worried about Rebecca. As captain, I must worry about everyone who sails on *Shenandoah*. I cannot, in good conscience, invite parents to send their children sailing, knowing full well that one or more of them could go missing. Imagine how devastating that would be to a family. The risk is too great. We must have faith that God is watching over Rebecca and Melissa."

Tess drew her hand back. "Dad, God may have allowed them to travel, or maybe He didn't and it's just the cabin. I know you think God is all-powerful, but if you look around this world, even just this island, there's a lot of stuff God is leaving undone. So I find it pretty darn hard to believe He planned for Rebecca and Melissa to leave. Sorry, I know that ruins your whole theory. But I haven't seen a lot of God lately."

Andy and her dad sighed simultaneously. The black sheep had spoken again. "Tess, did something happen today?"

Her brother answered for her. "Yeah, Jim Hensley announced his fake marriage to everyone in the grocery store in front of his daughter, and Tess pitched a fit."

Captain Roberts nodded slowly. Tess could see the disgust on his face. "Hensley is not a good man, Tess. You know that. I'm sorry if his actions in front of Megan upset you. I have no respect for cheaters and liars, and he is, without a doubt, one of the worst on the Island. How is Megan holding up?"

"You should've seen her, Dad. Her face crumbled as that slime stood there lying to Tom Wilson. She finally told us all that her father was a liar and the marriage was a sham. I wanted to strangle him. What's wrong with men these days?!"

The warmth of her father's big, weathered hand calmed Tess at the same time the feeling made her long for a hand she could hold. A hand that fit hers, a hand she could squeeze as she walked the beach or a hand she could place hers in as she sat in the movies. Tears welled in her eyes.

"What is it, Tess? Those tears are not for Jim or Megan."

Tess wiped her eyes. "It's nothing, Dad. I'm just worried about Rebecca."

Andy broke into the conversation, clearly picking a touchy subject to get Tess away from the construction that was going to take place in the morning. "As if, Tess. Get real. The end-of-the-summer beach party is next Friday, you don't have a date, you found out today that Hawk isn't going, and you've been in a bad mood all day."

Tess snapped her head up, snatched her hand from her father, and glared at Andy. "You don't know what you're talking about. This has nothing to do with Hawk!" Tess pushed her chair back from the table and stormed out of the room.

As she turned the corner, her mom came out of the kitchen. "Tess, where are you going? Dinner's ready."

"I'm not hungry!" Tess hollered over her shoulder as she took the stairs two at time.

3

TESS SLAMMED HER BEDROOM DOOR. She marched across the room to her window and gazed out at the gardens below and the pile of wood she'd chopped. A gentle breeze whispered in through the opening and carried with it the scents of the evening tide and her mother's flowers. The combination was soothing. Tess exhaled the pent-up breath she'd been holding. "What's wrong with me?" she asked for the tenth time in as many days.

She'd been antsy lately, for weeks, if she was honest with herself. To be totally accurate, Tess had been in a funk since Rebecca left. She'd spent countless hours wondering why Rebecca had been the one to discover Cabin 8 was a portal to another time. Why had Rebecca traveled to 1775 and met the love of her life? Why hadn't Tess been the one to zip across time? She, not Rebecca, was the one who loved adventure. She was the one who needed a change. She was the one who should have gone. Not Rebecca. Another sign that God was on vacation, and He wasn't on Martha's Vineyard.

Tess and Rebecca had been friends since grade school. They had both attended Holmes Hole Elementary, although Rebecca was a year older than Tess and a grade ahead. They had always offset one another, even as children. Rebecca was calm and smart and an avid reader. Tess was wild, couldn't sit still in school to study or read a book, and was always eager to be outside. They had both loved sports, though Tess loved competition and had always wanted to play on a team, while Rebecca thrived as a runner and had been known to play a mean game of tennis. Somehow, though, the two had bonded as children on the beach, and the bond had held strong through every phase of their lives. Well, until last month.

Shoulders drooping, chin to her chest, Tess stepped away from the window and swiveled toward the collage on the left wall. Dozens of photos from years of fun were cropped and placed on a sailcloth-covered board that took up half the wall. Rebecca finishing the Boston Marathon. Tess jumping off *Shenandoah's* rigging at the fore yard into the cool summer waters.

With a sigh, she traced a finger over a picture of Rebecca and herself laughing at a party on South Beach three summers ago. Her chest tightened. "I wish you had taken me with you. Are you happy? Are you married? Is life good there? It's not so great here."

Tess dropped her hand and choked back tears. Rebecca was the lucky one. She studied her friend's face, all smiles and laughter. With the exception of Tess's straight brown hair to Rebecca's head of curls, their five-foot, four-inch athletic frames looked identical, which had worked in their favor the morning Tess pretended to be Rebecca so no one would know Rebecca had actually disappeared off the *Shenandoah* in the middle of the night.

Tess could still recall every word Rebecca had told her in their short time together. "You won't believe it, Tess. I couldn't believe it at first. Then it happened again and again. Every night I've been onboard sleeping in Cabin 8, I've traveled back in time to 1775. At first it was terrifying, and then I met Ben."

The mention of Ben's name had changed every feature on Rebecca's face. Her eyes had lit up, her smile widened, her skin glowed. Tess knew before Rebecca had spoken the words that her dear friend had fallen in love—true love, like her parents had, the kind that lasted and weathered all the storms of life and still felt passion.

"Oh, Tess, he's...he's...he's everything we talked about and then some. He's strong and smart and sexy and sweet and stubborn and bossy, and his fingers make me feel like I'm on fire. I can't imagine life without him. Say you'll help me go back. Please. It's not crazy, trust me. He's everything. I want to spend my life with him, every day, wherever he is."

Tess wouldn't have said no, even if she could have. She didn't doubt for a second that Rebecca's story was true or that she was in love with Captain Benjamin Reed. Tess hadn't felt jealous at the time, not one bit—or had she? She was happy for Rebecca, even as she worried for her father and the family business.

Captain Roberts had called home as soon as Rebecca had told him her tale. History was repeating itself in a way the Roberts family could not afford. When Tess had walked into the kitchen last month, her mother had looked incredibly worried. They'd sat at the breakfast table, and her mom had shared the news.

"There is no easy way to say this. The rumors Pete Nichols spread about Melissa five years ago are true. Rebecca just told your dad that she's been traveling back in time to 1775 every night and has fallen in love and wants to return tonight—forever."

"No way, Mom!" A flurry of thoughts raced through Tess's mind. Becca had time traveled. Becca had fallen in love. Becca was going to leave her. "Pete was right? I can't believe this!"

Her mom had squeezed her hand across the table. "Appears so, honey.

Rebecca said she has seen Melissa, and she's happily married to Isaiah Reed."

"The man who built the *Shenandoah?*"

"One and the same."

"What's Dad gonna do?"

"He wants you and Andy to get to the boat as soon as possible. He's drafting a plan."

Tess had stood, slightly shaken, yet aware that her dad needed help quickly. "I'll call Andy as I drive over. He's probably in town anyway."

Tess had pulled her hair back in a ponytail as she raced to her Jeep. Her dad couldn't undergo another Coast Guard investigation. Surely Rebecca knew that. Five years earlier, Melissa Smith, another teacher from Holmes Hole Elementary, had vanished off the *Shenandoah*. Most folks believed she had gone swimming in the middle of night and drowned.

The galley boy, Pete Nichols, had told whoever would listen that Melissa had traveled through time to Colonial Boston. Few people, if any, gave Pete any notice, including Tess's father. Nevertheless, the Coast Guard had shut down the Roberts' tall-ship operations for the rest of the year.

"And we can't afford that again," Tess said as she turned off the engine.

Andy pulled in beside her. "Can you believe it?" He'd called from the truck cab. "Sorry I didn't pick up your call. I was on the phone with Dad."

"This can't be happening again. Why Rebecca? And what is she thinking? She knows how much the last incident hurt Dad." Tess popped out of the Jeep, slipped the keys under the seat, and walked over to Andy.

"What do you think?" With her eyes, she begged her brother for a positive answer.

"Dad didn't sound too bad. Maybe there's a way out of this. Let's go."

Andy rowed and Tess fretted, taking her hair out of the ponytail and putting it back in six times before they reached the *Shenandoah*.

Later that night, they had put their father's plan into action. Rebecca O'Neill had gone to bed like everyone else onboard. Andy had rowed out with their dad's favorite bagels and donuts. Tess had been in the rowboat, hidden under a tarp. She climbed the chains and sneaked into her dad's cabin while Andy chatted with the crew and distracted their attention.

Come morning, Rebecca was gone. Tess had dressed in her friend's clothes and departed in the early morning light, pretending to be Rebecca heading off hastily to catch a flight out of Boston for a mission trip to a remote village in Africa. It didn't hurt that Hawk had caught a glimpse of "Rebecca" as Andy motored behind another boat and toward the dock.

Only the Roberts family knew that Rebecca had discovered Melissa was alive and well and living in Colonial Boston with her husband. Now Rebecca was gone, on a romantic journey too fantastic to imagine, and Tess was jealous after all—maybe she had been since the beginning. She wanted adventure. She wanted to travel. She wanted true love.

But staring at old pictures wouldn't alter the present. Tess straightened up and walked over to her closet. She changed out of her shorts and pulled on a pair of jeans and grabbed a sweatshirt. She glanced back at the images of Rebecca. "If you can do it, why can't I?"

She went down the stairs and turned right into the dining room. Andy was telling her parents something about the Bartlett twins. He looked up. "Hey, stranger, you hungry yet?"

Both her parents smiled at her. Tess felt a lump form in her throat. Could she really leave them? What if she got stuck there? What if going for a visit turned into a permanent stay? She would miss them all, especially her mom.

"Honey, are you okay?"

Her mom's voice exasperated her doubts. Tess feigned a cheery disposition. "Fine, Mom, just thinking. I'm going for a walk on the beach. Don't wait up for me."

Andy stood. "Want some company?"

A moment of panic surged through Tess before she plastered on a smile. "Don't you have a date or some young island nymph to cavort with?"

Andy winked. "Now that you mention it, I did tell Allyson Flanders that I might drive through Oak Bluffs tonight and see what was going on. Why don't you come with me?"

Tess pretended to shudder at the thought of tagging along with her brother as he hit the night scene in Oak Bluffs. "Are you kidding? A third wheel with my brother trying to pick up girls? No thanks, bro. You go knock yourself out, not that you are going to get anywhere with Allyson. She is most definitely not your type."

"What's wrong with Allyson? She's a fun girl." Andy pretended to look miffed.

Tess rolled her eyes and leaned against the doorframe. "There is nothing wrong with Allyson. She is, in fact, a rather nice person. I like her. She works hard, dates selectively, and teaches Sunday school, all of which do not qualify her as one of your typical dates."

"Geez, Tess, give a guy a break. I didn't say I was going to date her, just that I might swing through town."

"Exactly! Allyson is not the swing-through-town type!"

Her father laughed his rich, deep laugh, and Tess felt another pain of remorse sneaking into her thoughts. She had to get out of the house now before she chickened out. She walked over to the table, picked up a multi-grain roll, sliced it in half, and loaded it up with chicken.

"You make the best roast chicken, Mom. I'll take this with me." Tess walked toward the door, stopping halfway across the hall. "Sorry about earlier. I love you all."

"We love you, too, honey. Enjoy your walk."

Her father stood and picked up his plate. "Don't forget to be at the dock in the morning if you want to help with Cabin 8. Might want to think about coming home early and getting some rest. Both of you."

"Sure thing, Dad." Tess cast her eyes to the floor and moved toward the front door.

Once outside, she practically ran to her Jeep. She drove the few miles into town munching on her sandwich and trying to remember every detail Rebecca had told her.

"It's the cabin, Tess. Pete was right. Somehow Cabin 8 is a time machine."

"I had to be in Cabin 8 when I went to bed."

"I slept in the top bunk."

"The only time I traveled was when I was asleep."

"The night I took Starr to the hospital, I didn't go back to Ben."

"When I woke up in the mornings, it was as if no time had passed at all. No one even noticed I was gone."

Rebecca's comments were easy enough to follow. Tess knew she'd have to leave her dad and Andy a note, just in case time didn't stand still and she didn't make it back before morning. If they changed one board in that cabin tomorrow, she might never come home.

By the time Tess pulled into her parking space at the dock, her heart was pounding. She walked down the long wooden pier until she reached the small rowboat her family left tied to the dock. They had a few motorboats to transport students and visitors to their ships, but she knew better than to take one of the motors out and leave it tied to the *Shenandoah* when Andy and her dad would need it come morning.

She climbed down the ladder and into the small skiff. The evening air was still warm, though fall's chill was moving in, and cold nights would soon be the norm. As she rowed out to the *Shenandoah*, each stroke of the oar bringing her closer to a decision she wasn't all that certain about anymore.

Tess glanced back at the shore and saw the warm glow of lighted homes filled with Island families and a few remaining summer visitors. She turned back toward the *Shenandoah*, hoping she'd find the answers to her life in

Cabin 8, or beyond.

A big cloud drifted in front of the moon, casting an eerie glow on the *Shenandoah*. Tess tried not to laugh. The setting was becoming far too perfect for one of those two-bit, B-rated horror movies. Tess could just picture a giant sea serpent slithering under the water while the audience held their breath, waiting for her to be eaten. She shook her head and stroked on the oars a little harder until she pulled up alongside the *Shenandoah*.

Once she reached the bow, she called out just to make sure no one was aboard. There was no reply. The cloud inched across the sky, allowing rays of moonlight to filter through. Tess tied off the skiff to the mooring-ball before heaving herself out of the boat and onto the chain. She shimmied up as she'd done a hundred times over the years. Only this time her climb wasn't a game. She wasn't racing Andy or Todd or Jack, and there would be no diving after the climb. Tonight she was ascending toward a new adventure.

Her fingers grasped the iron, and taut muscles reached hand over hand as Tess climbed. Her sneaker slipped halfway up. Her legs gave out, and her arms jerked to save her. Pain ripped through her biceps. She found her footing again and pulled up hard. By the time she reached the cap rail, Tess was wound tight as a string.

She threw her left leg over the side and dropped down onto the deck. In case anyone was onboard, she stomped over toward the crew's quarters. "Hello, anybody down there?" Tess called into the hatch. "Hello? Hawk? Dave? Anybody?"

Silence. Tess exhaled and relaxed her shoulders. Ever so cautious, she walked over to the doghouses, the two small, private quarters barely big enough for a cot and table, yet coveted on a ship. She knocked loudly on the doors. When no one responded, Tess slid each panel open. Empty.

I'm alone!

The thought of being the only person on the boat filled her with relief and apprehension. It was now or never. She tilted her head back and focused on the moon. Clouds danced in front of the golden globe, and eerie shadows and streaks of moonbeams shot out in all directions—a fitting night to vanish into thin air. And she still had a few things to do before she could leave.

She walked down past the galley, pausing at the helm to look at the compass. Could she chart a course where she wanted to go? Was there a compass made that could guide her there and back? No, yet she wished someone could steer her on a course to a fuller life. At twenty-five, she felt lost at sea without a rudder. She was on her own and had a message to write. She went below into her father's cabin to find some paper and a pen.

18

Tess turned on the battery-powered lamp and sat at his walnut desk. She ran her hands over the chips until she found the gash she herself had chiseled fifteen years ago. She had intended to carve her name in his desk so he wouldn't forget her throughout the summer sails. Her father had walked in on her, at first angry and then wrapping her slight, ten-year-old frame into his big, burly arms and assuring her that he would never forget his little girl. Now she was the one leaving, and she didn't know if she'd ever make it back. She fingered the gash and felt a pang of guilt. With a heavy heart, she wrote her note.

Hi, Dad (and Mom and Andy),
Please don't be angry. I decided to go visit Rebecca. I'll be home soon, I promise. I had to get away for a little while. Don't change a thing, and I'll be back. Sorry.
Love you.
Your screw-up daughter, Tess

A tear rolled down her cheek. She wiped it dry and headed back up on deck. She strolled down to the tool chest and dug around until she found a flashlight, a hammer, and a small nail. Supplies in hand, she descended the companionway and walked slowly toward Cabin 8.

Few things were as peaceful as sleeping on *Shenandoah,* either alone or with her family. Tess had always loved and appreciated the many nights spent dreaming under the stars on the big boat. Everything about tonight felt different, though. Even the air felt heavy. If things went according to plan, nothing about this night on the boat would be the same. If her idea became reality, she wouldn't wake up and go home tomorrow.

Tess shivered as she clenched the flashlight, her nerves starting to unravel. She'd done many a foolish dare in her life, but nothing like what she was about to do. What if she didn't come back? What if she didn't find Rebecca? What if she ended up aboard *Shenandoah* during the Civil War?

Too many what-ifs to consider. Time to go.

The cabin door was open, as were all the others. Tess balanced the flashlight on the floor, shining upward, and then tacked the note to the door where her father and Andy would see it. She picked up the flashlight and shined it over the walls.

The room looked no different than any other bunk on the ship. Tess noticed the beds had been stripped after the last trip. She walked back down to the linen closet and found a sheet, blanket, and pillow. She hugged the pillow tightly as she entered the cabin. She shook out the sheet and laid it over the mattress, then placed the blanket on top. She held the flashlight in her left hand as she climbed up into the top bunk, where Rebecca had slept.

The light on the wall jumped around as her hand shook. She stretched out on her back, propped the pillow under her neck just so, and waited for something to happen. She ran her hands over the boards, feeling them as though for the first time, searching for a peephole or a magic button or anything to explain how Rebecca and Melissa were transported back in time.

Her fingers found nothing. She closed her eyes and waited—for what, she didn't know. The minutes seemed to tick by as though a drum was beating slow and steady in the distance. Ironically, with no one onboard to ring the hourly chime, even the ship's bell was mute. Tess willed herself to remain still and wait.

She squeezed her eyes shut and began counting to herself. After a while, she lost track of time and her count. The silence of the empty ship, the dark, late-summer night, and the wash of waves against the boat finally lulled Tess to sleep.

4

TESS FELT THE SHIP SWAY. She squinted through barely open slits, saw it was still reasonably dark, tugged the blanket back up over her shoulders, and tried to go back to sleep. She loved sleeping on a boat. Nothing, absolutely nothing, felt as good as rocking to sleep on the water as the waves lapped the sides of the ship and sea salts scented the air.

If she had her preferences, she'd sleep under the stars in a hammock tied between the masts. She'd been able to sneak that option in only a couple of times when she was on the boat alone in the off-season. Hammocks and sleeping bags weren't allowed on the *Shenandoah* because the kids were never permitted to sleep on deck.

If she had her way, she'd live on a boat. Maybe that was her problem. She wasn't meant to live on land, even an island. She liked it well enough—her mom's gardens, family dinners, hiking trails, days at the beach kicking it up, concerts in the parks, baking brownies in her mom's kitchen, double scoops of homemade ice cream whenever she wanted, which was pretty much daily. All that was well and good, but nothing compared to being at sea.

How many times had she asked her dad if she could captain one of the boats during the summer season? Dozens? Hundreds? Oh, she had her own twenty-six-foot, gaff-rigged English pilot cutter she'd named the *Consolation Prize*, but she wanted to Captain either the *Shenandoah* or the *Lady Katherine*. "Not enough experience" was always his answer. Well, how was she supposed to gain experience if he never even let her work as crew? Cursed again because she was a girl.

No one needed to point out to her that Jack, Todd, and Andy had worked on both boats since they were old enough to walk. Now Jack, the eldest and ten years her senior, captained the *Lady Katherine*, her dad had *Shenandoah*, and she was still working in the gift shop. Seriously, she was twenty-five years old. When would she get to live the life she wanted?

Tess kicked her feet under the blanket and mumbled under her breath. All through high school, she had asked and hoped to crew on one of their ships. The past two summers she had begged her father to let her work on the *Shenandoah*. She knew the boat better than anyone outside her family, even Hawk. She'd tried to reason with her dad that nothing could possibly go wrong as he would be onboard too. He went through his standard list of reasons: one woman, ten men, trouble in the making; she might intimidate the crew and set off a morale issue; no private bunk for her to sleep in.

The problems seemed petty to Tess. Seriously, who cared that she could work as hard, or harder, than any guy on board? She could tone it down until they knew the ropes and were confident in their skills. She could refrain from trying to teach them how to do it better and quicker. And she certainly wasn't looking to get into a relationship with anyone her dad ever hired on as crew. They were always nice guys, of course, but not her type. The only one she cared a fig about was Hawk, and he could barely manage to say hello to her, never mind carry on a conversation. No problem there.

So, that left the sleeping arrangements. Tess had suggested she could stay in her dad's cabin with him. He had laughed at her, literally laughed. He asked her, a chuckle still in his throat, if she really thought they would do well sharing a small room for ten weeks. Tess grudgingly had agreed it wasn't her best idea.

Then she offered the doghouses, two tiny, hut-like cabins on deck given to the first mate and cook. Surely the cook or Hawk, who was the first mate, would forfeit his doghouse and sleep with the crew.

The doghouse suggestion was probably her worst mistake in pursuit of a life on the *Shenandoah*. Her father, the indomitable Captain Roberts, put his foot down. He rarely lost his temper, and though he hadn't screamed at Tess, she knew beneath his rigid exterior he *was* yelling. "There is an honor to having a doghouse. You earn the privilege, Tess. I will not steal that right from one of my crew so my daughter can bunk with the boys. I will never, do you hear me, never be accused of nepotism. Your brothers earned their ways on the boats. I am sorry. I love you dearly, but you will not sleep in a doghouse on my boat without earning the privilege."

"Well, then, I'll work as the cook," Tess had hurled back at him.

His stern expression had given way to amusement. "I think we would all tire of cold cereal and brownies three times a day, as good as your brownies are."

"I can cook, Dad! Ask Mom. Just give me a chance. One week, one kids' cruise, and if I fail, then you can hire someone else. Please?"

He didn't scoff at her idea, just told her patiently but firmly that a crew worked best that trained together and started together from day one. He would not risk the cohesiveness of his team on Tess's questionable cooking skills. Tess hadn't bothered to suggest he hire her as first mate. She knew that job was taken.

As memories of that May afternoon ran through her mind, Tess found her anger returning. And as her blood pressure rose, she remembered where she was and, more importantly, why she had slept on the *Shenandoah*. She didn't even bother to open her eyes and glance around the room. She knew she hadn't traveled back in time. "Obviously, I won't see Rebecca today. She gets the dream and I get reality."

Tess felt the ship sway. *Shenandoah* was rocking pretty hard. She hadn't remembered any storms being forecast in yesterday's news, though a biggie must be sweeping in through the harbor, judging by the movement of the ship.

She was about to pull the covers over her head and have herself a good sulk when she heard footsteps on deck. "Great. Dad and Andy have arrived, and I'm about to be nailed once again."

The note! Tess felt her panic rise. By now they would've seen the skiff and surmised that she was onboard. She heard voices and knew they were getting closer. She had to get out of this cabin and get her letter off the door before either of them saw the evidence of her intentions.

She threw back the blanket and swung her legs over the edge of the bunk. Smack! Her feet hit the floor. "What?"

Tess looked down. Her feet were on the floor. Impossible! And she was in a cot. Impossible! Unless—

Tingles started in her toes, moved quickly up her legs, arched across her back, and rolled down her arms. Had she? Was she? Did she?

She stood cautiously, just in case the floor wasn't real or she was dreaming or sleepwalking. *Shenandoah* rose and fell. Tess stumbled backward and landed on the cot. She sat momentarily stunned. She knew that feeling, knew it well. *Shenandoah* wasn't in the harbor, she was at sea!

And that could mean only one thing. . . .

5

ANDY SHOOK HIS HEAD and chuckled as he stared into Tess's empty room. She was either up early, or she hadn't come home last night. He'd gotten in around 2 a.m. Her door had been closed, and he wasn't about to wake her then and tell her that Allyson Flanders just might be his type after all.

Last night had been fun, surprisingly so. He'd stopped into the Coop, planning to have one beer and chat with a few of the guys. Allyson had been there with Tricia and Phoebe, both of whom he'd gone out with—not dated, just gone out with. Big difference in Andy's book. Dating was serious, one on one, and he'd managed to avoid it since college. With two brothers married, he was in no rush to settle down and provide grandchildren. Going out was fun, casual, and easy.

Surprisingly, Allyson had been better than fun. He'd walked over to say hello, and Allyson had grinned at Tricia and Phoebe and then turned her smile coyly on him. "Am I next in line?"

Andy had cringed. He had a reputation for being a ladies' man, but any girl who'd gone out with him knew he wasn't a swinger.

"Relax, Drew. I'm just teasing," Allyson had said while sliding over in their booth so he could sit down next to her. The rest of the night had gone by so fast he hadn't realized how late it was until Johnny was hustling them out the door. Andy had almost asked Allyson to go for a walk on the beach. He'd come so close to spitting out the words.

Her long legs and pretty blonde hair had caught his attention weeks ago at the beach party on Squibby. Tess had noticed him casting glances in Allyson's direction throughout the night. With a taunting nudge, his little sister had dared him to talk with her. Something about Allyson, though, kept him at bay. He'd left Squibnocket with images of her blonde hair lifting in the breeze and her legs dancing in the sand around the bonfire.

Last night, though, it had been her smile and sense of humor that kept him at her table until closing. If he hadn't been so dumbfounded when they stood to leave, he might have been able to form the words and ask her out on a date. He'd stood there wondering exactly where all the hours had gone and what specifically they had talked about that had been so fascinating he hadn't realized it was time to go home. Tess would get a kick out of that! Hmmm, maybe he wouldn't say anything yet. Maybe he'd ask Allyson out first and see if last night wasn't a fluke.

Moving down the hall, he smelled his mom's French toast, a heavenly mixture of cinnamon and vanilla. He could almost taste the warm, delicious pieces as he descended the stairs two at a time.

"Morning, Mom. Smells great." Andy gave his mom a quick kiss on her left cheek and waited eagerly for her to pass him a plate piled with nirvana.

"Good morning, dear. Did you see Tess this morning?" She handed him a plate with four thick pieces. "Maple syrup is on the table."

"Nope." Andy poured a circle of syrup around his toast, being careful not to pour any on top of it. He knew the syrup was real and would be warmed, his Mom's special touch, but he preferred the taste of the cinnamon over maple.

Tess, on the other hand, drowned the toast in syrup. He never understood why she even bothered putting any bread on the plate. She should simply sit down with a bowl of syrup and a spoon for all she could taste the French toast.

The back door opened, and his mom walked toward the mud room. She said good morning to his dad and kissed him.

And that was the reason Andy had never gotten serious with anyone. He wanted a woman like his mom—someone who would put down whatever she was doing, walk over, and kiss him hello. Nobody he knew fit that bill.

Well, Allyson seemed like that kind....

His hand jerked to a halt midway to his mouth. *Now where in blue blazes did that thought come from?*

His father slapped him on the back. "Morning, Andy. Something wrong with your breakfast?"

"Huh?"

His father grinned. "Appears to me you're staring at your food when you ought to be eating it."

Andy put the fork down. "Lost in thought."

"Must have been some thought if you put down your mother's cooking."

Heat coursed through Andy, and he went from mildly uncomfortable to somewhat lightheaded. What had happened last night? He'd only talked to Allyson. What had she said that even had him thinking about her kissing him hello?

His father sat across from him at the kitchen table. "Where's your sister? I want to get an earlier start. I regret telling Hawk to meet us at ten."

Andy pushed all thoughts of Allyson to the far recesses of his mind. "I

25

don't know. I think she's already left. Probably at the boat, hoping to talk with Hawk."

He watched a shadow cross his father's eyes. Andy had seen that worried look many times over the years. "Do you think she's serious about Hawk? I know you've teased her a great deal, but is it real for Tess?"

Real? What a question. "I don't know, Dad. Tess doesn't seem to like anybody else, but she's barely spent any time alone with Hawk. I know for certain they've never gone out. Hawk has stayed as far away from Tess as possible."

Andy watched his father nod slowly, approval and respect on his face. His dad liked Hawk, worked well with him. And Hawk loved working on the *Shenandoah*. They'd made a good team the last three seasons. Neither his father nor Hawk would rock that boat.

His mom brought them each two more pieces and paused after giving Andy his. "Why won't he date Tess? Has Hawk said anything to you?"

"Mom, it's got nothing to do with Tess. There's just no way Hawk is dating the captain's daughter. He likes his job. If he had his way, he'd convince Dad to let him sail the *Shenandoah* year round. He's not about to mess up any chances he might have by going out with Tess."

His mother clucked her tongue. "That's absurd. Your father would never fire him for dating Tess, right, dear?"

Captain Roberts smiled at his wife, yet Andy could see the expression in his eyes did not match his smile. "My love, Hawk is right. It would be difficult at best for him to date Tess if the relationship worked. If it failed, and there were hurt feelings or an embarrassing situation, I would be caught between honoring Tess and respecting my first mate. As much as I want Tess to find someone to love, I don't believe she should set her sights on Hawk."

Andy almost laughed out loud as his mom's face scrunched up in exasperation.

Raising the empty spatula, she waved the utensil at his father, and spoke the words Andy had heard many times in the course of far too many conversations on dating and marriage. "As if love can be set? Are you forgetting how my parents forbid me to go out with you? I believe they told me you would never amount to anything, and I deserved better. Have you forgotten?"

"I have not forgotten, Katherine, nor do I believe you shall ever let me. We proved them all wrong. Tess, though, is a different story. I like Hawk. In another situation I'd say he was perfect for Tess."

His mother returned to the table, carrying her own plate. She kissed his father on the top of his head before sitting down. "There, now, you've said it yourself. He's perfect for her."

"Don't go twisting my words, Katherine. I said no such thing."

"Oh, yes you did," she replied, winking at him before she took a bite of her breakfast.

Andy loved these interactions between his parents. The warmth and affection radiated from both of them: his strong, yet very soft and womanly mother and his gruff, hardworking, fair, and loving father. They were each other's perfect mate, a balancing half to the other.

Just as Allyson had fit him last night. *Oh, gosh, not again with the Allyson thoughts!*

As his parents continued bantering about Tess and Hawk, Andy drifted into his own world, shoving thoughts of Allyson back as they tried to creep forward. He had no idea how much time had passed when his mother reached for his plate to clear the table and his father announced they were leaving in five.

*

They reached the dock at nine. Hawk was waiting for them, pacing.

"What's wrong, Hawk?" his father asked.

"The little skiff is gone, Captain."

His father grinned. "I believe Tess has already made her way out. She left home before breakfast and her Jeep's here."

Andy suddenly had a sinking feeling. What had Tess said yesterday about wishing she could visit Rebecca? Did his parents know where Tess was last night? Did she really leave before breakfast? Or had she...? He couldn't finish the last thought.

"Dad, let's go find Tess and come back for the lumber."

Whether his father heard the urgency in his voice or not, Andy couldn't tell and didn't care. He had to make sure Tess was on the *Shenandoah*, their *Shenandoah*. The three of them climbed down into the motorboat. Andy took the wheel and started the engine.

Hawk cocked his head when Andy gunned the throttle, and the boat lurched forward. Andy saw Hawk's amused expression and knew the first mate probably figured he had partied too much last night. "Tough night, Andy?"

Andy ignored him, trying to remember what Rebecca had told them about her time traveling. Did she have to sleep in the cabin at a certain time of night? Was it a certain bunk in the room or just a bed in Cabin 8? He couldn't remember. The minutes to the ship seemed to take hours.

Finally he came alongside *Shenandoah*. Hawk spotted the dingy first, and they tied off. Hawk hoisted Andy up the side. He called out for Tess as he positioned the ladder and hooked it into place for his father and Hawk. "Tess! Where are you?"

Any fool could see she wasn't on deck. His father's brow furrowed. Andy saw the worry and frowned.

"I'm going down to my cabin to see if, by any chance, she slept in my bed," his father said.

"I'll check the girls' cabins, and Hawk can check the boys' end," Andy added.

His heart was racing. He remembered Tess's rash comments about Rebecca in the truck yesterday. Would she do it? He'd kill her! Their mother would freak. He took two steps down the companionway and jumped to the floor. He all but sprinted to Cabin 8, knowing if Tess was anywhere on board, that was the first place to look.

He saw the note before he could read it. Lunging for the paper, he tore it off the door. He knew, even before he opened the cabin door, that Tess wouldn't be there. Thumbing the latch, he threw the door open.

"No!" he screamed.

6

ANDY STORMED INTO THE CABIN. The top bunk had a pillow and linens on it, and he could see the indentation from Tess's head. He placed his hand where his sister had been only a short time ago. The pillow was cold—not a trace of human warmth. The sinking feeling in his stomach dropped through the hull of the ship, down to the ocean floor. Tess had been there, not that morning, but last night.

A deathly quiet settled in the room. His sister was gone. He knew to the very marrow of his bones she had disappeared, though to where he hadn't a clue. He inched his way along the bed.

A faint yellow circle glowed on the starboard wall. He reached across the top bunk and grabbed the flashlight, probably the last thing Tess had touched. Andy fingered the on/off button. If he turned it off, would Tess know? Could she see the light? How long ago had she left?

And where had she gone? Was she with Rebecca or lost in time? Could she find her way home? Would she come home?

"Andy?"

His father's gravelly voice jerked him back to reality. Andy turned and met his dad's eyes. Andy held out the note and watched his father's face crumble as he read it.

A barely audible "No" escaped his lips.

Hawk stood in the doorway with a puzzled expression. He had no clue. No one on the crew did, Andy knew. The mystery of Cabin 8 was a family secret, at least until now. Melissa Smith's disappearance had been explained by the Coast Guard as accidental drowning. Rebecca O'Neill hadn't actually disappeared. She'd skipped town and gone to Africa to be a missionary—at least, that's what everyone thought. Tess's vanishing, however, would be impossible to explain, especially to Hawk.

"Is Tess okay?"

The gruff Captain Roberts eased down onto the bottom bunk, the letter shaking in his trembling hands. He passed the note to Hawk. Andy watched the first mate scan Tess's writing and shrug. The words would mean nothing to him.

Hi, Dad (and Mom and Andy),

Please don't be angry. I decided to go visit Rebecca. I'll be home soon, I promise. I had to get away for a little while. Don't change a thing, and I'll be back. Sorry.

Love you.

Your screw-up daughter, Tess

"I don't get it. Didn't Rebecca go to Africa or Ethiopia or some remote village to work as a missionary?"

"No," Andy replied.

Captain Roberts stood, waiting for Hawk to pass him the note. He clasped a hand on Andy's shoulder. "Let's go up on deck. Hawk deserves an explanation, and we need to make a plan before I tell your mother."

Andy looked down at the flashlight and pushed the button to off. He shouldn't have blown off Tess's comments yesterday. He shouldn't have gone out last night. He shouldn't have teased her about Hawk. There were so many things he shouldn't have done, and now he hadn't a clue what he should do.

The three men climbed up the companionway. Captain Roberts headed toward the helm. Andy knew his dad would think better, and feel better, with the wheel in his hands and his eyes on the sea. He couldn't imagine how his father was going to break the news to his mother. Telling Hawk would be easy. He might be shocked, but he wouldn't cry. His mom, on the other hand, was going to die. He could still hear her gut-wrenching sobs after her mother had died ten years ago. His mom had grieved the loss for months.

He could imagine her reaction to this news. Tess was her only daughter. Yes, they'd had their share of battles over the years. As sure as June follows May, they'd butted heads more than a few times, but his mom loved Tess with every beat of her heart. And if he got his hands on his sister again, Andy was going to strangle her for putting them all through this.

At the moment, though, he had to help his dad disclose the family secret to Hawk. Andy leaned against the three-foot-high roof of the captain's quarters opposite the helm. Hawk followed suit. His father gripped the wheel with two hands, gazing past the ship and on up the hill toward town and down the road to where Mom would be.

A wave of sympathy surged through Andy. Tess was gone, for God only knew how long, and his dad probably blamed himself. And soon, all too soon, he would have to tell his wife that their daughter had chosen to leave them.

Andy was about to speak when his father cleared his throat. "Hawk, there's no point in beating around the bush. Tess did exactly what she wrote.

She went to visit Rebecca, though not in Africa."

Captain Roberts paused, a shadow passing over his eyes. Hawk waited patiently for him to speak. Anyone who knew the captain, especially those who had worked for him, knew he was a man of few words, and when he did speak, it would behoove you to listen. He'd earned the respect of sailors and landlubbers. He could be direct, not always as gentle as some might like, but he spoke words of wisdom.

He ran a hand through his thick, white hair. "Rebecca came to me last month and told me she was traveling to 1775 every night."

Hawk stood up in a huff. "You have got to be kidding me...all those rumors...Mike's accusations...Tell me you're joking!"

"I wish I was, Hawk. I understand why you're angry. No one meant to lie to you. The truth had to be kept a secret. Rebecca didn't tell anyone except the family. Nor did I. She told me on Friday night, the last night of the Holmes Hole cruise. She confessed that she had fallen in love with Captain Benjamin Reed and that she intended to, or wanted to, return to 1775 that evening and remain there."

"*The* Captain Benjamin Reed? You're telling me Rebecca fell in love with *Shenandoah's* Captain Reed?" Hawk began to pace as he absorbed the news. Andy wondered if he'd felt something for Rebecca or if his expression was merely one of disbelief and fury.

His father's hands relaxed on the wheel. "Yes, the Captain Reed who sailed as a privateer for General George Washington."

Hawk shook his head. "That's absurd."

"If only that were true, son. Why don't you have a seat, and we'll explain to you what we know?"

Hawk walked over toward Andy and leaned back against the rooftop, his arms crossed over his chest, his jaw set. "Does this have anything to do with Melissa Smith?"

Captain Roberts nodded. "As incredible as this is going to sound, it appears Cabin 8 is some sort of time-travel portal. I can think of only one possible explanation, and even that is a stretch for me. Years ago, when I had the *Shenandoah* rebuilt, Cabin 8 was reconstructed with every original board put back into the exact location as when the ship was first built in 1770. Now, though I have no idea how, the cabin has the ability to transport people between the past and the present."

A gull flew overhead, squawking loudly and startling the men. Andy looked up and noticed a flock of birds following the *Island Home* as the ferry left the harbor to cross Vineyard Sound to Woods Hole. The *Shenandoah* rocked in the wake of the large passenger ferry carrying more Island residents than tourists this time of year.

Hawk ignored the waving passengers. "So, Tess has gone after Rebecca?"

He asked a logical-sounding question. All three men ignored the improbability of what they were discussing.

"It appears Tess decided to visit Rebecca. We can only pray she found her. Honestly, Hawk, I don't know if Rebecca made it safely back to Captain Reed. That Friday afternoon, I called home and talked through the situation with Katherine. We formulated a plan. Friday night, Andy sneaked Tess onboard *Shenandoah,* and she stayed in my cabin. Rebecca made a show of coming up to speak with me. She brought some of her clothes, and she and Tess talked. In the morning, Rebecca was gone. Tess dressed in some of Rebecca's clothes, put on a ball cap, and Andy pretended it was Rebecca he was rowing to shore in the early morning hours."

Hawk turned toward Andy. "I remember that morning. You left around six. I wanted to talk to Rebecca, to say good-bye, but you sent me to get coffee. I made it up in time to wave as you slipped in behind another ship. So that was Tess in the boat?"

Andy looked his friend in the eye. He knew he shouldn't feel guilty. He had done what needed to be done. Still, he had lied to Hawk. "Sorry, Hawk. There was no other way to cover for Rebecca. We couldn't go through another Coast Guard investigation, and we sure as heck weren't going to announce to the world that our ship was a time-travel machine."

"Let me get this straight. Rebecca is now living in 1775, presumably married to Captain Benjamin Reed, and Tess has gone to visit her. Where is Melissa Smith? Did she really drown?" Anger crept into Hawk's voice.

"I believe Rebecca is with Captain Reed. I pray she is. As for Melissa, well, there was never any reason to contest the Coast Guard findings. I had no clue she was alive until Rebecca told me she'd talked with her. Five years ago, when Melissa went missing at sea, I believed she had drowned. I never considered another option, and I certainly didn't believe the rumor Pete Nichols was spreading about Melissa traveling back in time to Colonial Boston. Seems Pete knew or believed something none of us did. Rebecca confirmed Pete's story in more ways than one."

Hawk's eyes grew wide. "No way! The whole week Mike Natale grilled Rebecca about Melissa, she never cracked, never flinched, never once even looked guilty. I didn't take Rebecca to be such a skilled liar. Guess I misjudged her in a major way."

Andy winced. Captain Roberts shook his head. "In all fairness to Rebecca,

I don't believe she saw Melissa until her Thursday night travels. The good news is that Melissa is healthy, happy, and married to Captain Reed's uncle."

"You're kidding, right? Isn't he the man who built the *Shenandoah?*"

Captain Roberts nodded. "One and the same."

Hawk rose slowly, a scowl replacing his usual smile. "Unbelievable!" He faced his friend, a dozen questions and accusations revealed in his eyes.

Andy held his gaze. "Yes, to say the least. And now Tess has followed them, or we hope she has."

"What do you mean, 'you hope she has'? You know Rebecca and Melissa landed in the same location."

Andy walked over to his dad, placing a hand on his back. "Sort of. We know they both ended up on the original *Shenandoah* in Colonial Boston. They arrived years apart, and not on the days they actually left our *Shenandoah*. Tess could be anywhere at any point in time. For all we know, she's landed in the middle of another war."

Silence settled over the ship like a dark fog. The three men avoided looking at one another. Andy cleared his throat. "I don't know if this matters, but Tess elected to go. Rebecca and Melissa traveled unknowingly."

The silent fog engulfed the three men. Hawk reached over and picked up Tess's flashlight from where Andy had set it on the rooftop. He flicked the button from off to on and off to on. He rolled the small beacon of light in his hand before he passed the last item Tess had held to Andy. "All the more reason I should go after her," Hawk said matter-of-factly.

Big-brother mode kicked in, and Andy moved toward Hawk. "What? No way! I'm going. I'm the one who needs to bring her home."

"Andy, your mom's going to freak when she finds out about Tess. Think, man. You can't go."

Captain Roberts stepped around the wheel. "No one is going. Andy, I will not risk you chasing after Tess and losing you both. And, Hawk, I could not, will not, ask you to go. We must have faith that Tess will return tonight, just as Rebecca did each night."

Andy dropped his eyes to the deck.

"What is it, Drew?" Hawk asked.

"Rebecca told us she returned each night because she slept in the cabin on the other side. Tess knows if she leaves the cabin, she doesn't have to come back. I don't think Tess plans to come back tonight, Dad. Sorry."

The look on his father's face confirmed Andy's beliefs. "I suspect you're right, Andy. Tess is determined to have her adventure. I should have dismantled that cabin weeks ago. Your mother is never going to forgive me."

Hawk walked around the helm and laid a hand on the yawl boat. He looked out over the expansive sea stretching beyond the harbor and over Vineyard Sound. "Please, tell Katherine I'll be going after Tess. I'll bring her home in the morning if possible. Hopefully, this will be merely a bad memory by tomorrow night."

Andy saw it then, a flicker in Hawk's eyes of something he couldn't quite identify. Maybe the first mate cared more for his sister than he'd let on. Maybe he'd fallen for Tess that first day two years ago when Tess had fallen so hard for him. Best not to think about that—one Tess problem at a time.

Captain Roberts motioned for Hawk to stand behind the wheel. "I've trusted you with this ship. You've never let me down, Hawk. You're the best first mate a captain could ask for. Your job is here, on this vessel. You have no obligation to chase after Tess."

Rosy color crept up Hawk's neck. "I know that, Captain. I feel it is my place. Neither you nor Andy can go. It's me or no one, and someone has to talk some sense into Tess. I want to go, sir."

Captain Roberts paused, then said in his gravelly voice, "Okay, then. Let's meet back at the dock at eight o'clock. There's nothing to be done here today."

The boat ride back to the dock was quiet, the engine the only sound.

The three men shuffled toward the parking lot, the sand crunching under their feet. Andy cringed with each step. The warm late-summer day was lost on him. The sun was still rising, the day barely begun, yet he'd had enough. It wasn't close to lunchtime. His mom wouldn't be expecting them until later, much, much later.

"Dad, what are going to tell Mom?"

"The truth, Andy, the truth. Your mother will know as soon as we walk in the door."

Before climbing into his truck, Andy opened the door to Tess's Jeep. As he suspected, her cell phone was in the center console, as was her wallet. She, like so many Islanders, never locked a car or the house. He left the cell and picked up the blue leather wallet, then held it up.

His dad nodded, then faced Hawk. "Do what you need to do to prepare, in case, and we'll meet you back here later. And, son, if you change your mind, I won't think less of you. I wouldn't have asked you to do what you've offered. I am grateful, more than words can express. But I have no idea where you'll go or if you'll be able to come back. There is no guarantee. Don't take this lightly."

"I understand what's at risk, Captain. I'll square away a few things on my end as you suggested, just in case."

7

"I DID IT!"

Tess let the reality of the situation soak in. She sat on the cot and followed the rhythm of the boat with her body. She tried to assess how high the seas were. The boat was cresting, but with little movement within. Tess could feel small surges as *Shenandoah* rose and fell, but the movement was so slight she could easily stand or walk about the cabin. She figured the seas must be relatively calm and the wind fairly steady.

She also figured she must have slept well into the morning if the boat was underway. Her father hardly ever sailed *Shenandoah* before ten in the morning and only on very rare occasions had they ever gone out at night. Two hundred years ago, if in fact she had traveled just as Rebecca had to July 1775, sailing at night would be risky, but many vessels traveled in the dark, following the North Star with no lanterns or lights to distract the navigator.

Unless...

Tess rubbed her palms over her denim-clad knees. Unless George Washington ordered Captain Benjamin Reed on a secret mission. Tess knew *Shenandoah's* history. Her father had drilled the ship's life into his children's heads until they could spout her missions and journeys in their sleep.

Although the ship's logs from the summer of 1775 through all of 1776 had either been lost, destroyed, or gone missing, her father had searched and found some answers, at least enough to speculate and teach Tess and her brothers some sailing history a few nights a week before bed.

Where Captain Roberts had speculated, Rebecca had helped to fill in a few blanks with previously unrevealed facts. According to Rebecca, Benjamin Reed had been enlisted personally by General George Washington to serve undercover in the newly established Continental Navy only days before Rebecca had left the Holmes Hole kids' cruise for good.

All Tess had to do was figure out if she was actually on the *Shenandoah* and where in time she was. She didn't recognize the cabin she was in. It resembled an ancient doctor's office with its pungent smell of alcohol. Maybe Rebecca was on the boat as a nurse? She surely had seen and mended enough cuts and bumps and the occasional bout of lice during her few years teaching at Holmes Hole Elementary.

If Rebecca was on board, life would be perfect. Tess's feet itched to move. Her brain willed her body to be cautious. She wasn't accustomed to being patient. After a full five minutes of listening to the sounds of nothing out of the ordinary on the boat, Tess decided to make her move.

She opened the door to the cabin and poked her head out into the hallway. Nobody was in sight, although she heard voices and smelled biscuits or bread and something meaty cooking in the galley. Her stomach growled, reminding her that she hadn't eaten since the tiny chicken sandwich she'd thrown together as she walked out of her parents' house the night before.

Tess felt a moment of regret as she imagined her mom's response when she discovered her only daughter was gone. It was too late now, though, and her mom would understand when she explained it all when she got back....*if she got back.* A small knot twisted in her stomach.

The passageway was narrow, like the one on her *Shenandoah*. The ship felt familiar yet strange. Too much of what she saw was different—the wood looked and felt odd, bumpy and rougher, the doors were in the wrong place— and still there was something unmistakable. She moved slowly, her heart pounding, wondering what or who she would find onboard. She stopped short to the right of the galley opening, where she heard two men talking.

"The sky's too gray for June. An ominous sign for sure, Jonah."

"Could just be a storm, Adam."

"A storm it is, though whether of nature or of man we have yet to know. Could be hours of wait ahead before we know from whence it comes."

Jonah? Adam? Tess recognized those names. In the short time she'd talked with Rebecca that Friday night only a month ago, her friend had mentioned Ben's younger brother, Jonah, and the cook, Adam. Perfect! She'd made it back to sometime where Rebecca might be. Even if Rebecca wasn't there, somebody had to know her and where she was.

As she was about to step forward, though, a chill ran down Tess's spine. *What if I've come back before Rebecca? What if they haven't met her yet? They'll think I'm a stowaway!*

Tess pressed herself flat against the bumpy boards and held her breath. Adam had mentioned a storm. Was she the storm? Or was she about to be caught up in a storm and tossed at sea or worse, lost at sea? Her mind raced. *Forward or back?* Make herself known, or hightail it back to the cabin and wait for evening to come so she could return to the present? She didn't know much at the moment, but she knew one thing for certain: she wasn't a coward.

As she considered her options, an image of Hawk at the helm entered her mind. She had seen him there many times. She had whispered his name on a breeze, hoping he would turn toward her and call her name. His lazy smile and bright blue eyes never once turned her way. A stab of rejection tore through her once again, as it always did when Hawk ignored her. She blinked the image away, buried her wounded heart deep within her chest, and stepped into the doorway.

"Excuse me," Tess said, "do either of you know Rebecca O'Neill?"

The knife in the cook's hand fell to the floor. The young man, presumably Jonah, stumbled backward and fell against the ladder. The two men, one in his early twenties and the other older, probably in his sixties, judging by his gray hair and the character lines on his face, stared at her, jaws dropped, eyes wide as they regained their balance.

The older one, whom she assumed was Adam, shook his head. "Not again. Lord God almighty, You cannot be sending us another one."

Adam bent and picked up the knife off the floor. He brushed his hands on the once-white apron now stained with grease and streaks of red that must have been from the beets being sliced on the tiny counter. He kept his eyes on Tess, which made her feel like an insect under a magnifying glass. She watched him set the knife in the sink. The silence made her anxious.

"I'm sorry to startle you. I was hoping to find Rebecca. I've missed her, and things weren't going exactly—" She paused, realizing the two men were still staring. "Well, never mind my life back home. I wanted a bit of adventure and decided to find Rebecca before, well, um, before it was too late."

"A storm for certain," the cook stated over his shoulder to Jonah. He took a step in Tess's direction and extended his right hand. "Adam Greene, miss."

Tess shook his hand. "Hi, Adam. Tess Roberts. I'm Rebecca's best friend. I thought I might come for a visit."

"A visit? Is that what you ladies in your time call your travels? Well, Miss Roberts, Mrs. Reed is not onboard, though I am sure she will be pleased to see you."

Jonah stood stock-still, mouth gaping. He appeared to be in shock. Tess smiled, trying to put him at ease. He finally cleared his throat, a dry, scratching sound, and swallowed hard before pushing off the ladder to stand up straight.

Adam cast him a glance over his shoulder. "Let me introduce you to Rebecca's brother-in-law. Miss Tess Roberts, the speechless waif behind me is the captain's younger brother, Jonah Reed."

Jonah grinned and winked, clearly embarrassed yet able to flirt with the best of them. Tess knew instantly why Rebecca was so fond of him. His smile was contagious, boyish, impish even, yet inviting in an *are-you-single-let's-*

have-drinks kind of way.

"Welcome aboard, Miss Roberts. Jonah Reed at your service," he said before making a goofy bow. As he straightened, he winked again. "I hope Rebecca mentioned me."

Tess laughed. Jonah would be dangerous if he was a few years older. "Yes, Jonah, Rebecca did say something about Ben's little brother being cute and sweet."

Jonah clutched his hand to his heart in dramatic fashion. "Cute and sweet? You compare me to a young girl? You wound me, Miss Roberts, and you have yet to become familiar with my charms."

More laughter rang in the small room as Adam joined Tess in obvious delight at Jonah's performance. "Oh, I believe Rebecca told me all I need to know about Ben's baby brother. Now, where is that handsome brother of yours who stole my friend's heart and forced her to travel across time?"

Adam clapped a hand on Jonah's back and let out a deep chuckle. "I think the lady has declined the young whippersnapper."

"I may be twenty-five at home, but I'm far too young for him today, a couple of centuries to say the least." Tess giggled and her apprehension drifted away like seabirds riding the wind. "Speaking of time, what year is this?"

"1776," Jonah said as he joined in the laughter. Mischief gleamed in his eyes. "I would be happy to introduce you to Ben, if you are so inclined."

Adam looked over his shoulder at Jonah. "Perhaps Miss Roberts should change her attire before going up on deck?"

Jonah nodded, and both men appraised Tess's blue jeans and sweatshirt. She squirmed slightly under their stares. "Too bad, but I didn't bring anything else. This will have to do. Let's go."

Tess tried to walk past Adam. He held up a hand.

"Pardon me, Miss Roberts. I do believe Mrs. Reed has some dresses on board. If I recall correctly, her chest is in Captain Reed's quarters."

"Well, that won't work then. We'll have to go on deck just to get me into Ben's cabin to change. Really, I'm fine. These are my favorite jeans. If I'd given it a little more thought, I might have worn a sweater over my T-shirt instead of a sweatshirt, but I'm good."

Adam shook his head. "Miss Roberts, while I am pleased to know that you are comfortable, I am more concerned with your appearance before the crew. Men will question your attire."

Reality hit Tess where it hurt. Adam was right, but she had no desire, absolutely none, to wear a dress. She slumped against the wall. Why did everything have to be so difficult?

Jonah smiled at Tess. He seemed to sense the rapid shift in her mood. "We shall do our best to go unnoticed and have Miss Roberts appropriately dressed before the breakfast bell."

Adam nodded and moved aside so Tess could walk through the tiny galley and follow Jonah up the three ladder rungs and out onto the deck. He untied his apron and hung it on a peg near the door. "I believe I will join you. Ben might have a few words to impart that I do not wish to miss."

8

TESS STEPPED OUT OF THE GALLEY and onto the deck. Goosebumps rose on her arms under her sweatshirt and spread down to her legs. She sucked in her breath. She was standing on the *Shenandoah*. THE *Shenandoah*.

Her father would be so jealous. Well, after he killed her for leaving the family, then he'd be envious. The top deck looked much the same, though Tess guessed the cannons were functional as opposed to the decorative ones they had on their ship at home.

The clouds moved away from the sun. Tess squinted as she looked up at the sails. They were beautiful—crisp white sailcloth filled with wind and carrying the *Shenandoah* across the sea. Gosh, if her father could travel back in time too, he would be in his element.

"She is beautiful, is she not?" Jonah asked.

"Is she ever! I've heard stories about her since I was a little girl. Our boat is very similar, but this is even better than I'd imagined as a kid."

"Rebecca shared with us tales of her life on Martha's Vineyard and your friendship. She explained that your father owns the *Shenandoah*. Ben was impressed his ship is still in existence."

Tess smiled. Her father had worked hard and spent a lot of money to restore and remodel the original *Shenandoah* to the magnificent vessel she was in the twenty-first century.

"My dad couldn't save the whole ship. She was so far gone when he bought her that he finally had to relinquish his dream of restoring the original. He did everything possible to transform her into as close a replica as he could." Tess ran her hands over the wood framing on the galley roof.

"And, as I'm sure Rebecca told you, he reused every board that was salvageable, and we have one cabin, Cabin 8, that is fully restored." Tess paused, turned slightly, put both her hands on the ship's rail to her left, and grinned. "And magical. Cabin 8 is absolutely magical. I almost didn't believe it when Rebecca told me, but it must be true because I am not dreaming and you seem real enough. I hoped when I sneaked onboard last night that Rebecca wouldn't have made this up."

Adam inched by Tess, shaking his head. He stood beside Jonah, the wind to his back, and looked sternly at their visitor. "I don't know about magic,

Miss Roberts, but you are here in the same fashion Rebecca and Missy arrived. Does your father know where you are?" The cook's tone reminded Tess of her father's when she had disobeyed her mother as a child.

Tess hung her head. "Probably."

"Probably?" The tone sounded harsher to Tess's ears.

"I left him a note. I'm sure he's found it by now."

"I see."

She hated that phrase and Adam's implied accusation in those two brief words. "I doubt you do see. He was going to change the boards in the cabin, and then Rebecca wouldn't be able to come home. I missed Rebecca. And I needed an adventure."

Tess slammed her hand down on the cap rail. "The Island was driving me crazy. The guys are idiots, and Hawk won't give me the time of day. I've had so many bad dates I'm about to swear off men for the rest of my life. Last month, I made a nice shrimp dinner for Matt Falco, and do you know what that idiot did? He complained because I left the shells on, and then he refused to eat my food. I've had it! I can't do what I want to do because I'm a girl. And why should Rebecca have all the fun?" Tess jammed both hands onto her hips and stared at Adam.

The older man's jaw had dropped during her tirade. He closed his mouth and nodded. "That does clarify your situation." His words were softer and his eyes sympathetic.

Tess realized she probably sounded like a petulant child, but that was just too bad. She couldn't explain to these two men what her life was like and what men were like in the twenty-first century. How could she possibly explain her last date? When they had stopped at the Cumbies to buy some drinks and she'd asked Jerry for a Snapple, he'd returned to the car and handed her the iced tea along with the receipt. She'd gotten out of the car and walked home.

She couldn't explain a convenience store. She couldn't explain Snapple. She couldn't explain cars, and she sure couldn't explain what motivated Jerry to hand her a bill for $1.39. Hmmm, she probably couldn't explain spending $1.39 on bottled iced tea either.

While she considered what words might convey her dilemma, Adam clapped a hand on Jonah's shoulder and pointed toward the helm twenty-five feet away. "I believe it is time to introduce our guest to the captain."

Tess and Jonah followed Adam's gaze and discovered they had an observer. Tess grimaced. He'd probably heard her ranting, which might explain his cross expression. Whatever his problem, and even without the smile she'd heard so much about, Tess instantly understood Rebecca's physical attraction to Captain Benjamin Reed.

Ben stood as tall as Andy, with slightly broader shoulders and darker, almost black hair. He was handsome, though at the moment he didn't appear too friendly. His rigid jawline was clenched so tight he reminded her of Severus Snape in *Harry Potter*, to say the least.

Tess figured his bite couldn't be as bad as the one her father would give her when she returned. She inched forward, waiting for Jonah to take the lead.

"His bark is all bluff. I shall stay by your side, so fear not."

"Thanks, Jonah. I'm used to fierce captains and their occasional annoyance with me."

Adam chuckled. "Your statement does not surprise me. Would you be your father's only daughter, Miss Roberts?"

Tess laughed. "Oh, yeah. I'm the one and only and, trust me, my parents wouldn't want another girl if she was anything like me."

Jonah offered his arm. Tess stared at the bent appendage for a couple of seconds, then realized he meant to walk her formally to his brother. "Aww, how sweet."

"Twice in one day the young lady has called you sweet, Jonah. Perhaps you do remind her of a young child."

"'Tis pleasant to be thought of." Jonah nodded at Tess and patted her hand resting on his arm.

Tess chuckled. "Rebecca didn't say enough about you, Jonah."

"I believe you noted she was short on time." Jonah looked sideways and winked. "Are you ready to meet the captain?"

Tess appraised the man standing with his feet shoulder-width apart, arms crossed, apparently waiting for her approach. They'd gone only about two yards from the galley during her tirade about Island life. The two dozen feet between them and Captain Reed loomed before Tess like a dare she couldn't refuse. "Bring it on."

"Excuse me?" Jonah asked.

"Bring it on, you know, or I guess you don't know. It means that I'm ready, willing, and able."

"I have never heard Rebecca utter that particular phrase. I must remember to tell her to 'bring it on' the next time she asks me to fetch Ben at the dock."

"Um, probably not the right wording. It's more like when..."

Adam interrupted. "I believe you are stalling, Miss Roberts. You can explain when and how Jonah should 'bring it on' after you meet Captain Reed."

Tess swallowed hard. Adam began to walk toward Ben. Jonah escorted her until they stood a few feet from Rebecca's husband.

"Brother, may I introduce you to Miss Tess Roberts, a friend of your wife's. She has come for a visit."

9

TESS COULDN'T DECIDE if Captain Benjamin Reed was throwing daggers at her with his brown eyes or if he was sizing her up. Several moments had passed since Jonah had introduced her, and the good captain hadn't said a word.

"Brother, did you hear me? Miss Roberts is a friend of your Rebecca's."

He scowled at her. The man, whom she hadn't even spoken to, had the nerve to scowl at her. The already gray sky seemed to darken with each second that passed.

"Aye, I heard you, Jonah."

That's it? No hello? No how are you? No how was your trip here? There was no way this was the same person Rebecca had gushed on and on about.

Tess reached the end of her patience rope, which her mother told her on many occasions wasn't very long to begin with. She extended her right hand. "It's nice to meet you, Captain Reed. How is Rebecca doing? I can't wait to see her."

Another second passed, then another and another. Tess felt the weight of her empty hand like an anchor pulling her down.

Adam cleared his throat. "I think you have shocked the captain, Miss Roberts."

He didn't appear shocked to Tess. Angry she would believe. Annoyed was possible, given his sour expression. Constipated would also be believable. For the third time in less than five minutes, Tess wondered what Rebecca could possibly see in the man standing before her.

She suppressed the urge to chuckle at her more comical thoughts. Better to respond to shocked than her options. "In that case I'll be happy to sail the ship home for you."

He didn't even crack a smile.

Jonah's laughter broke the silence. "I would like to see that."

Tess turned left and gave Jonah a saucy look. "Listen here, Jonah Reed, I could sail this vessel around the world if I wanted to. I know every inch of her from bow to stern to boom to mast."

"Actually, Miss Roberts, you know your father's ship." Captain Reed paused, glanced around the boat, and then spoke with a tone so chilled that shivers ran down Tess's back. "My *Shenandoah* is not yours, nor is anything else in this time and place."

Tess wheeled to face Ben. "Believe me, Captain Reed, I know all too well that *Shenandoah*, whether my father's or yours, is not mine. My father has lectured me enough. I don't need your two cents added to his three. I was merely stating a fact: I am fully capable of sailing her anywhere in the world."

Tensions rose. Neither spoke. Tess's temper spiked once again. He hadn't even seen her sail, and he was questioning her competency? Ha! Tess disliked the man on the spot. He couldn't be any ruder if he tried. Rebecca had to be desperate to be with this one. She was probably sitting in some shack, hoping to be rescued. Thank God they hadn't changed the boards last week. Rebecca could come back with her tonight and be saved from a life with this beast.

Thunder rolled in the distance. The sea was still fairly calm. Tess figured the storm was either going to be a mild one or was still too far off to do anything more than rumble. The day was merely beginning, and it didn't look too promising either way.

"Captain," Adam said, "I have breakfast to prepare. I believe Miss Roberts mentioned earlier that she has an affinity for the kitchen. Perhaps she could prove useful in the galley?"

Tess spun on her heel to face Adam. "I said no such…"

Adam gave her a look quite similar to the one Andy frequently flashed at her when he was conspiring for her benefit. His eyes narrowed and focused on her mouth, almost willing her to shut her trap instantly.

"No need to be modest now, Miss," Adam said.

"Ah, you're right, Adam. I would love to slice and dice with you."

Ben simply nodded, turned his back on Tess, blowing her off and ticking her off all over again. What was his problem, anyway?

Adam stepped aside to let Tess pass. "After you, Miss Roberts. I believe you know the way."

Tess chuckled. Every inch she moved away from Benjamin Reed lifted her spirits. Once she was below deck, she waited for Adam to give her instructions. "What would you like me to do?"

"Not a thing, Miss. I have only to finish the biscuits. The eggs are boiled, and the ham is prepared. The beets were being sliced for lunch. They can wait until after I have served the men their morning meal."

"Then why on earth did you want me to come help you?"

"I was only trying to help you, Miss. You and Captain Reed seem to have gotten off on the wrong foot. I thought a little distance would benefit all."

"What is his problem?" Tess demanded. "He has the manners of a mule, if that. Did his mother not teach him how to say hello? Seriously! I can't for the life of me begin to imagine what Rebecca sees in him. Thank God I came when I did. At least she can go home with me."

Adam stared directly into her eyes. "Your idea, Miss Roberts, is the captain's problem."

"What?"

"I do not believe you arrived here this morning intending to take Rebecca home with you."

"Not until I saw that ogre. He was so rude, I couldn't even ask for any of Rebecca's clothes, not that he would have let me touch anything. My adventure just became a rescue mission."

"The captain, I feel, is concerned that you arrived with the intent to take Rebecca away from him."

"Oh, please."

Adam opened the oven door, lifted the tray of biscuits, and placed the pan on the middle rack before addressing Tess again. "I ask you to place yourself in the captain's shoes for one moment. A woman from his wife's past, or future, arrives on his ship out of nowhere. It could be possible someone sent you to bring her back. If you were the captain, and you loved your wife and your, um, family, you too might be cautious of the surprise visitor."

Tess leaned against the doorframe. "So that's probably what he meant when he said nothing in this time was mine. I should go talk to him. If I tell him I only want to visit with Rebecca, maybe he'll lighten up. What do you think?"

"A grand idea." Adam picked up a long wooden pizza board—at least that's what it looked like—and slid it under the biscuits to remove the hot pan. "I suggest you wait until after breakfast. I will call the crew in approximately five minutes. It might be best if you gave yourself more time to dispel the captain's fears."

Tess walked to Adam and kissed him on the cheek. When he blushed, she recalled from a tour to Plimoth Plantation that men and women did not have PDAs two hundred years ago. She chuckled at the thought of explaining public displays of affection to a sixty-something man in 1776.

Her stomach growled again. "Can I help you with anything while I wait? I'm starving and I'd love to speed up the process if I could."

Adam grinned, his color returning to normal. "You may carry the platters of ham and eggs to the tables. If any of the crew descends, return to the galley. I have no idea if the captain has told them of your presence as of yet."

Tess cringed. She hadn't thought of that. How would they explain her arrival?

46

10

WHILE THE CREW ATE BREAKFAST IN THE SALOON, Tess consumed every morsel of the ham and biscuits Adam had left for her in the galley. She listened as Captain Reed explained that a friend of Rebecca's had dressed as a man and joined them yesterday while they were in port. A situation they were unaware of until this morning.

"We are a few days from home. This shall inconvenience our voyage only slightly. Miss Roberts braved a treacherous journey to visit my wife. She will be resting today. Tomorrow afternoon, the good Lord willing, we will disembark."

Tess couldn't see the captain, but she could hear the strain in his voice. Maybe the crew would believe the "resting" comment, but she knew the man wanted her gone...and the sooner the better. She really needed to talk with him and try to smooth things out.

Adam returned to the galley and allowed Tess to help with the dishes and clean up. When the kitchen was clean, Adam thanked her for her help. "Now, Miss Roberts, I believe would be an appropriate time to talk with Captain Reed. Let me determine if he is at the helm alone."

"Great. Thanks."

Her neck muscles tightened across her shoulders. Tess rolled her head to relax her neck and upper body. She hated feeling anxious. What she really hated was talking to anyone when she had to express her feelings. She'd never been any good at it. It seemed like such a girly thing to do, and blabbing on about her emotions was something she'd avoided most of her life.

Tess preferred action over words any day of the week. And action was easy to find and even easier to create, especially if one threw in a dose of danger. Danger meant anxious excitement, not a sick knot in her stomach or tightness across her back.

While she rounded her shoulders to stretch her delts and traps, Adam came down the ladder.

"Captain Reed is at the helm. I did not tell him of your desire to speak with him. Whenever you feel ready, you may depart at your leisure."

"Better to get it over with. The sooner, the better. Putting something off has rarely worked out well for me."

Adam smiled. "I would beg to differ. I do believe actively waiting on the Lord is best. However, in this situation, I agree that you have given yourself sage advice."

Tess climbed up the three rungs and glanced over to her right. Ben Reed was standing at the helm, no one else in sight. Opportunity was knocking, whether Tess wanted to answer or not.

She approached Ben slowly and quietly. He had yet to realize she was moving toward him. She studied his expression. Maybe Adam was right. He did look stressed. She could see the worry in his tight jaw and the distant, sad look in his eyes.

When she reached the end of the cabin roof, Tess stopped. About ten feet separated them physically. Still, she felt the centuries between them stretch those ten feet into what felt like an impassable abyss.

He sensed her presence, or perhaps heard her internal monologue, before she spoke a word. Tess was still trying to figure out how to start the conversation when he turned and scowled at her.

"You are to return below deck."

Tess bit her tongue, literally. She swallowed her sarcastic retort and thought about what Adam had said. Rebecca wouldn't have fallen in love with this jerk if he really was a jerk.

"Look, I didn't come here to bring Rebecca back."

He raised an eyebrow and straightened, clearly not believing her.

"It's true," Tess said, tossing her hands in the air. "I was just so fed up with my life. I couldn't figure out what I wanted to do and everything I wanted to do I wasn't allowed to do, so I decided to visit Rebecca. Believe me, if Hawk had agreed to go with me to the beach party next Friday night, I wouldn't be here right now. But, nooooooo, he won't do that because I'm the captain's daughter, and God forbid the first mate date the captain's daughter. Which is ridiculous!"

Mid-rant, Tess wagged a finger at Ben, though not so much at him as at men in general. "And there really isn't another guy I care to date on the Island. You'll have to trust me on that. If you had seen Jim Hensley lying like a slime ball in the grocery store yesterday, you would totally understand what I'm saying about finding a good guy. Does that explain things? Do you see why I just needed to talk to Rebecca and hear her tell me that one day, someday, hopefully in this decade, well, my decade, I would get to sail around the world with Mr. Right?" Tess drew in a long breath.

Captain Reed's mouth gaped open as if he was about to speak, but no words were coming out.

When Tess was able to stop chuckling, she sympathized with Rebecca's eighteenth-century husband. "Don't feel bad. I have that effect on the men in my family, too. So long as you get the point: I'm not here to ruin your marriage or snatch Rebecca or move in for the short or long term. I only need a little adventure and a major break. Are we okay now?" Tess extended her right hand.

Ben closed his mouth and then, just as quickly, broke into a smile. "Rebecca tried to explain how a woman in the twenty-first century could be independent and equal to a man on a variety of levels. I believe I now understand how this could be possible." He covered the distance between them with his hand outstretched.

"Well, I'm hardly equal to a man," Tess said as she shook his hand. "If that were even partially true, then I would be my father's first mate instead of Hawk, and I'd get to sail *Shenandoah*. Perhaps, since you've been enlightened to Women's Liberation, you'd consider hiring me, Captain Reed?"

"I am sorry, Miss Roberts, but General Washington would relieve me of my duties instantly if I hired a woman."

Rich, deep laughter followed. Tess couldn't help but join in. Tensions between them eased, and a billon questions raced through Tess's mind.

"How is the war going? I was never much of a history buff. I know the *Shenandoah's* history by heart, but the school stuff went in one ear and out the other. Does Washington drop by often? Have you had him over for dinner? Rebecca thought it was beyond cool when she met him."

Captain Reed shook his head and chuckled. "Nay, Miss Roberts, His Excellency General Washington hath not crossed our paths again. Though our contribution is faithful and our mission dear, I believe he has greater concerns to which to dedicate his time than dining with a privateer."

"Forget the war." Tess waved her hand. "I know how it ends. Tell me about Rebecca. How is she? When did you get married? Where does she live?"

Ben's face softened. Tess saw his deep love for Rebecca reflected in his eyes. "My wife is well. She has adapted to life here, though I regret she does wish for a few of your conveniences from time to time."

"Ha! I bet. Probably craves a Scottish Bakehouse gluten-free brownie or some froyo at Tisberry. Does she ever mention me or talk about the Island?"

A wave of sadness washed over Tess. All the talk of Rebecca reminded her why she'd come in the first place. Sailing on *Shenandoah* was great, but she wanted to spend time with her friend. She missed her more than she'd thought possible.

"In August," Ben began slowly, perhaps noting that Tess's energy level had dropped to zero, "when we were planning our wedding, she spoke of you throughout the day. She wanted you present when we pledged our lives to one another."

Tess glanced out over the water, avoiding eye contact. "Did she have a maid of honor?"

The question hurt. The role would have been hers. They had joked and dreamed about boys and weddings since they were little girls. Tess would have suffered willingly with the dress selections and, with little or no complaints, wearing a dress. Now Becca was married and she'd missed the whole event.

Ben waited for Tess to face him. "I know she wished for your presence. She expressed her heartache on several occasions. I regret you could not share the day with us, Miss Roberts. As your presence was not possible, Rebecca asked my Aunt Missy to stand with her. Uncle Isaiah stood by me."

Tess absorbed the news. "That makes sense. Melissa was the closest to home, and she would've understood anything Becca might have been feeling. I can see that." her mood brightened. "On the plus side, I didn't have to look like a cupcake in some poofy chiffon thing. Not that Rebecca would have done that to me. What did she wear?"

Adam meandered over during Ben's explanation of who made what portion of Rebecca's wedding dress. The cook stared long and hard at the sky. Tess followed his gaze. Dark clouds loomed in the distance. She'd been listening to Ben, engrossed in stories of Rebecca, and she hadn't noticed the sea had picked up a little chop.

"Storm's coming, Captain."

"Aye, it is, Adam. I hope to keep the wind at our backs long enough to get around the shoals of Cape Ann and tuck into the harbour."

The two men surveyed the world around them like scientists. Adam's eyes focused on the movement of the clouds. "We have time—a day, I reckon."

"I believe you are correct, Adam. Tell the men to batten down the hatches and secure the cannons and equipment."

Tess stretched taller. "I can help. What would you like me to do?"

"With all due respect, Miss Roberts, I cannot allow you to assist the crew. I believe you to be as capable as you say, but circumstances forbid you the opportunity to prove your skill. Please understand. We are at war and *Shenandoah* is in service, however secret her missions." Tess thought his eyes were begging her not to make a scene or launch into another tirade about the fairness, or unfairness, of her life.

"No problem, Captain. I'll just sit and enjoy the view, if you don't mind."

50

Ben's shoulders relaxed and his smile broadened. "By all means, Miss Roberts. I imagine you are quite comfortable at sea."

"Nothing better in all the world. Now, I'll leave you to your work. You don't happen to have any books on board, do you?"

"Of course, Miss Roberts. I should have offered sooner. I shall have Jonah bring you the Good Book momentarily."

"Awesome! I love a good book."

Ben nodded and then glanced at her blue-jean-clad legs. Tess saw the analytical look in his eyes and knew he wasn't looking her over. She knew what he was thinking. She remembered parts of Rebecca's story all too well. And then there was Adam's comment earlier. Her jeans were short-lived.

"And perhaps Jonah could also bring you one of Rebecca's dresses. I understand your attire is appropriate in the twenty-first century. However, I feel the crew would be considerably more comfortable if you were dressed according to our custom."

Tess rolled her eyes. She had been afraid he was going to say that. Now she'd have to wear a dress, another girly item she'd avoided like the plague. She couldn't remember the last time she'd worn a dress. She'd even gotten away with wearing a pantsuit to her oldest brother's wedding two years ago. Probably not an option in Colonial times.

"A dress, huh? Sure, why not? Since I'm not going to be the first mate in my time or yours, I might as well admit total defeat and put on a dress. Has Rebecca mentioned pictures to you? Too bad you don't have a camera. Rebecca would love a picture of this!"

Ben nodded, and they both laughed. Tess decided her little adventure might be turning into a grand adventure.

She sat on the cabin roof, awaiting Jonah's return, dreading the dress and hoping whatever book Ben considered "good" would take her mind off whichever of Rebecca's dresses she would soon be sitting in.

The sky was getting darker. The whitecaps were larger and more frequent. Tess reminded herself that June storms were rarely hurricanes and *Shenandoah* had obviously not been crashed upon the rocks, as her father owned the ship more than two hundred years later. Comforting herself as she felt the ship rise and fall on the dark water, Tess didn't notice Jonah come up from the companionway.

"A dress and the Good Book," Jonah announced, passing Tess the items in his hands.

Tess did her best not to laugh. "The Bible, huh?"

Jonah shrugged. "Did you not say you'd like to read the Good Book?"

"Um, yeah, I did. I forgot you called the Bible the Good Book. I was thinking along the lines of Robert Parker, Phil Craig, or Cynthia Riggs. A local mystery to pass the time of day."

"The Good Book is the only book we have onboard, Miss Roberts. If you are yearning for suspense, allow me to guide you to a fantastic story." Jonah reached for the Bible and opened to Genesis 37. "Joseph's story is one of my favorites."

Dress in one hand, open Bible in the other, Tess was no longer convinced Rebecca was living the good life. Trying to sound more pleased than she was, Tess pasted on a smile and opted for a perky tone. "I guess I should change before I start reading. Thanks, Jonah."

Her new friend smiled back at her. "My pleasure, Miss Roberts. I would love to stay and discuss Joseph's trials and faith, but a storm is approaching, and I must attend to my chores. Until later." Jonah bent slightly at the waist, then headed toward the bow.

Tess looked longingly at the men securing the sails and lines and collecting any loose items on deck. She wished she could help. Same feeling she had back home two hundred years later on her father's boat. With a sigh, she shifted the dress and Bible to her left hand and went below deck to change and read in the makeshift bunk Jonah had arranged in a supply room.

11

ANDY STARED OUT AT THE *SHENANDOAH*. Her lines were sleek and radiant, even in the moonlight. She was one of a kind, at least these days. No electricity, no heat, no modern gadgets to distract you from the glory of being on the water. Just wind and sail. And she was fast. On a good day when his dad wanted to fly, *Shenandoah* could reach eighteen knots. He often wondered who would sail her when his dad retired. In forty years, his father hadn't missed a cruise. Would he hand the wheel over to him, which wasn't really in Andy's long-range plans, or would Hawk get the honors? Would Hawk even be back to captain any boat?

The water shimmered under the nearly full moon. *Shenandoah* looked beautiful resting there on her mooring ball, barely moving on the evening's still waters. All looked calm, but Andy knew it was only a surface calm. A serpent could glide through the seas searching for a ship to latch onto and pull under without causing a ripple on the surface. Andy knew the peaceful black hull of *Shenandoah* was exactly like still ocean waters: inside or underneath there was more activity than the mind could imagine, and some of that activity could sink a boat or get you killed.

Hawk would be in Cabin 8 now. Andy didn't know how Hawk was going to sleep. As composed as Hawk always was, he had to be a little undone, contemplating his future in the past. His parting words, "Relax, Andy. I'll be back tomorrow morning with Tess, whether she likes it or not," did little to ease Andy's mind now.

There were so many what-ifs: what if Hawk didn't find Tess, what if Tess refused to come home, what if they couldn't come back? What-ifs crept up Andy's back and wrapped around him like an octopus encompassing its prey. He tried to move, and his chest constricted. His mother had been tranquil when they left. She'd prayed and put her trust, and Tess's life, in God's hands.

Yet he had seen the spark of fear leap into her eyes when they first told her Tess was gone. He had watched his father pick up her five-foot, three-inch body and hug her to his chest. His mom had sunk into his arms like a waterlogged boat settling into the ocean floor. If Tess didn't return, his mother's heart would break. That fear drowned him now. He fought for air while his lungs burned. "God!" he begged in a silent scream.

Seconds later his muscles loosened, and air seeped into his lungs. "Thank You," he muttered, without conviction, yet well aware he had received help.

His mother would have assured him exactly where that help came from. She had found her strength falling back on or, as she would say, "running toward the Lord." He admired her faith and he believed, though he'd never relied on prayer or God as his parents did. Maybe it was an age thing. Or maybe his mom knew something or had something he didn't.

At the moment, though he was grateful to be breathing easier, he wasn't thrilled with God for letting Tess go where she shouldn't have gone. What kind of parent would allow his daughter to go on some stupid, crazy, out-of-this-world adventure where she could possibly get herself killed? And was God watching out for Hawk? His mother had prayed for them all, but what did Hawk believe? Andy had never asked him, and Hawk had never said. Now he was chasing after Tess, though certainly not in the way Tess had hoped, and who knew if either of them was going to make it back.

Andy started the engine. He backed up down the short dirt path to the dock and headed toward Oak Bluffs. "I need a drink!"

A dozen more what-ifs entered Andy's mind during the ten-minute drive to OB. He knew he should find a couple of friends and chill. Instead he turned onto Circuit Avenue and pulled into a space right in front of the bar. Summer was good for business. The other three seasons were good for parking. During the tourist season, he wouldn't have found a spot in town. Andy sat in the truck, quite aware that it might be better if it was August and his truck was parked somewhere else. For a moment he considered going home. Then he thought of Hawk—whether he was sleeping or even still on the *Shenandoah*.

Cursing Tess for probably the umpteenth time in twelve hours, Andy walked into The Shipwreck, an appropriate name for the sleazy place. He hated the bar, had been in the place only twice, and both times against his better judgment. Instinctively he knew the third time was not going to be a charm. He smelled the cigarette smoke as soon as he walked in the door. *Well, I didn't come looking to talk or to socialize.*

He'd chosen the hole intentionally so he could drink and be left alone. He didn't plan to see anyone he knew, at least not that he wanted to talk to.

He'd told his father he was going for a drink. He hadn't mentioned where. As if his parents didn't have enough to worry about, they'd both be shaking their heads if they knew he was at The Shipwreck. Oh, they weren't under any illusions that their youngest son didn't drink. They just expected him to have standards. The Shipwreck was all its namesake suggested...and more.

Andy walked over to an empty barstool. He hovered there for a minute, indecision the better part of his thinking. His mind raced. He had yet to figure out if he was more worried about Tess or more angry at her for leaving. Now Hawk was on the boat, or maybe he'd already left, or maybe he didn't go. Maybe he wouldn't leave. Maybe the cabin took only women.

His fist hit the bar and heads turned. Not the place to slam things around. Fights were as common as drunks in The Shipwreck. The bartender sauntered over. "Take it easy, pal. You're not the only guy in the joint."

Andy met his eyes. "Right, sorry. I was thinking about something else."

"Must be a woman. Everybody in here is thinking about a woman, one way or another. Take Jim over there, caught cheating again."

Both men looked down the bar. Bile rose in Andy's throat as he remembered how upset Tess had been in the grocery store when Jim Hensley had lied about being married. He was part of the reason Tess had left, and now he was sitting there drowning his sorry self in a pint of beer. Andy's fist clenched. He should get up and walk out. Now.

"Give me something dark, on tap."

The bartender drew his beer with precision, just the right amount of foam atop the dark amber liquid. He placed the mug on the counter and waited.

Andy picked up the thread. "So, what's Jim's story this time?"

A toothy smile cracked the bartender's lined face. "Seems his fiancée found out he's been messing around with her predecessor. He's on his fifth beer, and he ain't stopped whining yet. With Jim, it's always somebody else's fault."

Andy nodded. "I've heard that. He's passed it on to his son too. We had that boy on a boat for two weeks and had to let him go. Bad attitude every which way 'til Sunday."

"I ain't surprised. Jim's not an example anyone would want a kid to follow."

Andy was about to expound on the Hensley family when his brain kicked in. He took a sip of beer instead. His mother had taught him better than to gossip. He put down the beer and tapped his fingers on the bar. *Where was Tess? Would Hawk find her? Would he find her in time? How much time did they have?*

Andy wasn't sure Rebecca's journeys were similar. Rebecca had told them that time had stood still while she traveled. Tess had been gone for twenty-four hours, and the day had moved with the same pace as any other day. What did that mean? Was Tess trapped? Had she been gone longer than he knew, and she'd already decided to stay?

Andy pushed away the beer. Fire was burning his belly, and a glass of beer wasn't going to put it out. He had to get out of there and away from the sorry likes of Jim Hensley. He slapped a ten down on the bar and nodded to the bartender.

"Where's your sista? I gotta thing or two to say to her."

Andy froze in his tracks, halfway to the door, halfway to safety. He turned around and faced a drunken Hensley, six-foot-two and at least fifty pounds overweight with threadbare clothes bursting at the seams. He wasn't worth the time or energy. "Go back to your beer, Jim."

A couple of guys in the corner stepped closer. Andy cursed himself for walking in the door in the first place.

Jim staggered toward him, poking a finger into the air. "She shoulda kept her mouth shut. Megan shoulda kept her mouth shut, too. Nobody's business what I do. All those women are…"

"Save it, Jim." Andy's blood was boiling. He needed to get out of there. He backed up, keeping his eyes locked on Jim.

"Next time I see Tess, I'm gonna let her have it. Meddling woman got no business talking to my daughter. You tell her I—"

The first punch hit Jim on the underside of his left jaw, and he stumbled sideways. Andy vaguely heard the cheers of the other drunks. He kept his hands up in front of his face and moved closer to the idiot who'd pushed his buttons.

A few mugs banged on the tabletops, something that must have seemed like encouragement to the cheating drunk. He smiled and then all hell broke loose. Jim charged, staggering as he swung.

"If you ever come near my sister, I'll beat the living—" Andy didn't finish his threat.

Jim hit the floor belly-up with both feet in the air. Andy felt people grabbing him as he bent to pick Hensley up for another go. Two guys had his arms and pulled him back toward the bar.

"Break it up!"

Andy felt the veil drop and consciousness return. As the fog cleared, he wiped his brow with the back of his hand. "I'm fine," he said, shaking off the two guys holding him back. He made eye contact with the bartender. "I'm leaving. Sorry for the trouble."

The bartender nodded. A fellow near the exit opened the door and stood to the side as Andy left the scene, never once glancing back at Hensley. A short walk, and he climbed into his truck and slammed the door shut. He noticed the blood on his knuckles. "Well, that was stupid!"

He reached in the back seat for the bagel bag he'd tossed there yesterday morning and fished out a napkin. With any luck his mother wouldn't notice. His father wouldn't be pleased, but he wouldn't say anything. His mother didn't need the stress.

"Idiot! I'm an idiot."

Cleaned up as well as he could with leftover napkins and spit, Andy drove home. A vision of Jim Hensley tumbling backward and landing with a loud thud on the hardwood floors flashed through Andy's mind and brought the first smile to his face in hours.

"Couldn't have happened to a more deserving man."

12

"WHAT ARE YOU DOING? GET OFF THE BED!" Tess pushed at the man sitting on the edge of her cot. In the darkness of the supply room, she couldn't see who had come in. But she hated being awakened. It usually meant she was in trouble for something.

"Nice to see you too, Tess. Glad to know you aren't letting strange men into your bedroom."

Tess shot to an upright position. Her heart stopped. Could it really be him? She took a breath, and her heart began to race. "Hawk?"

"In the flesh. At least I hope so." The blue-eyed blond examined his arms and hands. "Everything seems to be attached."

Hawk stood as Tess reached for her sweatshirt on the floor. She pulled it down past her head, smoothed the thick cotton over her T-shirt, and swung her feet to the floor.

"What are you doing here? Did you follow me? I checked the boat. No one was onboard when I set off on this adventure," Tess growled at the man she'd been in love with for the last two years.

She didn't want to sound hopeful. She didn't want him to know just how glad she was to see him. Or how disappointed. She knew, even before he answered, that he hadn't come for her. Not really. Not like she wanted him to.

"This," Hawk said, waving his right hand around the room, "your little disappearing act, is not an adventure. This is another of your hare-brained schemes that is causing your parents more worry than either of them deserves. Even Andy is stressing out over this one." He peered down at Tess, bossy as ever. "Thank God you were in the first room I tried. Now we can go back to Cabin 8 and end your family's worry."

As her eyes adjusted to the dim light in the room, Tess glimpsed the anger evident on Hawk's face. His mouth was drawn tight, his ever-present smile nowhere to be seen, and his eyes were narrowed…at her.

Her backbone stiffened. "No one asked for your opinion. Go back where you came from."

"I intend to do just that, Tess, and I'm taking you with me."

"In your dreams, Hawk! I'm not going anywhere with you. So find a corner to sit in all day until you can travel your egotistical self back to

Martha's Vineyard."

Hawk shook his head. "Look, Tess, I didn't come here to fight with you."

Tess wanted to scream. Or cry. Her heart hurt. Hawk was too close and still too far away. "Well, you didn't come here for any other reason either."

"Yeah, Tess, I did. Andy found your note. The captain nearly had a heart attack. Andy wanted to come and bring you home, but I volunteered instead. I didn't follow you. I came so your brother wouldn't have to. Your parents don't need to be worrying about two of their kids lost in time."

She winced. Regret tugged at her heart. "Tell them I'm sorry. I don't want anyone freaking out about where I am. Tell them you saw me and that I'm fine. I just needed a break, okay? I'll be back in a few days. I want to see Rebecca, that's all."

"I'm not going back without you, Tess." Hawk squared his shoulders and stretched a little taller into his six-foot frame.

Maybe it was a natural reaction to her defiance, but Tess thought he might be trying to intimidate her with his size. Wouldn't work.

"Ah, well, yes, you are. 'Cause you're not staying here with me. This is my trip, and it's a solo journey."

Hawk stepped forward. "I promised your father I'd bring you home."

Tess stood and glared up at Hawk. "Guess you'd better un-promise him, then, because I'm not going back with you."

The tall blond began pacing in the small space. Tess watched with some amusement as he took two strides forward, spun on his heel, and took two strides back. "Why, Tess, do you always have to be so difficult?"

Her fists clenched. She wanted to hit something, preferably Hawk's thick skull. "Why is it, Mr. I'll-Do-Whatever-Your-Father-Wants, that I'm the one being difficult? Has it occurred to you, or anybody else for that matter, that I'm over eighteen and can do whatever I want, when I want, where I want?"

"Grow up, Tess. All you do is what you want. It's always all about you. Does it even cross your mind how your mother might be feeling right about now? What if you got stuck here? What if you can't go back? What if she loses her daughter—forever? Did you even think about her?"

The punch hit her in the gut as if Hawk had physically plowed his fist into her stomach. Tess reeled back and sat on the cot. She hadn't thought about the what-ifs...not exactly. The possibility of getting stuck here hadn't fully crossed her mind. She'd written the note so they'd know where she was, but she hadn't considered not going home. She'd told them she was coming home. She intended to go home.

Tess pinched the blanket between the fingers of her right hand and worked it back and forth. "I won't leave *Shenandoah*. I'll stay on the ship the whole time I'm here. Melissa and Rebecca remained here because they got off the boat. Rebecca told me she had to leave the ship and sleep on land. I won't. I promise. And as soon as I see Rebecca, I'll come home. Just go back tonight and tell my mom I'll be there soon."

"I'm not going to argue with—" Hawk paused at the first clang. He listened as the next two familiar clangs grew louder.

Hawk and Tess smiled at the same time. Tess felt her stomach flip.

The first mate turned his head toward the door. "Guess Old Bessie hasn't changed her morning noises in the last two centuries."

Tess nodded. "She woke me up yesterday. I thought I was dreaming. It's not our Bessie, but they are definitely related."

When Hawk focused back on Tess, most of the anger was gone, though determination still radiated from his eyes. "If the stove's on, the crew is up. I hear what you're saying, Tess, I do. I'm sure you miss Rebecca. But I have to bring you home tonight. I have to."

Tess shot to her feet. "You didn't hear me. So let me try this again, slowly. I. Am. Not. Going. Back. With. You. Is that clear? You don't own me, and you can't boss me around. You're not the first mate on this *Shenandoah*."

Tess sidestepped Hawk and hurried toward the door. Hawk slammed his hand against the upper right corner and closed off her escape. She felt the nearness of him right to her core. Every single time it was the same thing—her body melting and vibrating in some chemical/emotional reaction. She tried to exhale, but it came out like a whimper.

Hawk's expression softened. Clearly he had no idea what she was feeling. "Don't argue with me, Tess. This one time you are going to do what somebody else tells you to."

Every inch of her body went rigid at his words. Tess fumed. The man was as dumb as a box of rocks if he thought he could order her around. She shouted across the six inches between them, "Get out of my way, Hawk! You can't force me to do anything!"

Footsteps hurried down the hall. "Miss Roberts, are you okay?" Adam called. "Open the door or call out if you need assistance."

Hawk frowned. "You never cease to draw attention to yourself, do you, Tess?"

"Shut up, Hawk, and open the door or I'll scream."

Hawk shrugged. "Whatever, Tess. Have it your way for the moment. I'm sure Captain Reed will see things differently." He stepped back, and Tess swung the door open.

60

Adam eyed Tess like a grandfather, then caught sight of Hawk. A flash of concern went off in his eyes. "From the sound of your yelling, Miss Roberts, I presume you did not invite a friend to join you."

Tess moved her head from side to side, her eyes shifting to the floor. "I didn't invite him, and I want him to leave. Now!"

The cook stepped into the room to stand beside Tess. "Young man, you had best have an excellent explanation for the reason you are in a room alone with Miss Roberts."

Hawk walked three strides toward Adam and extended his right hand. "I do, sir. My name is Hawk, first mate on the *Shenandoah*, and I've come to bring Tess home. At the captain's request."

After a moment of hesitation and a glance in Tess's direction, Adam shook hands with Hawk. "Adam Greene."

"Nice to meet you, Adam. Is Captain Reed at the helm?"

"Aye, he's on deck, though I doubt your arrival will be welcome. Is there anyone else expected to arrive?"

"There better not be," Tess said.

"There isn't," Hawk assured them.

Adam motioned to the door. "Then now would be the optimal time to introduce you to the captain. Miss Roberts, after you."

13

ADAM WAS HOT ON TESS'S HEELS as she inched her way toward Ben. The deck felt more like a tiny cabin floor than the open expanse she loved. She knew the pending conversation wasn't going to go her way. Hawk would play her father as the captain, and Ben would nod. As her feet slugged along at a snail's pace and Adam kept bumping into her heels, Tess played the scene out in her mind.

There was simply no way she'd be able to convince Ben that her father had given her permission to be here. She could lie, but she wouldn't. Not because she hadn't—God knew she had told many creative stories to get out of trouble in the past—but this time Hawk would be right there to point out the truth. Knowing Hawk's resourcefulness and, let's face it, overcompetent nature, he'd probably smuggled her note across the time line and would wave it in Ben's face to prove she'd sneaked off in the night.

Fact is, she'd already confessed as much to Adam, so now she'd have to stand there and listen to Hawk tell Ben how irresponsible she was and how worried her parents were, and Ben would send her packing. She knew there was no way some bloke from the eighteenth century would grasp the "It's My Life" concept Bon Jovi sang about so perfectly.

In the fifty or so feet they'd walked from the companionway to the helm, Tess's heart had grown exceedingly heavy. She couldn't even look up at Ben when they stopped. She heard him groan, though.

"Adam, please, for the love of all that is holy, tell me I am imagining the man by your side."

Hawk tried to move past Tess, but Adam put out an arm to stop him. "My apologies, Captain. The man is real. Let me introduce Hawk, first mate on Tess's *Shenandoah*. I believe he also knew your wife."

Ben brought his right hand to his forehead and massaged his temples. "Tess, you look downtrodden this morning. Am I to surmise you are not pleased with Hawk's arrival?"

A dozen smart retorts emerged in Tess's mind. She desperately wanted to say Hawk was the rain on her parade, that his showing up to drag her home had ruined her grand adventure, and seeing him ticked her off to no end, but she knew Ben was already annoyed.

"I didn't invite him. I didn't tell him I was coming. And I wish he would leave."

A strong breeze rustled the sails, making a loud clapping. Captain Reed called orders to the crew, while Tess waited impatiently for his verdict.

Ben shifted his focus to Hawk, who looked all too eager to spout off his views on Tess's comments. "You have arrived uninvited on a privateer vessel in His Excellency's fleet. What brings you here, Hawk? I pray it is also not to visit my wife."

Hawk grinned, then glared at Tess. "I have come at Captain Roberts' request to fetch Tess and bring her home. Her mother is worried, and her father is, well, concerned, to say the least. Tess is a headstrong, selfish—"

Tess elbowed Hawk in the side. "No one asked for your opinion. I know all too well how you feel about me, and I don't need you polluting Ben's mind with your parochial views of my life."

The stern of the ship grew quiet. The crewmembers on deck turned to see who was yelling. Jonah made his way over to Ben's side. Adam wore a slight grin, and mischief lighted his eyes.

Hawk ignored Tess and moved closer to Ben. "Look, Tess shouldn't be here. I just want to stay until evening and then bring her home with me. I'm asking for your help, one captain for another."

Ben glanced at Adam, who nodded. Then the captain glanced between Tess and Hawk. "Can you tell me, Hawk, how Tess managed to travel here in the first place? It was my understanding from Rebecca that Captain Roberts was going to change your boards out the day after Rebecca returned to me. Am I to conclude this has not happened?"

Hawk looked Captain Reed in the eye. "With all due respect, sir, Captain Roberts had a day to change over and prepare for the last school sail of the summer. We hardly had time to get all the linens washed and replaced, never mind refurbish a cabin between Saturday afternoon and Sunday evening."

Tess thought Ben appeared exceedingly impatient. She was rather enjoying watching Hawk take some heat. Thunderclouds were moving in, and Tess couldn't help but consider what a bolt of lightning would do to Hawk. She rubbed her hands together in small satisfaction and waited for Ben's next question.

"And in the eleven months since? No work has been accomplished?"

"Eleven months? No kidding? Rebecca's been here eleven months?"

Ben nodded. "By my calculations, we are this thirteenth day of June 1776, and my wife arrived in July 1775."

Hawk shook his head. "Well, yeah, I guess eleven if it's June and she arrived in July. Only a month or so has passed back home." Hawk paused. "It was mid-September last night, and Rebecca left in August."

Tess wondered if Hawk was thinking what she was thinking: how much time, if any, had passed since she left home.

She pushed aside her troubled concerns and tuned back into Hawk's explanation. "We finished the kids' cruise, then started the breakdown on *Shenandoah*. The sails had to be cleaned and stowed for the winter, the gear and portables taken ashore. It's a process, believe me, especially when Captain Roberts oversees every inch of work to the minute detail."

The first roll of thunder extenuated the importance of Hawk's story. "When he suggested remodeling Cabin 8 to add an extra bunk, I thought he was crazy to squeeze another person into that space. Now I get it, but at the time I couldn't understand the rush. We ordered the new boards for Cabin 8, Rebecca's cabin, and the boards took a good two weeks to arrive."

Tess stepped between Ben and Hawk, softening her knees to adjust to the waves. "You would be impressed, Ben. They had to wait for the boards because Dad called around to see who had the quantity and quality of antique wood to replace and match the original boards in Cabin 8. My father has kept the look and feel of *Shenandoah* down to the smallest details." She took a breath and glanced around at the ship her family now cherished two hundred years later.

"If I could take a picture back to him and show him how closely he's matched the look and feel of the ship, he'd probably forgive me for taking off. Heck, he might even thank me." Tess swiveled toward Ben. "You don't happen to have a camera onboard, do you?"

Ben laughed. "Sorry, Tess, I do not. Though Rebecca has explained the advantages of owning such a device."

Hawk's laughter cut a caustic sting in Tess's heart. "Don't get your hopes up, Tess. Picture or no picture, your father is livid. You'll be lucky if he doesn't have you keelhauled." Hawk smiled, clearly enjoying the image and Tess's sudden discomfort.

Tess rolled her eyes at him. "Read my mind, Hawk, read my mind."

Ben cleared his throat. "Excuse me." He eyed Jonah, who had tiptoed over next to Adam. He glanced at Tess and then Hawk. "Obviously, you two are at odds. The situation before me has changed, Tess. I appreciate that you miss Rebecca and desire to visit with her. As I am returning from a mission and then on my way home for a brief visit, I saw no reason not to accommodate you. Now, however, a different issue has arisen."

No, no, no, Tess was screaming inside. She knew where Ben was going, and it wasn't good. And it was all Hawk's fault.

"Tess, I believe Hawk has come on behalf of your father. Therefore, I cannot allow you to stay here." Ben looked apologetic, but she was past apologies.

Tess stamped her foot. "Hawk is not the boss of me! He can't force me to go back with him. I won't!"

"Tess!" Hawk yelled.

Adam leaned over toward Jonah. "The clouds are getting darker. Reckon I was right about that storm, after all."

Jonah tipped his head back and took in the graying sky. "I believe you were right, Adam. If we were a day ahead, we might make it home tonight. With a fair wind, and my brother at the helm, we'll round Cape Ann and perchance see Boston by nightfall."

"I remain uncertain that Mother Nature is the only storm brewing." Adam clasped a hand on Jonah's shoulder and shifted their focus back to Ben and the two guests.

Tess wished Adam would keep talking so Ben and Hawk wouldn't.

The captain wore a mixed expression of amusement and frustration. The tension between Tess and Hawk was palpable. A wise man knew the tension had another origin. Ben was smart and tread cautiously. "I agree, Tess. This man cannot force you to return to your family."

Tess flashed a smug smile at Hawk.

"However…"

Her smile faded as soon as the word left Ben's lips.

"Hawk has come on behalf of your father. I cannot and will not ignore my responsibilities as captain to see to your safety and to respect a fellow captain's request. If the situation were reversed, I would wish for my daughter to return home immediately as well."

Tess felt like a cartoon character with a bright red face and steam coming out of its ears. She was furious—at Hawk, at Ben, at the world, and at God, who without a doubt was not helping her or even cutting her some slack. "So you're kicking me off the ship, is that it? I should start swimming for shore now?"

Ben almost chuckled. "No, Tess, I would never throw you overboard. Nor will I allow Hawk to forcefully remove you from my ship. I am, however, going to respectfully ask you to depart with Hawk this evening. You are Rebecca's dearest friend. She will be disappointed she did not have a chance to visit with you. However, I would be doing her and you a disservice if I did not do what I think is best for everyone. Do you understand my position?"

Tess dug her toes into the wooden deck. She stared at the boards beneath her and wished she could disappear between the cracks and float off into space where no one would tell her what to do. She knew Ben was doing his job, but it wasn't fair. She didn't want to go home yet. She hadn't even gotten to see Rebecca. She hadn't even had an adventure at all. One day on the *Shenandoah* was not her idea of a vacation. Hawk had ruined everything.

She felt four pairs of eyes waiting for her response. The cracks between the floorboards shrank from view as she lifted her face to Ben.

Tess barely choked out the words, "I get it." She spun on her heels and came face to face with Hawk. "Are you happy now? When will you get tired of trashing my dreams?" With both hands she shoved him out of her way and ran toward the bow.

"Tess, wait," Hawk called.

*

Adam stepped in front of Hawk. "Let her be, young man. It is none of my business, but there seems to be more between the two of you than her father's request to bring her home." Adam gazed past Hawk to Ben and lifted a brow at the captain.

Ben nodded in return and smiled. He noted that Hawk's interest was centered on Tess climbing on and over the windlass and cap rail to get onto the bowsprit.

"Take an old man's advice and leave her be," Adam advised Hawk. "For reasons I do not know, and I suspect you are oblivious to as well, Tess chose to visit her friend. She knew there were risks involved, yet she took those risks to be here. Clearly she had her reasons. Now she must return home, she has not spent time with Rebecca, and you appear to be the last person she wanted to see this morning." Adam gave Hawk a long look. "The young lady deserves some time to herself. Would you not agree, Captain?"

"Aye, Adam. Tess is not pleased with any of us at the moment. Her mood yesterday was much more enjoyable," Ben said.

Jonah winked at Ben. "I will go cheer her up."

"No, Jonah. You too shall leave Tess alone." Adam's tone carried an edge of finality to it. "I could use your assistance in the galley. The crew will want breakfast, and I have nothing prepared."

Jonah and Adam walked away from the captain and first mate. A weak ray of sun escaped through the gray clouds. Small white caps were forming on the crest of the waves. Tess sat on the bowsprit in silence.

Ben motioned for Hawk to join him at the helm. Hawk peeked over his shoulder toward the bow before following Ben.

The captain waited until he had his attention. "A storm is moving in. We had cloudy skies yesterday, but today promises to yield foul weather. We will sail after breakfast. Perhaps you would like to work in the crew, take your mind off Tess?"

"My mind isn't on Tess," Hawk snapped back a little too quickly.

Ben grinned. "I stood in your shoes once, not too long ago."

Hawk gave Ben a blank stare. "I don't know what you're talking about."

Ben dropped the topic of romance, or lack thereof. He knew Hawk had feelings for Tess, and he'd been in that same denial with Rebecca. "I remember when Rebecca arrived. She seemed fragile and lost, yet strong and capable at the same time. Though they are quite different, Tess reminds me of Rebecca."

Hawk laughed, sharp and short. "Tess? Fragile? You don't have a clue. Tess hasn't had a fragile moment in her entire life. If you knew what she did for fun, you'd give up that idea right quick. She's reckless and pigheaded and fearless. No one would ever call Tess soft. Look at her now, sitting out there as if the waves aren't rocking the boat."

Ben glanced at Tess. A shaft of sunlight poked through an ominous thunderhead and illuminated Tess's solitude on the bowsprit. Her head was hung. He could not tell if she was crying, but she was sad and hurting. The waves were picking up, but his wife's best friend was in no physical danger. And Hawk was showing his hand, whether he admitted to his feelings or not. "As you said, I do not know her well, but she appears fragile to me. I wish Rebecca were here. I think Tess needs a friend."

Both men stood in silence and contemplated the woman at the other end of the boat. Ben guessed Hawk had decided long ago not to have feelings for the captain's daughter. Rightly so, but he figured Hawk had lost the battle somewhere along the way. As for Tess, her heart was on her sleeve. Ben decided to tread lightly between the two. He studied Hawk out of the corner of his eye.

The tall blond stood pensively, his thoughts guarded, his expression absorbed and worried. His eyes were narrowed and far away, beyond where Tess sat. Ben wondered if the first mate could truly see the woman before him.

Time would tell. For the moment, breakfast would be served and the ship would need to be readied for the coming weather. And soon he would have to ask Tess to go below deck for her own safety.

14

ANDY FLIPPED BACK THE COVERS, swung his long legs over the side of the bed, and groped around the floor for his phone. With his modern-day flashlight substitute in hand, he reached for his clock, an old-fashioned analog with a round face and absolutely no glare from red digital lights. With no desire to focus on the tiny numbers on his phone screen, he pushed the center button on his cell and aimed the green light to illuminate the clock face: 5:16 a.m.

Time to call Hawk. Time to find out if the first mate was still onboard *Shenandoah* and would answer his phone, or if the call would go to voicemail because Hawk was gone, too.

One ring. Two rings. Three rings. Four rings. No Hawk. Andy hung up and dialed again, just in case Hawk was sleeping and didn't hear the cell. Four rings later, the call went to voicemail.

Andy left a message. "Hawk, it's Drew. If, by any chance, you're sleeping and not doing the Jules Verne thing, give me a call when you get this."

Andy punched the off key and tossed the phone onto his pillow. He yawned and stretched and stood to make his bed. Pulling the white sheet back up, he folded the top over and tucked it all in under his mattress. He plumped the pillow and laid the cell on his navy comforter as he lifted the right corner and tugged the whole down mess back into place. The cell didn't make a sound, not a ring, not a beep, not a call, not a text. He knew, with part relief, part dread, that Hawk wasn't going to call him back, at least not today.

Reason number eighty-six why he hadn't slept well. He hadn't lost any sleep over his fight with Jim Hensley the night before, and his body felt no worse for the wear, but today his heart felt heavy, and he dreaded going down to breakfast. He simply didn't want to face his parents, especially his mom, and any questions they might have about Tess and Hawk.

One valuable trick he'd learned in high school from his older brothers was the use of his mother's rose trellis on the south side of the house. Last night he'd climbed up and slid as quietly as he could across the roof before prying open his window with a screwdriver. Two steps onto his floor and he sunk into bed. He hadn't even used the bathroom…didn't want to risk his mom knocking on his door ten minutes later. She'd never be any wiser he'd taken the Mother Nature route instead.

Now, however, he knew she'd be up in half an hour, and he couldn't leave before he talked to them. Well, he could, but his father hadn't raised him to slink away from a battle—physical or emotional. He rubbed the palms of his hands over his eyes, momentarily easing the throbbing behind his thick skull.

If only he had listened to Tess harder or paid closer attention to how she was feeling…. He could have gone with her two nights ago when she said she was going to the beach, insisted on going even, and then she wouldn't be missing now.

Tess had been gone for at least twenty-four hours, probably more like thirty. Hawk had been gone at least six, depending on when he'd fallen asleep in the cabin. He didn't even know if Hawk had found Tess or where they both were. And there was nothing he could do about any of it.

Andy left his phone on the bed and walked down to his bathroom. He needed a shower, a steady stream of hot water to burn away the dread and pain building inside him.

Fifteen minutes later, feeling clean and slightly more alive than before, Andy donned a pair of jeans and a rugby shirt, grabbed his cell phone, and headed downstairs. He heard the legs of a chair scrape across the floor. At least one of his parents was up early. He slowed his pace, willing his cell phone to ring and for Hawk to say he'd snatched Tess, jumped into the time machine— ha! ha!—and they were already home.

As he neared the kitchen, he heard his parents talking. Their voices were hushed, lower than the normal morning conversation. And he didn't smell food. His mother wasn't cooking. He paused in the hall, wishing the next three steps would bring a plate of pancakes and his sister at the table, drowning the delectable disks in way too much maple syrup.

When he reached the kitchen doorway, his heart filled. His parents were sitting side by side, his dad's large hands covering his mom's smaller ones, and they were praying. His mom was quoting one of her favorite psalms, number forty-six. Andy had heard it many times in his life, but never before had it seemed so fitting.

His dad squeezed her hands as she finished before he added on Philippians 4:6, the verse his mom had cross-stitched and hung in his dad's cabin on the *Shenandoah:* "Do not be anxious about anything, but in every situation, by prayer and petition, with thanksgiving, present your requests to God."

His mom looked up and smiled at Andy. "Come join us."

He walked over, hugged them both, and then sat down on the rustic pine chair to his mom's right.

She reached for his hand. "Heavenly Father, You have told us that where two or more are gathered in Your name, You are here with us. Lord, please watch over and protect Tess. Guide Hawk and keep him safe. And please, Lord, bring them both home in one piece. Amen."

"Thank You, Lord. Amen," his dad said.

All Andy could think to say was a measly, "Um, amen." He wanted to say more, he felt more, but the words failed him. He'd attended church at Christmas and Easter and maybe once during the summer, basically when his father gave him a look that said no more excuses, but he wasn't into it anymore. He wasn't as bad as Tess, questioning God's presence and all, but he didn't feel the fire he'd felt when he was thirteen and had just given his life to Christ. Seventeen years later, he'd forgotten what it was like to drop to his knees or lift his hands.

His mom must have sensed his inner turmoil. She patted his hand. "It's okay, Andy. He knows your thoughts. He hears your unspoken words."

Andy nodded.

"Tess is well cared for. I trust she will be home. I don't know when or how, but I know God is in control."

"How, Mom? How do you know that?"

Her eyes softened. "I've raised four children and sent a husband off to sea over a hundred times. I have prayed over and for all of you. Through every trial, every storm, God has been faithful. I trust Him now."

Captain Roberts leaned over and kissed his wife of forty-two years softly on the mouth. "She is a tower of strength, son. Anyone who said women were the weaker sex hasn't had a woman praying for him."

They all laughed, and his mom rose to make breakfast.

His dad turned toward him, nodding at Andy's cell phone. "I take it Hawk did not answer his phone?"

"No, he didn't."

"Let's hope he's found Tess, and he can convince your headstrong sister to come home."

His mom cracked a dozen eggs and beat them until they were light and fluffy. She turned on the gas stove and melted a wedge of butter into the pan. Andy watched her movements, precise and thoughtful. He knew she was thinking about Tess, but he could tell she wasn't worried. He had underestimated her.

"Can I have cheese in my eggs, please, Mom?"

She glanced over after she poured the eggs into the pan. "Andy, in thirty

70

years, have I ever served you scrambled eggs without cheddar cheese in them?"

He knew she was making a joke, trying to ease his concerns. He didn't disappoint her. "Well, Mom, I do remember that one time a few years ago when you were so mad that I left Melody Crawford at the beach without a ride home that the next morning you refused to cook me any breakfast, never mind put cheese in my eggs."

"Hmmmph," she said, moving the spatula through the eggs. "Don't you forget it."

Andy grinned at his dad. "I won't. But when Tess gets back, could you serve her pancakes without any maple syrup or butter? For a month? Maybe two? I'm just saying."

15

ANDY DROVE INTO TOWN feeling lighter than he had in the last forty-eight hours. Although he was headed to the dock and would soon motor out to the *Shenandoah* to confirm that Hawk had vanished in the night, the morning with his parents had calmed him.

He felt their peace, a peace he had grown to envy as an adult. In his teens, he'd been pretty sold out on church and youth group. Jesus, God, and the whole church thing had worn thin in college. None of his friends at school believed, or if they had, they hadn't shared it with him. Partying and sports and girls had been much more exciting.

Over the last few years, Andy had felt an emptiness he couldn't explain. He still enjoyed a good time, though he rarely drank more than two beers. And, though rumors might say otherwise, he'd discovered dating and casual sex weren't all the movies and magazines and books made them out to be. He went out with a lot of girls—Lord knew Tess never let up on counting how many—but that's all he did these days. Date.

"Maybe I'm getting old," Andy mused as he voiced the thought that had been creeping around inside his head all summer long. He knew the truth, even if he wasn't ready to admit it to anyone. He was ready to settle down, more than ready. He wanted what his parents had. Their marriage. Their kind of family life. And maybe their faith.

As he drove into the tall ship parking area, an image of Allyson Flanders came into focus. Andy couldn't help but smile. She had captivated him the other night...well, all summer long if he was going for honesty. Allyson was different. She didn't flirt with her gorgeous body. She flirted with her mind. And, for the first time in his life, Andy admired a woman for her values and intelligence over her legs and other physical features.

He smacked his hand on the steering wheel of the truck. "Not now. Fantasy Land will have to wait."

Andy stepped out of the truck, tossed his keys into the cup holder, and headed toward the dock.

"Running late today, hey, Drew?" Tim McCourt called from the coffee shop across the street. "Guess you're all glad the season's winding down."

"Still got a few weekend sails and a bit of work to do on *Shenny*. Catch ya later, Tim." Andy knew he'd been short, but he wanted to get on the water. He all but jogged to the end of the dock.

The little skiff was gone, which was only one more sign that Hawk hadn't rowed back to shore this morning. He climbed down the ladder and dropped into the eight-passenger motor dory. The engine started on the first pull, and Andy sat down and maneuvered through the harbor, past the *Lady Katherine* on her mooring ball and beyond to the *Shenandoah*.

As Andy motored around *Shenandoah*'s sleek, black hull, he caught sight of the little skiff tied off on the mooring ball. Hawk must have shimmied up the chains, just as they assumed Tess had. Andy pulled up next to the smaller skiff. "Might as well join the club," he mumbled and began to climb the chains.

Once on board, Andy wasted no time going below deck. He turned around at the companionway, took two steps backward down the ladder, pushed off, skipping the last four rungs, and then dropped to the floor. In less than a minute he reached the door to Cabin 8.

Without hesitation, he opened the door. Just as he thought, the bunk was empty. "Hawk?" he called out, not expecting a response. "Hawk," he shouted.

Nothing.

Andy walked the length of the ship fore and aft, below and up on deck. He searched the crew's quarters and his father's cabin. He found Hawk's cell phone on his father's desk, on top of the ship's log. The meaning wasn't lost on Andy. There would be no record of this trip. Hawk was not onboard.

He stood at the helm, looking out over the water toward town. The air was warm, the perfect late-summer day. There were still plenty of boats in the water, the ferry was still transporting tourists to and from the Island every day, and all the shops were still open.

Somewhere in town, Allyson was either walking down the street or already at work. She would be smiling at friends and strangers, and right now he could use one of her smiles. He wouldn't tell her about Tess or Hawk, he wouldn't tell her about Cabin 8 and the bizarre time machine on his father's ship, and there was no way he'd tell her he needed one of her smiles. He'd just stop in, say hello, allow the warmth of her smile to reach his bones, and then he'd go home and tell his parents Hawk was off to Neverland too. And maybe a minute with Allyson would make the rest of the day a whole lot better.

The thought boosted Andy's spirit. He rested both hands on the cap rail and lowered his head. "Okay, God, they're in Your hands. I'm going to trust You. I'm going to believe that You will bring them both home safely."

Andy straightened and walked over to the bosun box. He extracted an orange oil rag and went back down to Cabin 8. He took Hawk's cell phone out of his pocket and put it on top of the orange rag in the middle of the floor. No way Hawk would miss it when he returned.

With a roll of his shoulders, Andy shifted his thoughts back to Allyson. He climbed up the companionway and walked toward the bow. As he pictured Allyson, a smile emerged on his face. He slid down the chains and hopped into the boat, the weight of the world no longer on his shoulders.

16

TESS SAT ON THE COT AND CURSED THE WEATHER. She wanted to be out in the sun, her face to the breeze, her hair flying out behind her as *Shenandoah* crested the waves. Instead, the seas were getting rougher by the hour, the sky was dark, and Ben had told her to stay put until the ship was secured. One more man who didn't think she could lift cargo or tie secure knots as well as the men in his crew. She tapped her left foot in annoyance and attempted to picture where they were on her father's antique colonial maps.

Just before Ben had banished her to below deck, he'd pointed out the Twin Lights as they went around Thacher Island. "Are you familiar with the Twin Lighthouses, Tess?"

"Yes, we've sailed by them numerous times."

Ben nodded. "They have been dark for almost a year. July last, three militia companies sailed to Thacher Island and shattered the lighthouses' glass and lamps and commandeered all the oil. They brought Captain Kirkwood, the lighthouse keeper who had worked the lights since they were built in 1771, to shore and, alas, ordered him gone. A bittersweet victory for us, as the lights were British built and operated, yet they served a mighty useful purpose for those of us at sea."

Oh, how Tess knew those facts about the beacons once nicknamed "Ann's Eyes." Her father had taught them all from childhood that a sailor should know every lighthouse and its signal pattern along every route they would ever take. And she knew the lights marked the Londoner, a partially submerged reef only half a mile offshore and a hazard for ships.

With some satisfaction, Tess elaborated on the history for Ben. "They fixed them shortly after the Revolution and then, about a hundred years later, rebuilt them. Only one of the Twin Lights operates today, ah, in the twenty-first century, but there are now four other lighthouses along Cape Ann." She could have gone on and told Ben that visitors to Thacher Island had to sign up weeks in advance to take a tour of the lighthouses, but he didn't appear the least bit interested.

She changed the topic to Gloucester Harbor. "Three of the lighthouses built after the Revolution are in Gloucester Harbor. There are now two right at the entrance, less than half a mile apart. There's another one farther in the harbor on Ten Pound Island. As weird as this is going to sound, a little over a hundred years from now, in the summer of 1880, a famous American painter will pay the lighthouse keeper to stay at Ten Pound Light. Winslow Homer will paint a ton of seascapes from the harbor, and they'll sell for over $100,000 each in the twenty-first century. A few have sold for over a million dollars."

Ben had taken in the information, but other than a look of shock when she mentioned the selling prices of the paintings, he hadn't asked any questions. Tess wondered how he could stand to have a chance to know the future and not ask. Right now, sitting in the bunk, feeling the waves rock the ship, she would love to know where they were, where they were going, and what was going to happen to her.

She tried to remember the coordinates of the shoals and ledges along the northern coastline years ago. Every sailor for centuries knew Cape Ann could be treacherous, despite the deep water. The times had definitely made sailing easier. Buoys marked most of the bigger rocks and hazards where Tess sailed at home, and there was extensive navigational equipment available, even on the smallest of ships. Ben wouldn't have that luxury.

The wind lashed the rain against the ship, pounding the exterior of Tess's cabin like a drum. A loud drum. She was beyond tired of being ordered below deck. She listened to the thunder and wondered if lightening was illuminating the late afternoon sky. Her cabin was nearly dark. The rain must be pouring down from the heavens. She slid back against the wall as the ship's bow rose on a building crest. She grabbed the edge of the cot and prepared for the plummet. *Shenandoah* hit hard at the bottom of the wave. The impact rocked Tess smack into the wall, her arms and feet in the air.

They had passed the dark lighthouses about an hour ago and were still at full sail. Tess couldn't gauge how much progress the ship was making in the rough water. Many sailors and captains relished heavy weather. The ship often sailed faster, it was definitely more exciting, and the crew got an opportunity to "show their stuff" and work as a team.

Perhaps they could make it into Gloucester Harbor and ride out the storm. Even Brace Cove would provide some shelter if they couldn't make it around the bend. The trick would be getting into the Cove during the storm and in the dark of night. The entrance was deep enough, but narrow, and the rocks to the left and right could be a huge problem if a wave tossed them off course for even a minute.

Tess felt the bow rise again. This time she pressed herself against the wall and waited for the fall. When the ship leveled out, she reached her hand out to steady herself and stood. She needed to get up on deck. If they were in for a nor'easter, she wasn't about to ride it out being slammed around a small cabin until her stomach felt like it wanted to heave all its contents. She looked at the pail Jonah had placed in the corner and decided there was no way she was going to sit there long enough to need it.

Her jeans and sweatshirt were folded at the head of the cot. Hawk had appreciated her donning a dress after breakfast, but it took her only a split second to decide to change out of Rebecca's dress. It took another ten minutes to finagle the row of buttons down the back and free herself from the yards of material. With gratitude to whoever had left a jacket hanging on the peg, probably Jonah, Tess slipped into the oilskin and opened the door to freedom.

She moved slowly down the passageway, walking with her legs wide and her hands on a wall to stabilize the rocking. Once she got a grip on the ladder rungs, she felt 100 percent better. Being in the hole was for the rats, as far as Tess was concerned. She climbed carefully up the companionway, pushed open the hatch, and poked her head out. Hawk was fifteen feet away with his back to her, tying off some rigging.

She pulled herself out of the hatch, slid back the lid, and leaned against the cook's doghouse. The five-by-eight-by-six-foot mini-cabin/wooden tent was the closest solid wall on deck. She knew better than to slide open a door and sit in the cook's or the first mate's private quarters. Private meant exactly that: private. The little doghouses weren't much to look at, but they were a place of honor for the man who earned one.

Frigid, gray-black water slapped at the sides of the boat, soaking the crew near the cap rail. Hawk was drenched from head to toe. He'd removed his sweater, and the back of his white cotton shirt clung to his skin, outlining his well-muscled back and sending shivers of an altogether unwanted kind down Tess's spine. She averted her eyes and peered under the boom to search the stern for Ben.

The waves were still reasonable, though they had felt much worse below deck. Tess knew that was common. Once you could see a storm, it hardly ever felt as bad as it did in a bunk. The temperature had dropped about 10 degrees in the last hour. She knew it was June after Ben's comment about Rebecca being here for ten months, but it felt more like late March. She spotted Ben standing at the helm, holding the wheel in two hands, calling out orders to the crewmembers working near him.

The winds weren't yet at gale force, but she felt the storm building. They had to be near a harbor on the windward shore. They just had to be. She wanted to ask Ben but didn't dare move. Hawk was bound to notice her sooner or later, but the longer she went without one of his piercing, condescending glares, the better.

As if he read her mind, Hawk stood, turned, and locked eyes on her.

She thought he swore under his breath. He wasn't one to use language, even back home, so she had to be wrong. She'd heard her father comment on what he called "Hawk's maturity" a number of times. It was one of the many reasons he respected Hawk so much. But looking at him now, with his eyes boring holes in her head and his mouth drawn into a thin, taut line, she guessed his thoughts weren't something her father would want to know or hear.

He resembled a steamroller heading toward her, ready to flatten her in two seconds or less. Unfortunately, the rain wasn't hard enough to drown out his yelling as he strode the five steps between them. "Don't you ever listen, Tess? This isn't some school cruise. See the swells? This is real, not some stunt you get to pull off. Do you think you could get that through your stubborn head?"

Fury rose inside Tess. The storm wasn't that bad, at least not yet, and she did know what she was doing, not that Hawk would ever see or admit that. "I am perfectly capable of working on this ship in any kind of weather. When are you going to get that through your thick skull?"

Hawk's strong, calloused hand grabbed her wrist. "I'm taking you below."

Tess yanked her arm back and slid sideways along the doghouse wall. Two seconds later, a wave slammed the ship. Hawk, already off balance from her tug, careened into Tess. His body covered hers and pressed her against the wall. He quickly threw both his hands on either side of her shoulders and pushed himself six inches away from her as *Shenandoah* rode the surge.

The distance wasn't far enough. Despite the wind and rain, Tess could feel his breath on her skin. Heat spread across her face and down her neck. Her stomach flipped for the first time that day, and she knew it wasn't the storm.

Her heart pounded. She hadn't been this close to Hawk since the first day they'd met. Face to face, body to body, she couldn't breathe. Though oxygen was important, she'd skip inhaling to wrap her arms around him and feel the muscles in his back tense under her fingers. What she most wanted, though, was to brush the damp hair out of his eyes.

The last notion was her undoing. Her gaze followed the path of her thoughts and connected with his brooding blue eyes. Her breath caught in her throat. She hoped like crazy that he couldn't read her mind. She wished even more that he would lean in and kiss her.

Seconds passed. Neither spoke a word. Neither moved.

Tess resisted every urge to touch him. Her breath was shallow. Her body temperature was rising. What was Hawk thinking? Tess wanted to search his face for answers, but she couldn't break away from his stare.

"Hawk." A voice pierced the howling wind. "Hawk!"

Tess turned her head.

"Hawk!" Adam was standing ten feet away with an urgent look on his weathered face.

Hawk shook and cleared his head, then stepped back from Tess.

Adam didn't miss a thing. He winked at Tess before addressing her first mate. "We need to shorten the sails. We've got to reach Gloucester. Ben thinks we can get there in less than hour. We might slip into Brace Cove if the seas are forgiving. If the waters are too rough to find the channel, we shall head around the point and into Gloucester Harbor. Either one will provide protection to ride out the storm."

Tess moved a few feet toward Adam, keeping her right hand on the doghouse wall. "I can help reef the topsails and the outer jib. I can work the rigging."

Hawk spun on his heel. "You're going below. Now!"

Tess shook her finger at Hawk. "Don't tell me what to do. I'm just as capable as any man here, and you know it. I've sailed on the *Shenandoah* many times, more than you have."

Tess turned pleading eyes toward Adam. Salt water sloshed across the deck, hosing down her feet once again. Every man topside was soaked, even those with oilskins. There was no point trying to stay dry when there was work to be done. And she could man the lines and lower the sail, by herself if she had to. Her father had bragged many times that they never reefed, but that wasn't completely true. Tess knew there had been school trips when *Shenandoah* had been caught in heavy wind and her father had ordered the sails reefed, or lowered, for the safety of the students.

Adam must have seen the determination, and hopefully knowledge, in her eyes. He nodded at her briefly and faced Hawk. Over the gusting wind he asked, "Can she reef the sail?"

Hawk stammered, "Well, of course. She's a Roberts. I never said she couldn't. That isn't the point. I don't care if she can lower the sail, fire the cannons, and man the helm all at the same time. She needs to be someplace safe where I don't have to keep an eye on her. My job is to bring her home to her family. In one piece."

Tess clenched her fingers together and made a fist. "Keep an eye on me? Ha! How about you leave me alone? I've managed to sail every ship I've captained just fine without you. And I know her. I've been out in every kind of weather on *Shenny* with my father."

Hawk met her steely look with a belittling smirk. "Last time I checked, you've never worked as crew on or captained the *Shenandoah*. Now isn't the time to start."

The painful truth of his words shot through Tess and tore her heart. With practiced skill, she swallowed the bitter facts and put on a poker face. Hawk knew better than anyone that she'd wanted to crew for her father for years, but if he was looking for a reaction, to see if his bullet had hit its target, Tess wasn't going to give him the satisfaction.

Glancing down at her wrist, she rolled the elastic band over her hand and held it between her teeth. With both hands she gathered her soaked tendrils into a ponytail and tied it off. She turned toward Adam and then glanced over her shoulder at Hawk. "Who are you to tell me what I can and can't do?"

Tess took a step toward Adam, her hands on her hips. She felt the ship rise once again. Widening her stance, she bent her knees to absorb the motion of the rolling ship. "Show me how and where I can help. *Shenandoah* is long and stable. Hawk knows as well as I do that she will not capsize in these waves. We might get tossed about, but the captain's concerns are the rocks, the reefs, and shoals. We need all capable hands on deck, and mine are as capable as his." Tess pointed at Hawk as she spoke the last sentence.

Adam whistled high and shrill. Tess and Hawk straightened as though they were reporting for naval duty. "You both have much to learn. Lesson one begins now. Teamwork is vital to the survival of a vessel in a storm—any kind of storm. Now you will work together to furl the topsails and the outer jib."

Hawk appeared ready to launch into one of his many thoughts on why Tess shouldn't be on the *Shenandoah*...this one or her father's. "Adam, I just don't think—"

"Hawk, time is of the essence. Consider the lesson an order, young man, and perform the job well."

Tess smiled from ear to ear. Hawk scowled at her. Adam gave them both a look that said they had better put aside their differences and crew the ship. Then he headed toward the bow.

Hawk cocked his head to the left. "Follow me. And hang onto the cap rail."

Tess gritted her teeth. Any sarcastic response would only tick him off more. And she was working as part of the crew now. Who cared what Hawk did or said?

They inched their way down toward the foremast. Tess kept one hand on the railing because she wanted to, not because Hawk had ordered her to. She noticed six men working the lower brace and another four on the sheets. She hoped no one was up in the rigging but didn't waste time checking.

As they went by the third cannon, a wave broadsided the ship. Tess held fast to the rail as the icy cold sea showered her. She spit out a mouthful of salty water. "Great!" she yelled.

Hawk glanced over his shoulder and smirked. Tess didn't care. Let him laugh. She watched the salt water slide through the scuppers and back out to sea. A storm was raging, and she was on deck. She was about to reef the sails.

At last she was on the *Shenandoah* as an official member of the crew. Wiping off the water with the back of her forearm, she continued toward the bow with a smile, the likes of which she hadn't known in months.

17

WIND AND RAIN LASHED THE SAILS, SHIP, AND MEN. In the blackness, Tess tried to guesstimate the course they were on coming into the harbor.

"Keep your eyes starboard, men," Captain Benjamin Reed called out.

"Starboard" was then relayed down both sides of the ship as the wind swallowed all but muffled human sound.

Tess trusted Ben. He'd gotten them this far, and the ship had certainly survived for her father to buy it over two hundred years later. Yet, for a moment, an inkling of doubt flew through her mind. *What if I've changed history by coming here? What if Ben doesn't know Gloucester? What if we run aground on Dog Bar or Round Rock and rip open the hull?*

Tess wiped her hand across her dripping eyelashes, trying to clear her vision and her mind. Ben must surely know this route. She'd bet on it. Still, she offered up a quick prayer and watched carefully as he commanded the skilled crew around Webber Rock and the southern point of Gloucester Harbor under reduced sails. Tess knew if they were sailing this same pass in her day, the Eastern Point Light Station, the 2,250-foot breakwater in front of the lighthouse and Breakwater Light would be to the starboard, guiding them safely past Dog Bar Reef and its buoy and into the harbor.

Lightning flashes lit the western shore. Tess breathed a sigh of relief. The distance felt right. They had attempted one pass into Brace Cove after the sails had been reefed. But the waves had been too rough, and Ben had determined the risk of crashing into a rock wasn't worth another attempt. With the winds howling through the rigging, the crew, including Tess, had followed Ben's orders and brought *Shenandoah* around Cape Ann.

The rain was coming down in a steady wall of water. Visibility was next to nothing. A lighthouse would be a godsend, but none would be built that night or for years to come. Flashes of lightning helped guide the crew far enough westward of Dog Bar and Round Rock Shoal.

"Captain!" The first mate, William Barton, called out, moving quickly from bow to stern. Blue streaks lit up the dark sky, and Tess caught sight of the cause of the concern in Will's voice. Up ahead, closer to Ten Pound Island, she could barely make out the outline of at least one other anchored ship. For certain there were many family boats tied up along the shore and docks, but

Tess knew without being told that the ship in front of them had entered the harbor for the same reasons as *Shenandoah* had—to ride out the storm. Without a flag flying, and in the midst of the storm, no one could determine if they were Patriot or redcoats.

Adam stood to Tess's right, beside Ben, as the anchor lowered. The cook pointed in the direction of the other boat. Lightning flashed, illuminating the darkness for another split second. Tess saw then what Adam had probably been looking for: a second ship. Off the port side of *Shenandoah* were two ships anchored within yards of each other, clearly friendly with one another. The question at hand was whether they were friend or foe to the *Shenandoah*.

Gloucester had always been a Patriot port. The only skirmish Tess could remember was in August of 1775 when the HMS *Falcon* attacked a few schooners in the harbor. The townspeople rallied and sent the *Falcon* sailing back to England. She couldn't remember any battles in or around Gloucester in June of 1776. But Captain Reed didn't know what Tess knew, and there was no telling how much Hawk knew.

Ben ran a hand roughly through his dripping wet hair. Tingles of fear crept down her back. *Shenandoah* was safe, structurally at least, sheltered in the inlet. But Ben didn't look relaxed, not by a long shot.

"We have no choice, Captain. The Good Lord will keep us safe," Adam said.

Ben shook his head. His narrowed gaze and the lines on his forehead revealed his worry, and the storm had nothing to do with it. "There will be no rest tonight, Adam. The crew can sleep in shifts of eight for two hours. The others shall remain on anchor watch. Until we discover the allegiance of the two vessels, we shall be on guard and at the ready."

Hearing his words, Tess felt her first real moment of fear. Rough seas and thunderstorms had never unnerved her. Guns, however, were a different matter. Ben was prepared to fight. More than prepared, he seemed to expect it, and he wanted the men ready to attack or defend. She tried to see through the blurring windswept rain. Without two lanterns each at the bow, stern and midship, she wouldn't be able to spot Ben and Adam, and they were standing right next to her.

"I will give your orders to William. He can select the first eight to go below," Adam said. As if on cue, eight bells signaled the end of the second dogwatch, or twenty hundred hours.

A strong wind whipped Tess's ponytail into her eyes, causing her to stumble into Ben. He grabbed her shoulders and helped her stand. "Are you stable, Miss Roberts?"

Tess grinned while pulling her hair out of the string and braiding it. "Hawk wouldn't say so, but I'm fine. Wasn't expecting to be slapped in the face. Where is Hawk, by the way?"

Ben pointed toward the bow. Tess followed his gaze, able to see about six feet, maybe seven, through the haze of rain, and Hawk wasn't that close. "He was lowering the anchor with Jonah and the men. I suspect he shall be about to find you soon."

Tess whirled around toward Ben. He wore a smile, which ticked her off big time. Even in the current danger, her priorities were her priorities. Hawk was an annoyance and nothing more. That's what she wanted everyone to believe, herself included. "I wasn't looking for him, not like I wanted to see him or anything. I just wanted to know where he was so I could avoid him and whatever inclination he would have to boss me around."

Ben chuckled. "Of course."

The icy rain did little to cool the flush creeping up Tess's neck.

Men can be so utterly annoying. Even when they're right.

Aloud, she said, "The seas are calmer here in the harbor. I think I'll go below deck, if that's okay with you, Ben."

The captain nodded. "Yes, I believe that would be wise, Miss Roberts. You may rest, if you can, until morning."

"It's only eight o'clock, but it's been a long day. I'm a sound sleeper onboard. Feel free to wake me if you need help." Tess moved cautiously across the slick deck. The ship rolled slightly in a steady rhythm she had grown accustomed to while standing. She reached the companionway, slid back the hatch, and placed her hands on either side of the ladder.

"Miss Roberts," Ben called out, "do you know how to fire a weapon?"

A sharp trail of fear threaded down Tess's spine and back around to her heart. She was glad Ben couldn't see her through the downpour. "Yes, I can. My father taught us all to shoot. He said if we sailed, we should be able to fire a rifle as well as a flare gun."

Ben said nothing for a moment. Tess waited to descend the stairs, inhaling a long slow breath.

"Good," was his matter-of-fact reply.

Tess moved slowly down the companionway, one rung, then another until she reached the bottom. Only then did she exhale.

18

THE DAY WAS FINALLY OVER. Monotonous paperwork had filled the daylight hours. Heading to the Y for an hour and a half had allowed Andy to do something both productive and physical. He grabbed a white towel one of the trainers had placed in a stack on the counter. When he had mopped the sweat from his brow, he tossed the damp rag into the basket on the floor and downed the rest of his Gatorade.

"You chasing demons, or they chasing you?"

Andy pivoted to find Brian Walker finishing up his sets on the Roman chair. "Hey, man, didn't see you. How's that gorgeous new wife of yours? She ready to divorce you and run off with me?" Andy joked.

Brian laughed, low and deep. "Way you were running over there, doubt she'd catch you, even if she could tear herself away from her manly man."

Andy shrugged. "Just trying to keep up with your animal physique."

Brian waved him off, and Andy turned to leave. He had spent twelve waking hours killing time, at least it had felt like killing time. On the other hand, he hadn't moped around or worried himself sick over Tess and Hawk.

The forty-five minutes of running and equal amount of time weightlifting had been the best thing he'd done for himself since he rolled out of bed. *Hmmm, maybe not the best thing.* He grinned as he bent over and reached for his keys in a wall cubby. The thirty or so minutes he'd spent with Allyson had been the highlight of his day. Every second had felt...well...great. And when she could no longer ignore the people in the store, Andy had wanted—no, needed—to ask her out to dinner.

Twice in one day. Thank God Tess wasn't around. If she knew he'd intentionally sought out Allyson twice in twenty-four hours, Tess wouldn't have let it go. Andy chuckled. He wanted Tess home, the sooner the better, but maybe God did have a plan after all, and perhaps that plan was to give him a chance to date Allyson at least once without Tess putting her two cents into every move he made.

Andy jogged lightly down the stairs of the gym and out into the cool evening air. He glanced at his watch. It was just before six, and he'd told Allyson he would pick her up at seven. A shave and a shower and he could make it to her house with time to spare. He climbed into his truck and pulled the clipboard and papers off the dashboard and put them on the passenger seat. Andy shook his head. He'd better allot five minutes to clean out the cab if he wanted Allyson to sit beside him, and he definitely wanted her close.

He started the engine and switched on the radio. Allyson had mentioned a station on satellite that she listened to. He scrolled through until he found her station, The Message. The radio screen flashed the current song's title: "God Gave Me You" by Dave Barnes.

"Is that a sign, God?" Andy asked aloud.

Whether it was or wasn't, Andy held his finger over the preset button, thinking about dinner, Allyson's company, and her laughter. He grinned and then pushed down hard for a few seconds to set the station permanently on The Message dial. Allyson would appreciate listening to her music whenever she rode in the Chevy.

19

ANDY DRUMMED HIS FINGERS ON THE STEERING WHEEL in time to the music. The song was catchy, something called "Move" by a group named Mercy Me. He didn't know who they were, couldn't even sing more than a few words, but he liked it.

He listened to the lyrics. "I've got to hold it steady. Keep my head in the game. Everything is about to change....This turn is getting heavy, but I'm not about to cave....I just might bend, but I won't break....When life won't play along and right keeps going wrong, and I can't seem to find my way...I'll keep dancing anyway...."

"Gotta move, gotta move to a different beat." Andy sang the words he'd learned after the first chorus, jamming to the music as he drove.

He could get used to Allyson's station. He pictured how pleased she might be when she heard her music playing, and he nodded. He loved her smile, not only how her mouth looked so inviting, but more how her eyes laughed and danced when she was happy. If he never saw her lips move, he would know Allyson was smiling just by looking at her eyes.

The song changed as Andy turned onto Lambert's Cove Road. He opened the mirror on the visor and glanced at his reflection. He looked okay. No food in his teeth after inhaling a bowl of his mom's pasta-veggie salad to tide him over and take the edge off of his hunger. He ran his fingers through his hair, still slightly wet, but drying quickly. Tess said he was good-looking. Rebecca had chided him many times, calling him a dashing, yet dastardly, rake. Those two were less than unbiased. He just hoped Allyson liked what she saw.

He slid the mirror shut and flipped up the visor, slowing as he neared the turn onto the long, dirt drive at Osage Meadow Farm. The pastures were empty, the horses bedded down for the night. Andy pulled in next to the barn and walked over to the cottage Allyson rented from the Stewarts.

"Hey, Drew." Allyson called as she stepped out onto the porch.

Andy sucked in his breath. She was in a dress. Granted, he'd seen her in a dress earlier at work, but she'd changed into something else. Something soft and feminine. Something not at all work-like. Something altogether gorgeous.

He stood perfectly still and stared at her. A moment or two passed, and Andy said nothing. Just gazed.

The sky-blue color of the dress made her eyes bluer than usual.

"Oh." Allyson ran her right hand over her dress, her smile shrinking. "Am I overdressed? You did say dinner, right?"

"No. I mean, yes, dinner." Andy stumbled over the words, still gawking, his reaction surprising him and confounding his senses. "Wow, this really is a date."

Allyson cocked her head slightly to the left. "You did ask me out, right?"

Andy faltered. "No. Yes. I mean, yes, I asked you out. You just look so, so—nice. I wasn't expecting…you had on that pink dress earlier, so I, well—" Andy stopped speaking when he heard her laughter. Her enjoyment at his discomfort registered quickly. "I guess I just made a complete fool of myself. Wouldn't Tess love to hear this story?" Andy said.

Allyson walked down the two steps and eased across the grass in her heels, her laughter and sparkling eyes getting closer as she approached. She stopped two feet in front of Andy and grinned. "I've never known you to be a fool." She laughed again and started toward the truck, tossing over her shoulder, "Though I do think Tess will enjoy hearing about this."

Andy jogged up beside her, ready to open the door. "Good thing she's away for a few days."

Allyson climbed into the truck. "I didn't know Tess was going off Island."

Andy kicked himself as he walked around and got in. He shouldn't have brought up Tess. How was he going to get out of this one?

"Neither did I. But you know Tess. She does whatever she wants." He heard the annoyance and worry in his voice. He'd have to change the subject in a hurry.

"What is it? Where has Tess gone?"

Where has Tess gone? Ha! A loaded question if ever there was one. If only Andy could tell Allyson. He would love to talk with someone other than his parents. He didn't want either of them to know he was more than a little worried that Hawk wouldn't be back with Tess tonight.

Tension started to creep across his shoulders and around his neck. Andy shrugged it off, trying not to let Tess ruin his first date with an amazing woman. He was already going to kill his sister, so he'd just wring her neck a little harder for distracting him from Allyson.

The gearshift rested in reverse, Andy's right foot still on the brake. "Hey, let's forget about Tess and her disasters tonight and just have a good time. Deal?"

"Deal." Allyson smiled.

Andy's heart warmed and melted in one fluid second.

They drove in silence for a few minutes. Still distracted, still angry, Andy thought about Tess and Hawk. *God,* he prayed silently, *please watch over Tess and Hawk. And get them out of my head tonight so I can be with Allyson. Thanks.*

Allyson grasped the radio button. "Mind if I turn this on?"

Andy almost blushed as he realized her station would come blaring over the speakers as soon as she pushed the button. "Sure."

He watched her face as the music came on, and surprise and pleasure registered in her eyes. "Oh, I love this song!" was all she said, all she needed to say, before she started singing. "'When the waves are taking you under, hold on just a little bit longer. He knows that this is gonna make you stronger, stronger.'"

As they neared the Vineyard Haven-Edgartown Road, Andy asked, "What are you in the mood for? Any place special you'd like to go?"

"I love just about anything," she said, then scrunched up her face. "But no eels or squid or slimy stuff."

Andy stayed on State Road and headed toward Oak Bluffs. "How about Dolce Vita?"

Allyson's eyes widened. "I've never been there. Do you think they're still serving outside?"

Andy smiled at her. He'd called Carlton, the chef, just to be sure they could be served on the side patio. Nice to have friends in the right places, though he wasn't going to mention it to Allyson. She could figure out that the restaurant was open only Thursdays through Saturdays now, but she wouldn't know he'd asked for a personal favor—to be served under the stars. He played it cool, having already looked like a lovesick puppy when he picked her up. "We can eat outside."

"Great." Again, her eyes lit up when she looked at him.

Andy smiled at her.

September made for easy parking in Oaks Bluff. In the summer months, Andy would have been lucky to find a spot at the end of Circuit Avenue after driving the circle four or five times. Tonight, he pulled right into the second-to-last spot on the strip, jumped out, and walked around the truck to open the door for Allyson.

She put her hand in his and stepped down. "Thanks, Drew." And then she smiled again.

Andy soaked it in. If they went home now, it would have been a great evening. He knew it was only going to get better.

September on Island had always been a favorite time for Andy. The weather was perfect, the tourists were nearly gone, he had free time to relax, and his favorite places remained open. Dolce Vita was a personal as well as a family favorite. They would close soon for the winter months, but tonight the lights were twinkling in the terrace garden, the outdoor bar was still open, and Carlton was creating culinary masterpieces in the kitchen.

They sat on the side deck, elevated above the tables below and able to take in the stars and the moon, the plants and flowers, the lights glowing around the perimeter, and even the activity moving on the sidewalk and in the street outside and beyond the hedge.

"It's beautiful, Drew. I've always wanted to sit in here and just watch the summer people eat and laugh. I've heard the food is amazing."

Andy nodded. "Carlton is a master. There isn't a bad choice on the menu, except for those who don't eat slimy things. You might not appreciate the oysters."

Allyson playfully whacked Andy with her menu, and they both laughed. He ordered a bottle of wine and asked their waiter if Carlton would whip them up some crab cakes.

"I take it you know the chef?" Allyson said.

"We've done some sailing together. His wife is a friend of my sister-in-law, too, so I see them at family parties. Good people."

The crab cakes arrived, followed by a salad made with Island greens and local goat cheese. Allyson told Andy about work. Andy avoided talking about the dock, the ships, and the *Shenandoah*. They laughed. A lot. And Andy realized one dinner would not be enough. While they waited for their entrées, he asked Allyson about her off-season plans.

"I don't know yet. The gallery will close after Veteran's Day. I'm still trying to decide whether to head south for the winter or not. Do you have a suggestion?"

Don't go, his heart screamed. *Stay here,* was what he really wanted to say. Again, he played it safe. "We can probably rule out any job that involves fishing, cleaning fish, clamming, cooking calamari, or the like."

He laughed as she jutted out her chin and tried to look indignant. She met his gaze. "I will have you know, Andrew Roberts, that I just so happen to love to fish. Granted, I don't clean them, but I will cook them once someone else has done the dirty work."

Now it was Andy's turn to be surprised. "You fish?"

She chuckled. "Yes, Drew, I fish. I can even bait my own hook and cast my line off the jetty in Menemsha."

Before he even thought about the words, Andy said, "Would you like to go tomorrow morning? The Derby starts on Sunday, so we'll still have a shot at a quiet stretch of beach. Or we could go out in one of the motor boats if you'd rather be on the water."

She was smiling again, that warm invitation that seemed to start in her heart, appear in her eyes first, and then somehow turn up the corners of her mouth. He could look at her smile all day long.

"That would be awesome. I'd need to be back by eight-thirty so I can get cleaned up and open the gallery a little before ten. What time do you want to meet?"

Andy wondered if her heart was racing, too. Did she feel the need to be with him as much as he wanted to be with her? If he could, he'd talk with her all night until it was time to go fishing. "How about I pick you up at five? We can drive up to Quansoo and see what's biting."

"Sounds perfect, Drew." Time flew while they ate and talked. Allyson twisted the blue and green watch on her left arm. Andy glanced down at his. It was already nine. He'd better get her home if they were going to get up in a few hours and hit the tide right.

"Would you like some dessert?"

Allyson shook her head. "No, thanks. I'm stuffed."

The waiter brought the bill. Andy stopped by the kitchen to thank Carlton and introduce Allyson. As they walked through the door into the night air, Andy took her arm and guided her down the front steps. When they reached the sidewalk, he didn't want to let go. He held out his hand and watched in amazement and gratitude as Allyson placed her small, tanned hand in his.

When they arrived at his truck, Andy opened the door and helped Allyson in. She squeezed his hand. "Thanks for a wonderful evening, Drew."

He squeezed back before letting go. He drove slowly to her cottage, savoring her presence and listening to Allyson sing the songs she loved. When he walked her to the front door, Andy hesitated. He wanted to kiss her good night. He needed to kiss her good night. He just couldn't decide whether to make the move. Something held him back. Something about her. Something special.

For the first time in his adult life, Andy felt awkward at the end of a date. He racked his brain for an intelligent comment. "Thanks for going to dinner with me. I had a great time."

Allyson beamed at him. "Me too, Drew. It was heavenly—the food and the company."

Andy shoved his hands in his pockets. He felt like a sixteen-year-old boy on his first date. He didn't know what to do, just knew that he wanted to kiss her but felt instinctively that he shouldn't make that move. His right hand clenched over the cell phone in his pocket.

"Hey," he said, a sane thought finally entering his mind, "why don't you text me in the morning when you're up and about? If you oversleep or are too tired, I won't come barreling down your drive, waking you up on a Friday morning."

"Don't you worry about me, Drew. I'll be up, dressed, and have a thermos of coffee made to take with us." Allyson winked at him. "But I'll text you just to be sure you're awake."

Andy laughed, took his hands out of his pockets, and waved the cell phone at her. "Sounds like a plan."

They stood immobile. Andy searched her eyes for some hint of what she wanted. Too many girls were throwing themselves at him because he was thirty and available, or maybe because of his dad's business. Allyson wasn't like that. And her eyes were bright and happy looking, but he had no idea if that meant she wanted a hug or a kiss or a handshake.

He was just about to step forward and give her a hug when she leaned over and kissed him on the cheek. "See you in the morning, nice and early."

Andy backed away, keeping his eyes on her as Allyson turned and walked into her house. "Nice and early," he said to her back as he placed his left palm over the spot she'd kissed on his cheek.

He drove home in silence, thinking about his perfect evening and the woman who had just stolen his heart. Pulling into his driveway, he realized Tess and Hawk had never even crossed his mind.

20

"I'VE GOT ONE!" Allyson let out a shriek of excitement. She dug in her heels as the rod bent toward the sand. "He's huge!"

Whatever she had on the line had taken hold and was now pulling her toward the surf. Andy stepped in behind Allyson. He reached his arms around her and placed his hands over and under hers on the fishing rod. He felt her muscles straining as she hauled back on the line, then released and reeled in a little bit more. He braced both feet deep into the sand and tried to take some of the weight and fight of the bass striper into his arms. He liked the feel of Allyson close to him, of his arms around her. He could get used to fishing like this—

Andy's old, round alarm clock shook on the bedside table. He rolled over with a grin and pushed the button on the back to stop the incessant ringing.

"Sweet!" he exclaimed before tossing back the covers and swinging his legs over the side of the bed. Two weeks ago, he would have freaked dreaming about Allyson. This morning, he liked the idea. A lot.

He tiptoed down the hall to the bathroom he'd shared with his brothers growing up. A quick shave and shower, and he was creeping down the stairs. His parents had been awake last night when he got home from dinner. His father had sat back with a mug of tea in his hands and listened as his mom squeezed out every detail of his evening she could. When he told them he was picking Allyson up this morning to go fishing, his mom's eyes had lit up.

"She's a nice girl."

Katherine Roberts was not a woman of few words. So Andy knew the short sentence spoke volumes. He'd said good night, wanting to get out of the kitchen before his mom said or asked anything else.

He spent an hour in the garage, checking his fishing gear, setting up the rods, packing extra sinkers, and tying on eighty-pound mono leaders in case a school of bluefish came in for an early breakfast. This time of year, they had a good chance of catching blues, and even a three-pounder could shred a normal leader. He set aside some frozen bait in a cooler. With a little luck, they'd catch a few small fish early on to cut and chunk. Better to use fresh bait, especially in September, when the fish could be choosy. By the time he'd finished in the garage, his parents had gone to bed.

Walking down the stairs, he smelled coffee brewing. *You're a saint, Mom.* When he entered the kitchen, he found a note resting atop a plastic box next to the coffeepot.

Good morning, Andy. I made blueberry muffins for you and Allyson. Please give her my best. Happy fishing. Love you, Mom.

He loved her blueberry muffins, but really? It was too early to think about whatever plans his mother might be concocting. He remembered all too well how she'd baked pastries and breads for two of his brothers' girlfriends. They were now his sisters-in-law. Somehow his mom had taken "the man" out of the old quote and twisted it to, "The way to a woman's heart is through her stomach."

He poured some coffee into a to-go mug, picked up the muffins, and eased out through the mudroom door as quiet as a mouse. It was dark, but he wasn't the only person on the road. Ed Whitcomb's rusted-out Chevy was filled with newspapers, and he was undoubtedly heading Up Island to deliver them to Alley's, the Chilmark store, and the gas stations.

A few minutes later, as Andy drove down Allyson's driveway, he couldn't contain his ever-widening grin. He'd seen her last night and was beyond eager to see her again this morning. A first.

She came through the front door before he had a chance to turn off the truck. He couldn't help but grin and nod. She had on a great pair of Orvis boots. The woman knew her footwear and, judging by the scuffmarks, she'd broken these in a long time ago. To top it off, she was carrying a pair of waders. He was impressed.

He opened the door, eager to jump out and give her a hand, but she waved him back in. She walked over to the passenger side of the truck and flashed him the prettiest smile he'd ever seen.

"Morning, Drew," she said as he lowered the electric window.

"Morning." He leaned across the seat and opened her door. "Want some help?"

"I'm good." She tossed her waders and jacket in the back seat on top of his jacket and the two pairs of waders he'd brought. She slid in beside him and placed a large thermos of coffee on the floor. As she buckled her seat belt, she noticed the plastic box filled with muffins.

"Aw, you shouldn't have. I didn't know you baked." Allyson was obviously in a good mood.

"Nothing edible," he said with a wink. "Mom said to give you her best." Andy was about to warn Allyson that the muffins were only the beginning, when he realized that he didn't mind if this was the beginning. Of something.

94

Allyson opened the box and inhaled the mix of cinnamon, sugar, and blueberry. "Yum! Crumble topping, my fave. I love your mom."

He refrained from saying, "She approves of you, too," and settled for the much safer, "She's a great cook."

"Her brownies are famous at church. She's says it's only because she uses real chocolate squares, but she's holding out. I've made the recipe on the chocolate box, and mine didn't taste like hers. Want to share her secret?"

"No can do. It's a family recipe. I'd be cut off and tossed out on the street."

Allyson snatched his mug of coffee from the console. "What about blackmail?"

Andy chuckled. Her blue eyes were sparkling with mischief. They were lucky he didn't drive off the road before he managed to tear his gaze away and shift his focus back to State Road. The fairgrounds looked particularly empty with the bare patches and worn areas from last month's fair. He thought it might be pretty sweet to walk around with Allyson next summer, maybe get her on the tilt-a-whirl so she'd be pressed up against him on the spins.

"Stakes aren't high enough with coffee. Torture might be your most successful route," he teased back.

She put down the coffee and then settled into her seat. He glanced over. She was tapping her index finger against her chin, another mischievous grin on her face. "Torture, huh? I'll give that some thought."

She looked so beguiling, sitting there trying to act wicked but just too darn nice to come close to pulling it off. Her reputation preceded her. He wanted to play along, though, wanted to watch the various expressions flash across her face. And wanted to be the man she was thinking about.

"I'll be ready for you," he jested, though he meant every word.

She sidestepped the innuendo. "And I'm ready to fish. Quansoo, is it?"

Andy nodded. "Let's give it a shot. We might have a good stretch of beach to ourselves, and if the fish are running, they'll be all ours."

"Sounds perfect. Music?" She turned up the radio and sang along as they drove three miles down the winding dirt roads leading to the beach access. Andy listened to her voice, enjoying her singing and the colors of the late-summer foliage.

By the time they'd staked a couple of rods in the ground and poured fresh cups of coffee, the early twilight glow gave off a perfect gray light to begin fishing. A few guys were working the surf to the left and right but down a ways from them. One of the last mornings for space and privacy. Once the Derby started on Sunday, the beaches and waters would be packed with men, women, and children hoping to win some money, a new boat, or a new truck. And everyone wanted to see his or her name on the leader board.

"High tide," Andy noted as he cast his first line. "Come to papa."

He watched Allyson cast with both hands on the rod, rocking back and arcing the line out over the water. "Nice," he said aloud. *Are you kidding me?* The woman next to him was smart, funny, great company, gorgeous, and she not only liked to fish, she knew how. Why hadn't he ever gone out with her before?

"All right, with a cast like that, we're not talking baiting a hook to catch some sunnies off the jetty in Menemsha. Who taught you how to fish?"

"My dad," she said, her eyes filled with love. "He was crazy about fishing. My brother John went, but he never really got into it. I couldn't get enough. I realize now that when my dad first started taking me, we let everything go. He assured me the fish weren't hurt. Every now and then, he'd land a good size bass and he'd ask me if I thought we should bring it home to Mom for dinner. He had a way about him, you know, that subtle difference between preaching to teach and leading to teach."

There was a good roll to the surf. The sand was cool but not cold. A beautiful woman was fishing beside him. Andy was in paradise. He sliced a small baitfish he'd caught and listened to her story. He wanted to know everything. "Sounds like a great guy."

"He was. He's probably looking down right now, rather pleased that I'm up and out fishing before going in to work." Allyson reeled in her line, checked her bait, and cast again.

The line zipped through the air and dropped thirty or forty yards offshore. Andy grinned. She had great form. And, he couldn't help but notice, she looked cute in waders with her blonde hair in a ponytail.

Some ripples skimmed across the surface near her line, then a few more. "Hang on, Allyson. I think we've got company."

Within seconds, the smaller ripples became larger ones as a school of stripers started chowing down. Andy grabbed the two rods in the sand spikes and reeled them in so he wouldn't lose one. He kept an eye on his favorite rod, which he'd jammed into the sand a few feet away so he could pull the other two in. Allyson had a lot of movement on her line. Somebody was thinking about taking a big bite. He picked up his favorite rod and kept an eye on Allyson.

She had a slight tug on the line, then it peeled from the reel. Allyson kept her body loose, letting the bass take off. After a few seconds, she put the reel in gear and waited for the line to go taut. The stripper fought the tension on the reel. Her body lurched forward before she planted her feet and got ready to land him. She lifted the rod and leaned back against the fish. Little by little, she brought him in.

Andy felt the first hit on his line and stepped toward the water. Whoever was on the other end decided he liked the bait. The water was beginning to look like a bubble bath with so many fish moving, fleeing, and feeding. Dinner was about to be caught.

Over an hour later, Allyson and Andy sat in their beach chairs, jackets off, sweat dripping, bottles of water in hand, two happy people with two fair-size stripers apiece on ice. Andy had lost one huge fish, a photo op that Allyson captured on her cell phone.

"Want to try again?" Andy asked.

"Let's leave 'em for the Derby. I'm happy with these boys." She patted the cooler and raised her bottle to Andy.

She looked happy. Her eyes were bright, and her cheeks were flushed with excitement and exertion. Andy marveled yet again at how incredible she was. And she was sitting beside him. Life was good.

They sat for a while in quiet companionship, enjoying the feel of the sun rising over water and warming the air. September had a summer feel with its warm, sunny days and the added bonus that the beaches were, for the most part, visited only by locals.

At seven o'clock, they packed up their gear and trekked back to the truck. A blue crab sidestepped over some rocks in the shallow stream under the bridge by the parking area. "He'd make a good appetizer," Andy quipped.

"How about another muffin instead?"

"What, you didn't enjoy the crab cakes last night?"

Allyson shook her head. "I loved the crab cakes. But he looks peaceful, and I'd rather not be the one to ruin his day."

"A muffin it is. Let's get this stuff loaded. I'm suddenly starving." Andy put the cooler in the back of the truck and tied on the rods. They shrugged out of their waders and wet clothes, then Allyson passed him a hot mug of coffee and a muffin. He ate the muffin in four bites before they headed down the dirt road, radio playing.

"Hey, since you wouldn't share the coveted brownie recipe, want to divulge a different family secret? Any clue what Tess is planning for the party next week? She's got more guts than I'll ever have."

What could Andy say? That his sister had pulled off her best stunt yet? That Tess was traveling the world—another world? Or that he didn't know if she'd be back next Friday—or ever?

"Tess has already done her stunt. Her unplanned vacation and no phone call or contact since is all the stunt we need." Andy knew he sounded angry, but Allyson's question cut into the pain he hadn't wanted to deal with the last few days.

"Oh, no. Sorry, Drew. Has anyone heard from her?" Allyson placed her hand gently on his arm as he continued driving.

Her touch radiated peace. Taking a deep breath, he exhaled his anxiety. He glanced down at her manicured fingernails, slightly dirty from the morning fishing. Her nonchalance about the sand under her nails was a quality he greatly appreciated. He wished it was August, and he was in a T-shirt. He'd probably feel even more relaxed if her hand was on his skin. Hmm, maybe not so relaxed, but good. Definitely good. He felt better already.

"No call. Just the note. Tess can be all about Tess when she wants to be," he said, the edge gone from his voice.

All too soon, Allyson lifted her hand off his arm and gestured toward the scenery they were passing. "I doubt she'll be gone long or go very far. Who'd want to be anywhere else than here in September?"

Ha! If she only knew. Not that he could casually bring up that Tess was more than a few miles away. She was centuries away, and they had no idea exactly where or what day it was. But if he did mention it and Allyson understood how crazy Tess's situation was, maybe she'd put her hand back on his arm. He sighed. Not today.

"I'm sure she'll be back for the party, full of stories and threatening some daredevil stunt." Talking about the party, Andy became acutely aware of the fact that he wanted to go with Allyson, not just meet her there.

The Fjord ponies were running in the field as they passed Tamarack Farm. One of the younger ponies was bucking like a bronco in a rodeo. They both laughed at his antics.

"Good to be him," Andy said.

"I'll say. And he doesn't have to go to work in two hours."

"You could play hooky," he said, half joking, yet hoping she'd say yes.

"I wish. Unfortunately, I need the job to pay the rent. Ask me in a couple months. If I haven't found a winter job, I'll have plenty of time to run around and kick up my heels." Allyson chuckled, but Andy heard the concern in her voice. He had to know someone who needed help in the off-season. There was no way he wanted Allyson heading to the mainland, or America as Islanders called it, for the winter.

He turned left onto Lamberts Cove Road. "Ah, speaking of kicking up our heels, can I take you to the party next Saturday?"

Her eyes smiled first. He saw her answer before she opened her mouth. What a beautiful thing.

"I'd love that."

"Great. Maybe we should go fishing that morning to have something fresh to grill on the fire. And who knows, we might catch ourselves a Derby winner." Andy kept his smirk to himself. He'd done it again, asked her out twice in one day.

"You've got a date. Two, actually." She nudged him slightly.

Andy didn't want to turn down her driveway. The day, the workday, was starting too quickly. He parked his Dodge and got out to help her. He reached into the truck bed and picked up her damp jacket and waders.

"Hey, want me to spray these down for you?"

"No, but thanks. I'm going to throw them in the horse washer in the barn tomorrow, and I'll hang them out to dry." She held out her left hand for the clothes. Andy looked at the thermos in her right hand. If he passed her the clothes, she'd have no arms left to hug him good-bye.

"Let me carry these to the barn for you."

"Better yet, walk with me up to the house, and I'll hang them over the porch railing." She looked back into the truck. "Mind if I take a blueberry muffin for lunch?"

Andy walked behind her and held the truck door open. "Take the whole box. There's plenty more at home."

She reached in for the muffins. "You're a prince."

"And you are easy to please." He closed the door and walked with her toward the house. He cut across the lawn and draped the damp waders and her jacket over the railing. She stood on the pavers at the base of the steps, waiting for him.

He walked over, staring into her eyes. "Thanks for the coffee and the great company. You sure you don't want a filet later? I'll be happy to drop one off at the gallery." He stopped three feet from her.

She took a step and closed the distance. "How about you bring a couple of filets over tomorrow night, and we'll grill them together?"

She was a mind reader! That was exactly what he wanted. "Can I pick up a bottle of wine to go with dinner?"

"Yes." With the muffins in her left hand and the thermos in her right, she leaned closer and kissed his cheek. "Thanks for a great morning, Drew. I'll be looking forward to dinner."

"Me too," he said as she stepped back. He wanted to draw her in to him, to hug her tightly and kiss her softly. Instead, he offered her a hand up the steps. "Have a great day. See you tomorrow."

"You, too. And don't cut yourself fileting our fish."

He laughed with her and then walked back to his truck. Another perfect date. The only flaw was having to say good-bye.

He hummed along to her music until he reached the intersection of Lambert's Cove and State Roads, then turned off the radio and headed left toward Vineyard Haven. He knew neither Hawk nor Tess would be there, but he had to motor out to *Shenandoah* and see for himself.

He dialed the home phone. "Hi, Mom."

"Good morning, Andy. How was your time with Allyson?"

There it was. Just like last night. In one sentence his mother had again given her approval of Allyson. She hadn't asked about the fishing, which his mom enjoyed as much as the rest of them. She hadn't asked if he was bringing anything home for dinner, which she would normally be planning the meal around. She had simply asked about his time with Allyson. Andy smiled with genuine affection. He loved his mother, and he loved the ways she loved him.

"We had a great time, Mom. Caught a few stripers. Twelve to fifteen pounders. Had one big guy on the line, but he wiggled free on the first run."

"We'll grill the fish tonight." She paused. Andy heard the longing in her silence and knew her heart was breaking. "Have you heard from Tess or Hawk?"

"I'm on my way to *Shenandoah* now. But, Mom, don't get your hopes up, okay? You know Tess. She's not about to get there and then come right back just because Hawk told her to go home."

Katherine sighed. "No, Tess will not be forced. I'd just like to know she's safe, that she's with Rebecca, and..." her voice choked up, "that she plans to come home."

Andy heard the tears when she spoke the last words. He didn't need to be in the room to know that his mom was fighting off a good cry. He wanted to strangle Tess all over again. And he would, given the chance. He might not kill her, but he had every intention of giving her a very large piece of his mind.

"I know, Mom. I hope she's safe too. But I'm gonna kill her when she gets back."

"I believe Jack spoke those exact words a few minutes ago. Your sister has given us all a good scare this time. Regardless, I'll be grateful when she's home."

"So will we. It's been a few years since Jack or I pulled Tess's hair or put a snake in her bed. I think we can cook up something in the next day or two before she gets back." Andy was doing his best to distract his mother. Though, if truth be told, he was going to call Jack and plan a little revenge on Tess. She was in serious need of some brotherly love, and he was the brother to dish it out.

His mom attempted a chuckle, and the mood lightened. "I'm laughing, Andy, because I trust that you will do no such thing. Though I understand why you and your brothers are annoyed with Tess. Call me from *Shenny*, please."

"Will do, Mom. Tell Dad I'm headed there now."

Andy hung up and placed his cell phone in the cup holder. If Hawk or Tess were back, they would have called. He'd left Hawk's phone on an orange oil rag on the floor in Cabin 8 so he would see it when he got back. And Tess's cell was in her Jeep, which he parked next to a few minutes later.

As he walked down the dock, he wished Allyson was still with him. He'd love to take her sailing before the weather changed, maybe at sunset, maybe this weekend.

He jumped down into the dinghy and started the motor. A search of the boat confirmed his earlier suspicions—Hawk and Tess were still gone. The trip out to *Shenandoah* was a waste of time.

The thrill of his morning with Allyson was wearing off, and that was one more thing he'd be taking out on Tess when she returned. He'd spent too much time talking about and thinking about his stubborn, very selfish sister. Now he had to call his parents and tell them Tess wouldn't be home today. He punched the throttle.

The dinghy splashed through the wake of the 8:30 ferry. Andy eased back on throttle, pulled alongside the dock, cut the engine, and tied off the boat. Before climbing the ladder to the dock, he looked back at *Shenandoah*, wondering where Tess was, what century, if Hawk was with her, what time of day it was there.

"Mom misses you, Tess. Come home."

21

TESS HEARD THE SCURRY OF FOOTSTEPS before she heard the knock on her door. She jumped up, remembering all too well Ben's final comments to her last night about knowing how to shoot a gun. She sprinted the three steps to the door.

She flipped the latch quickly but not fast enough for Hawk. Before she could say hello, Hawk pushed the wooden door wide enough to step through, entered her room, and then closed the door behind them. He strode forward and Tess backed up, a little too quickly, into the stack of supply crates.

"What the...?" Tess sputtered as her head cracked into a sharp wooden slat.

The urgency in Hawk's eyes silenced her impulse to yell or even whimper. "Tess, just keep it down and listen."

Wincing at the pain, Tess mumbled through her gritted teeth. "Fine. Go ahead."

She rubbed the bump forming on the back of her skull, slightly miffed at his tone, and more than a little nervous because Hawk was, for the first time since she'd known him, acting scared.

He paced a stride forward, a stride back, a stride forward, a stride back. "Two British ships are in the cove. We are hoisting anchor and setting sail immediately. Stay below deck and out of sight. There's a fair wind this morning, and we should be out of the harbor right quick."

"But I want to..." Tess didn't finish her thought.

Hawk shook his head without taking his eyes off of her. "Not today, Tess. *Shenandoah's* not flying a Patriot flag, but they'll figure out pretty fast that Ben is a privateer working for the Patriots. The last thing we need is to be spotted with a woman onboard. If they believe you're the captain's wife, which is the only logical option, you would be the first one they took hostage. No better way to assure our full cooperation than to take the captain's wife hostage. Got it?" Hawk stared her down and waited for her response.

"Fine. Okay. I get it. Now leave me alone." Tess pointed her index finger to the door to show Hawk the way out.

"You don't have to ask me twice," he said before spinning on his heel and shutting the door with a thud behind him. Tess dropped to the cot and sulked.

Hawk was right. She knew he was, but she hated it. She hated being stuck below deck once again even more. All the action was happening on deck. Where she longed to be.

The dankness of the storm had lifted, and the morning air smelled crisp. Judging by the light coming in through the porthole, the sun was rising. Tess could hear the men's voices as they got the ship underway. She felt the big ship tack left and then head for the channel past Round Rock and Dog Bar, then out into the open seas.

Adam would undoubtedly be making breakfast. The men still had to eat, especially after a long night of being on watch and full alert. Surely it wouldn't hurt anybody if she went down to the galley to talk with Adam.

She eased the latch and poked her head out, just in case Hawk had put a guard, or was standing guard, at her door. No one in sight.

Tess grinned and made her way to the galley. "Hi, Adam."

"Good morning, Miss Roberts. I was expecting you." Adam gave her a brief nod while he continued to slice big slabs of bread.

"You were?" Tess asked, trying not to sound surprised.

"Aye, I was. I suspect you are not accustomed to remaining below deck any more than you're accustomed to women being relegated to home and hearth."

"Ha!" Tess exclaimed before raising her hand chest-high and waving her finger at Adam. "Believe me, I'm quite used to men on a ship telling me to stay home or go home. My whole life I've wanted to sail with my father just like my brothers did. But do I get to go? Noooooo! No girls in the crew. And no one's inviting me into the kitchen either. Not that I want to be in the kitchen. I hate cooking. Such a waste of time when I could be..."

Tess closed her mouth when the words she'd spoken hit her ears. "Oh, Adam, I didn't mean that you were wasting your time in the galley." She winced, hoping she hadn't offended the man who had befriended her.

"No offense taken, Miss Roberts. The galley is where I belong. The Good Lord saw fit to put a knife, fork, and spoon in me hands when I was a young lad, and then He guided my feet to the boatyard. It has been an adventure, and I'm grateful each and every day."

Tess smiled. "You're lucky, Adam. You can do what you want. Women's lib may have arrived in the sixties, but I haven't seen any sign of it on my dad's ships. Title IX, women's rights, and equal opportunity employment do not, I repeat, do not exist in my home."

Adam frowned. "Though I have no understanding of your laws or ways, I suspect you are more independent than many women of your day. Would this be the case, Miss Roberts?"

Two hands moved aggressively in every direction, punctuating her words with dramatic flair. "Not the way you think! Sure, I take risks and do some crazy stunts—at least my brother Andy thinks they're crazy—but whatever I'm doing is only to prove to him and my father that I'm as tough and as able as any guy in his crew."

Adam put down the knife and reached for a crock of butter. He slathered each slab of bread with a huge amount of butter. Tess's stomach growled. Adam glanced her way. "Would this journey to visit Rebecca be another 'crazy' idea, Miss Roberts?" he asked and handed her a freshly buttered slice of bread.

Tess looked down at the wooden floorboards. "Maybe."

"Perhaps I am not the only one who does as I wish?"

"You're not going to get into trouble, though!" Tess took a bite of the bread and butter and relished the creamy, homemade taste while Adam grinned at her comment.

"You are correct in that statement, Miss Roberts. I shall not be facing any consequences for my honest employment. Though we might all still have a bit of trouble headed our way today." He looked up through the galley hatch toward the blue sky and beyond. Neither mentioned the ships Ben was hoping to avoid in the harbor.

Tess watched the old man move effortlessly in his kitchen. He assembled the sandwiches quickly, making Tess acutely aware of his words. She couldn't see where they were or if they were being followed. The fact that Adam was making butter sandwiches for breakfast instead of oatmeal or johnnycakes was probably a good indication that Ben wanted all hands on deck just in case. She wondered what Hawk was doing.

Adam gathered the slices of bread into a large wicker basket. "I must disperse these to the men, Miss Roberts. I shall check on your man and report back to you shortly."

Tess nearly choked on the last bite of her bread. "He's not 'my man,'" she yelled as Adam climbed up the galley rungs and onto the deck. She thought she heard him laugh.

22

TESS WAITED IMPATIENTLY IN THE GALLEY. Not for Adam to bring news of Hawk, mind you. She merely wanted to know what was happening on deck. When he passed her the empty basket, she knew immediately from the worry on his face that the news wasn't good..

"Adam?" Tess questioned after his feet were on the floor.

His brow furrowed. "I do not wish to worry you, Miss Roberts. However, ye'd best be aware that the ships in Gloucester Harbor were British, and one of them has given us chase. She will be alongside us shortly."

No sooner were the words out of his mouth than Hawk dropped through the hatch, skipping the three rungs on the ladder altogether. "Get to your room, Tess. We're about to be boarded." He paused. "And seized."

She wanted to argue on the pure principle that she hated being told what to do, but Tess saw the concern and urgency in Hawk's eyes and decided she would let him have his way this one time. Adam said nothing, yet she sensed his approval, which felt good, even if she didn't need it.

"What do you mean 'seized'? Who will take the helm of *Shenandoah* from Ben?" Tess followed Hawk out the galley and down the hall.

He didn't slow his pace to answer her. "The British captain will board *Shenandoah* and demand Ben step down. If they don't shoot a few cannonballs at us first."

Tess grabbed Hawk's forearm with her right hand. He paused midstride. "Is Ben going to shoot him?" she asked.

Hawk brushed her hand off as if she were an annoying fly. "Wake up, Tess. This is the eighteenth century. Men don't just knock somebody off even when they're at war."

Tess hated the sarcasm in Hawk's voice. "Well, then, what's the big deal? We're not flying any flags. How will they know we're American? We've probably got over an hour on them, so why not just try to out-sail them?"

Anger and impatience seemed to seep from every pore in Hawk's body. He clasped two hands on her shoulders and gave her a rough shake. "Snap out of it, Tess, will you? The big deal is we are about to be seized by the enemy. There is no outrunning them. Ben is going to lower the sails. The British captain will very nicely ask Ben and the rest of us to lay down our arms and submit to King George's rule."

"But—"

"No buts and no pranks this time, Tess. Your little adventure, this game you just had to play, has gotten very real and very dangerous."

"It's not my fault. How was I to know the *Shenandoah* was about to be captured? Nothing bad happened to Rebecca." Tess mumbled the last words and hung her head. She was scared, and she felt like crying, but she didn't want Hawk to see her fear or her tears.

"I'm not interested in the blame game, Tess. Suffice it to say, neither of us would be here if you hadn't sneaked aboard the *Shenandoah*."

Tess snapped her head up and met his blue eyes with a cold stare of her own. "I didn't ask you to come."

"No, you didn't." Hawk raised his arms slightly and lifted his palms toward the ceiling, rolling his eyes as he did so. "This was all about your needs. You up and left your family back home worrying sick about you. Which, as you well know, is why I came. It was me or Andy, and I was the better choice."

The mention of her family made Tess long for home. Stupid, arrogant Hawk was probably right. This was her fault. She wished her father would magically appear. He would know exactly what to do. And she could go home and be safe. Not that she would admit any of this to Hawk. No way, no how.

Instead, Tess pushed past Hawk and marched in to her bunk. "And the war's not my fault either. I think that was on the history books long before I decided to visit Rebecca." She turned to slam the door and came face to face with Hawk.

He didn't crack a smile, not that she'd expected him to. He glared at her, then slowly, with a hard edge to his voice, gave the orders. "Debating what is and what isn't your fault is a waste of time. You, of all of us on board, are in the most danger. A woman onboard is unheard of, according to Ben. He said for you to crawl under something and hide. Let's go down the passageway and find a safe place. There's nowhere suitable in this cabin."

Hawk held open the door. Tess hesitated.

"Today, Tess. Get moving. We've got minutes, not hours."

Tess walked by Hawk, wishing like crazy she could ram an elbow into his side. She opened the first door on the left. The room was tidy, probably in part because no one had really slept last night. There were twelve beds, but not one had space below to hide under. And the hammocks hanging from every other available space would be far too obvious.

She watched Hawk opening the footlockers. "No way! I am not climbing

106

into one of those."

He glanced over his shoulder. "I wasn't asking you to. I was looking to see how deep they were and if they were sealed in back. You might have been able to crawl through to a larger opening. No such luck."

Tess rolled her eyes and left the room. She walked across the hall. "Hey, Hawk, I found the slop room."

Hawk strode through the door, annoyance written between every pinched line in his scowl. "Tess, really, this isn't the time to sort through their clothing."

Ignoring his tone and presence, Tess began to open every chest in the small storage room. Slops, breeches, simple linen shirts, waistcoats, jerkins, stockings, knit caps, hats, bandanas, and great-looking pea coats were stored in various-sized wooden chests.

Unfortunately, not one of the trunks was empty. Tess closed the last of the chests and turned to face Hawk. "It was worth a look," she tossed over her shoulder as she pushed him aside and went back into the crew's quarters.

She heard him fall into step behind her, then felt him breathing down her neck. All the days and nights she had spent wanting to get close to Hawk, and now she only wanted him to go away. God was not amusing her, not one bit. When she'd asked over and over again for time with Hawk, this was not, even in her worst nightmares, what she'd envisioned. They entered the end bunk room. Tess shook her head.

"We need to keep looking. Maybe there's a closet." Hawk moved a step toward the door.

"Wait." Tess jumped up onto the bottom bunk in the right corner and climbed onto the top bed. With only four feet between the straw mattress and the ceiling, Tess bent low so she didn't hit her head again. She held onto the back rail of the bunk and peered over the edge. "Yes!"

"What?" Hawk asked.

"Just like our boat, the upper corner bunks are not flush to the wall because of the ceiling height. Have you ever looked at the bunks in Cabins 11 and 12? The backboard of the top bunk is about three feet off the wall. I thought Dad had designed it that way so a kid wouldn't sit up in the middle of the night and smack his head on an extremely low ceiling.

"Guess the idea has been around for centuries. It's the same here. There's a good three-foot gap between the bed board and the wall. I can just lie down in there and pull a blanket over me."

For a moment, Hawk smiled. And in that moment, Tess forgot he was being a jerk, she forgot they were caught in a war, and she forgot he was about to leave her alone in a dark room in a very small space.

"Good thinking, Tess." He smiled again.

She smiled back, momentarily lost in his blue eyes.

Hawk nodded. "Up you go."

The happy moment was gone. Hawk was all business once again. Tess inched slowly across the scratchy mattress and down into her tiny hiding place. "Do I need to pull the blanket up now?"

"You'd better. They'll be here in under an hour, and I don't know if I'll make it back down to warn you."

Tess reached for the nearest dark wool covering and lifted it up to her chin. She raised her head and looked at Hawk. "You can leave. I'll be fine."

Hawk pointed sharply at the hiding place. "Tess, stay there. Don't move. Don't make a sound until I come get you. If you don't hear my voice, don't you dare show your face or speak a word."

Tess shivered. "How long will you leave me here?"

For a second, Hawk's face softened. He shook his head. "I don't know. I haven't a clue what's going to happen. I'm sorry. Just stay put. Are we clear? Don't move."

"Crystal." Tess dropped down into the cubby and sighed. *Worst trip of my life!*

She listened for the sound of Hawk leaving. She didn't dare lift her head, in case he was testing her. Seconds passed. She didn't think Hawk had moved.

"Tess, your father might forgive me, but I wouldn't forgive myself if something happened to you. I'll be back to check on you as soon as I can. I promise. Okay?"

She didn't respond. He'd told her not to speak. He'd probably jump down her throat if she answered him.

"Tess?"

"I thought I couldn't speak," she whispered.

Hawk chuckled. "Good girl. It's a small miracle, probably one for the record books. Let's pray for another miracle. We need the HMS *Greyhound* to find another target."

Tess heard the door shut, and she closed her eyes. *What did he just say? What was the name of that ship? And did he mention praying?* She had to think this through. At least she had something to do while she waited for Hawk—or the enemy—to come and get her.

23

TESS STARED AT THE CEILING. Her brain was working overtime, and her toes twitched as quickly as her thoughts spanned one synapse to another. Was Hawk serious? His praying had to be a joke. When had she heard Hawk pray or talk about God? Sarcasm at the very least.

The *Greyhound*, however, sounded familiar. Tess knew she'd heard the name before, though she was certain there wasn't a *Greyhound* in any of the harbors on the Island. She knew every boat that sailed from the Vineyard. So where had she heard of the HMS *Greyhound*? It had to be from the past—the distant past.

Tess drummed her fingers on the wall to her right, albeit quietly so neither Hawk nor anyone else would hear her. *I know this. I know this! Cheese and crackers! Why can't I just remember exactly what and who the Greyhound was?*

Her father would know. If the *Greyhound* had ever been within sight of the *Shenandoah*, her father would know the story. *Think, Tess, think. It's 1776,* Shenandoah *is in service. What bit of history has Dad tried to drill into my head?*

"Oh, my gosh!" Tess bolted up, ducked just in time to avoid smacking her head on the ceiling, then crawled over the back bed rail and swung her legs across the bunk and dropped down onto the floor.

She hustled over to door, cracked it open, and peered into the hallway. No one in sight. She ran across the hall, threw open the slop-room door, scurried inside, and closed it tightly behind her. She ransacked the trunks to find a pair of pants that would stay on and a shirt that didn't look four sizes too big. When she pulled a small tunic over her head, Tess looked down to check the fit. For the first time in her life, Tess was glad she was barely a B-cup. The shirt was loose enough and her chest flat enough that she might pass for a teenage boy. For extra measure, she slipped into a short gray jacket. Not her best color, but she didn't exactly want to look good.

She couldn't find a pair of shoes or boots small enough to fit her. Looking down at her bare feet, Tess chuckled. "Thank God I didn't get a pedicure last week!"

She found a piece of rope and tied it around her waist to help hold up her trousers. If Hawk didn't start screaming at her and blow her cover, Tess figured she could pass for a galley boy. Pulling her hair into what she hoped was a manly looking low ponytail, she tied it back with a piece of twine she lifted off the nail on the back wall. She finished off her disguise with a black neckerchief she found in the nearest chest.

Hoping for the best, Tess opened the door and strutted down the hall, rather pleased with her new outfit. Within ten steps, she froze midstride. No man would walk as she was. She dropped her shoulders and hunched over slightly at the waist. She consciously took wider strides and did her best to saunter, without laughing, toward the companionway.

One look at the pot-bellied stove and Tess decided on an extra bit of insurance. She reached in and ran her palm along the bottom of the stove. Then she patted her soot-covered hands together and rubbed her rather nice-looking feet until they were appropriately grimy. Satisfied that no one would give her previously buffed feet a second glance, Tess swallowed hard and ran her dirty fingers over and through her hair, dulling any shine that might have caught Hawk's eye if he'd lingered long enough to notice. Filthy from head to toe, Tess ascended the ladder.

A knot formed in her stomach as she inched her way up. Hawk was not going to be angry. He'd be furious. Why did the man have to be such an overbearing jerk? He never gave her a break, nor would he ever acknowledge, without force, that she was capable. But this news couldn't wait. Ben had to be told who, or what, the HMS *Greyhound* was. And she was fairly certain Hawk didn't know. But she did, and what she knew, what her father had drilled into his kids' heads was the history of the *Shenandoah*. And what she knew now could save lives—American and British, hers and Hawk's and Ben's and Jonah's and Adam's and God knew who else. Rebecca would thank her, regardless of Hawk's response.

24

TESS STEPPED UP FROM THE COMPANIONWAY and onto the deck midship. She turned about, hoping not to see Hawk. Or hoping he wouldn't see her first. In the midst of the sails being lowered, the crew jostling about, and the HMS *Greyhound* approaching, Jonah caught her eye and walked over.

"Begging your pardon, Miss Roberts, but have you confused your clothing, or Rebecca's dresses, with that of a lad?" There was no jest in Jonah's tone. He was concerned and puzzled. He evaluated her attire from head to foot. A small grin reached his face when he saw her soot-covered feet. "Pray tell, did you fall into the coal bin?"

Tess held up a hand. "Shh, Jonah, don't blow my cover."

"Cover?" Hazel eyes rolled and squinted into a perplexed expression.

"Disguise, Jonah. My clothes are my cover, if you get my drift. And call me Roberts. I'm your new galley boy."

After a glance around the deck, Jonah asked, "And Peter Murdock shall be resigning from his position today?" Jonah was too tense to laugh, but Tess knew he had made an attempt at a joke.

She wasn't in the mood to laugh either. Her message was the only reason she'd come up on deck and defied Ben's explicit orders. "Listen, Jonah, I've got to talk with Ben without Hawk seeing me. Will you help?"

He twisted the knot on his bandana. "Miss Roberts, under normal circumstances I would be happy to assist you in any endeavor you were inclined to attempt. Your timing, however, is not suitable given our grave situation. I think you had best return below deck. The captain is preparing to…"

Impatience got the better of Tess. She heard the annoyance in her words before she could change her tone. "Jonah, I'm not an idiot. I see the ship. I also know what's going to happen. I know that this is the middle of June in 1776. Unless you're going to tell me it's a different year or a different month, then I have information Captain Reed needs to be aware of. As in I *know* what is going to happen. Now. Here. Today."

Whether it was her tone or her words, Jonah's expression changed instantly. Clearly no longer affected by her outward appearance or the fact that she was a woman, he stood straighter and instantly regarded her with the same look of respect that he gave his captain.

"Come with me, Roberts. I shall bring you to the captain and explain to any crew within earshot that they should refer to you as Roberts, our galley boy."

Tess sighed with relief and fell into step behind Jonah. No more than fifty feet separated her from Captain Benjamin Reed. Her stomach fluttered ever so slightly, but her eyes focused on Ben, willing him to see her and to remain calm, maybe even read her mind and understand her disguise.

"Jonah!" Ben yelled while looking directly at Tess.

Without flinching or backing down, Jonah stopped his brother before Captain Reed ordered Tess below deck—or worse. "Captain, Brother, the galley boy Roberts insisted on speaking with you. *He* has information about the approaching ship, information from her, ah, his father, your fellow captain."

Ben lifted an eyebrow when Jonah suggested Tess was their galley boy, but he no longer looked cross. Tess knew that Rebecca had shared vital information regarding the American Revolution with Ben and General George Washington at a time when she was a suspected traitor stowed away on the *Shenandoah*. Only a few weeks ago in her time, Tess had sat with Becca on her father's bunk and listened to Rebecca's incredible story. She remembered the day as if it was yesterday.

"Tess, you wouldn't believe it. I was standing there face to face with George Washington. You can't imagine what it was like to see him, and there I was, a prisoner who was about to sound like a crazy woman or a witch. But I had to tell them what I knew. I was afraid Ben wouldn't believe me, but everything inside me was screaming, 'Tell them about the guns and the battle at Dorchester!'

"So I did." Becca laughed, spinning her index finger in circles by her head to indicate how crazy she must have sounded.

Tess recalled the twinge of jealousy she'd felt, listening to Rebecca talk about President Washington. "Dad would probably give anything to have traded places with you."

"Yeah, he would've loved it. I would have given anything to have a camera or my cell phone. I wish I had a picture of Ben, too, so I could show you. He's, well, he's perfect, Tess."

Their time had passed too quickly, and then Rebecca was gone. Now, a month later for Tess, yet nearly a year having passed for Becca and Ben, Tess stood next to Rebecca's husband with a British ship about to threaten everything that mattered in this lifetime to her oldest and dearest friend, and

Tess was the only one who knew what would happen. At the moment, she was thankful that Rebecca and Melissa Smith had paved the way for twenty-first-century visitors.

Tess nodded at Ben and walked up beside him. In a voice just above a whisper, she relayed what she knew. "Captain Reed, there is no danger to you, the crew, or the *Shenandoah*. The HMS *Greyhound* sailed from England in early spring. She put into port in Halifax, Nova Scotia, on May 15, with a number of American prisoners on board, including Colonel Ethan Allen. The prisoners disembarked and remained in Halifax to be exchanged for British prisoners of war. The *Greyhound* set sail from Halifax around June 4 and is headed to New York."

Ben leaned down and spoke quietly so only Tess would hear. "I appreciate the history lesson, Miss Roberts, but have you information what shall occur today, in the next hours? What can you tell me of my men's safety and of my ship?"

Tess nodded. "Everything is going to be okay. President George Washington kept a journal during the war. He wrote about the HMS *Greyhound* capturing a ship off the coast of Cape Ann in June 1776. No one knew the name of the ship. My father often wondered, even made up a few bedtime stories for us, in which the captured ship was our *Shenandoah*. But no one ever knew—until now. This," Tess said, waving her hand toward the *Greyhound*, "is what George Washington wrote about.

"You've got no reason to worry. The *Greyhound* will seize *Shenandoah*. You will surrender peacefully, without any resistance. My father never mentioned anyone getting hurt, so I don't think you ordered anyone to fight off or attack the British when they boarded *Shenandoah*. Tomorrow or the next day a sloop will retake *Shenny*, and I'm sorry I don't remember exactly when, but the history books have no exact date. My father created different versions depending on which story he was telling at night, and your ship logs were either lost or destroyed, so we never had a clue *Shenny* really was the seized boat."

She watched Ben nod, his face pensive, his eyes intense, his pupils fixed on her. "Yes, specific logs have been destroyed. I could not allow any mention of Rebecca to be recorded throughout history. My father and I agreed that the logbook during Rebecca's time onboard had to be destroyed. Now I shall feel the same compulsion to burn the current log and any mention of you and Hawk before the full account reaches General Washington or anyone else. This would explain why your father could find no accurate remarks prior to or during these current events."

Tess was impressed. "My father had suggested as much after Rebecca went back. He never understood the missing logbooks until then. After that, it all made sense. Anyhow, without the exact date to give you, all I know is that pretty soon an armed American sloop is going to retake the *Shenandoah*, and you and all the men will sail home, cargo intact. You will send word to General Washington in New York, telling him what happened, and Washington will record your message in his journal."

Ben removed his hat and ran his right hand through his black hair. "Are you certain, Miss Roberts?"

"You can trust her on this, Captain. Tess knows the history of this ship better than anyone, except her father. Her brothers have told me that she learned *Shenandoah's* history until she could recite it at family dinners from memory, always to the delight of her father."

Tess's jaw dropped open. She couldn't believe that Hawk had just defended her, agreed with her, taken her side on something. She could only stare at him, dumbfounded. Hawk didn't so much as glimpse her reaction. He kept his focus on Ben, communicating his confidence in Tess with his solid stance by her side.

The captain nodded at Hawk, then turned his concentration back to Tess. "I am putting the lives of my men in your hands, Roberts. Is there further information you can or should tell me? Did your father relate to you specific details? I implore you to search your memory and consider what is at stake."

There was nothing more. Tess believed with all her heart that they were safe and would soon be rescued by another American ship. This was the only skirmish recorded that could have occurred between the *Shenandoah* and the British. If there had been one drop of blood shed, one injury, the slightest potential damage to her father's beloved ship, her dad would have drilled the information into Tess's brain until she could recite it forward and backward, awake or asleep.

Her father had taken his research seriously, traveling to England when she was in high school to visit the National Naval museum and read the old logbooks there. He'd found the logs of a few ships named HMS *Greyhound.* One of them had entries that coincided with the events off of Cape Ann in June 1776. No injuries or fatalities were recorded.

"I am confident that everything and everyone is going to be fine. Nothing bad happened. My father would have forced me to memorize every detail if something had gone wrong. I know I'm asking a lot here, but you can trust me. You will be safe."

Hawk moved to Tess's right side. She felt his presence surround her. He was with her—not beside her, but with her. She had expected him to be angry, furious, livid even. She had been prepared to stand her ground, to argue with him or tell him off. Now he was standing with her, and she couldn't find the words to ask him why or how.

She knew Ben was talking, instructing his crew and calling out orders. She sensed people moving about, yet all she could feel was Hawk standing next to her. His nearness filled her. She felt as though he was holding her hand, the warmth of his approval radiating throughout her body.

"Roberts. Roberts! Quit your daydreaming and help Murdock coil the lines."

Jonah was shaking Tess. His hands drew her away from Hawk. "Huh? What?"

Ben pushed Jonah aside and demanded Tess's attention. "Have you remembered something, Tess? Is there a detail you need to impart?"

She wanted to shrivel up and fade away. They were all looking at her, waiting for some intelligent comment. Heat rose from Tess's heart up her neck and across her cheeks. There was nowhere to escape. Why did she have to be a girl?

"Ah, nope. Sorry, I was just thinking about, um…" She squirmed slightly. There was no way she was going to tell anyone, especially with Hawk standing right there, that she was thinking about how wonderful it was to have Hawk by her side. "Well, talking about home got me thinking about my family."

There, now she'd lied…and less than successfully. Ben turned and strode toward the first mate, who was standing between the starboard cannons. She could have sworn he was grinning as he walked away. Hawk hadn't moved. Jonah was smiling.

I hate men.

"If you are done pondering your family life back home, perhaps you could assist Murdock with the lines." Jonah winked at Tess, then looked at Hawk. "When you have finished observing Roberts, I could use your help explaining to the men who the new galley boy is while we still have time."

Hawk cleared his throat as Jonah walked toward the bow. Tess noticed the flush of his cheeks and realized with immense satisfaction, and a good degree of wonder, that she wasn't the only one caught blushing.

She pivoted and walked toward the port side. The British were only moments away, yet she couldn't wipe off her grin. It was turning out to be a fantastic day.

25

TESS STOOD BETWEEN THE PORTSIDE CANONS. Across the deck, Ben talked with first mate William Barton, the only non-family member of the crew, other than Adam, who had been told who Rebecca truly was and where she had come from. Will glanced in Tess's direction a couple of times. He was nodding as Captain Reed pointed to the main mast.

Ben turned and went back to the helm. Will walked toward the bosun box, stopping once to talk with Adam, who appeared to agree with whatever Will was saying. Adam patted Will on the back and made his way past the crew flaking the foresail and around to where Ben stood. Jonah and Hawk followed Adam. Tess walked along the portside rail to hear what Adam and Ben had to say.

"A wise decision, Captain Reed," Adam said, all four men facing the horizon, watching the distance close between them and their enemy. Tess knew they had less than an hour, probably closer to thirty minutes, until the HMS *Greyhound* would be upon them.

Ben stood with his back to Tess, his hands behind him clasped around both ends of the spyglass. He shifted, brought his hands toward the rail, and raised the old-fashioned monocular to his right eye. Then he rotated it slightly in each direction and brought the glass and his hands behind his back again. "One vessel."

One ship made sense. Only the HMS *Greyhound* was recorded in President Washington's journal account of this conflict. One boat was good. One boat meant history was playing out as it should. One boat meant her message to Ben was accurate.

Tess couldn't see Ben's expression, but his hands were relaxed. There was a confidence to Ben that Tess both felt and saw. His strength was evident, not only in his build, but more so in the way he handled himself and his crew. The ship was under control. The deliberate actions of the men were a direct result of Ben's clear orders. But she also sensed the reverence and trust the sailors placed in their captain's command, much like her father's crew did. She felt safe.

Ben pivoted on his left heel and faced Adam, his profile a reflection of determination. He unrolled the leather around the two ends of the spyglass and held the pieces in his right hand. "Miss Roberts has revealed information that I believe to be true. Her words, the facts she speaks of with such conviction, resemble statements Rebecca once made in a similar situation. My wife spoke truth then. I reason Miss Roberts is doing the same. I am going to surrender. I pray my trust is not misplaced."

Ben didn't so much as glance at Tess, yet she felt the weight of his words. She wanted to defend herself but knew there was no need. She had given him facts—historical facts. She may not have been an honor student in American or world history, but she knew *Shenandoah's* past and any bit of speculation her father might have had about his ship. She also had Hawk's support.

She smiled, remembering that Hawk had vouched for her. Only a short while ago, he'd stood by her and stood up for her. Her heart filled as she recalled his words stored forever in her memory. Unconsciously, she stepped closer to Hawk.

Beyond the soundtrack playing in her mind, Tess heard Adam reassure Ben. "Our faith does not rest in the wisdom of men, Captain, but in the power of God." Adam paused. He lifted his eyes to heaven, then focused on the HMS *Greyhound.* "I believe Paul was familiar with troubles at sea. Would you not agree?"

Adam stood at an angle to Tess and the approaching British ship. Tess was surprised at how calm he appeared to be, externally as well as internally. Though she felt confident of the outcome, her stomach was in knots. War had always been in books or on television. Even the horrors of 9/11 had felt far away from her Island teenage life. This was real. The weapons on board both ships were real. The prickles of fear poking at her heart and mind were real. Fortunately, Hawk's presence was also real.

She stepped left and whispered to Hawk, "Who is Paul? What has he told Adam?"

Hawk leaned down and spoke softly to Tess, for her ears alone. "Paul is the apostle Paul. Adam quoted from 1 Corinthians chapter two."

Tess jerked her head back and looked up at the blonde demi-god standing next to her. He was a sailor with sun-bleached hair, calloused hands, and a smile that could melt the polar icecap. He was not a seminary student. She'd never seen this side of him, didn't even know he believed in God until this trip. She was gawking, she knew, but the man she'd crushed on for two years had just recognized a verse of Scripture that wasn't one of the top five.

Granted, most people knew at least the opening line from Psalm 23: "The Lord is my shepherd. I shall not want." Same with John 3:16: "For God so loved the world…"

Sports figures and inspirational speakers promoted Philippians 4:13 everywhere you went these days. Tess had seen numerous bumper stickers and T-shirts reading, "I can do all things through Christ who strengthens me." And anyone who had attended a couple of weddings had probably heard the full version of "Love is patient, love is kind..." from 1 Corinthians 13 and Matthew's "What God has joined together, let no man separate."

Those five were easy. But Hawk had recognized some random Bible verse instantly. Not only recognized the words but knew where in the Bible they were written. Hawk. *Shenandoah's* first mate. The guy she wanted to date and more. Tess couldn't help but wonder how she'd never seen or heard about this side of him. Before she could ask the questions on the tip of her tongue, Ben stepped in front of her.

"Are you certain, Miss Roberts? You have no doubt, no question in your mind as to the accuracy of the information you shared with me?"

Every inch of Tess's five-foot, four-inch frame straightened under Ben's stare. The slivers of fear dissolved as she heard her father telling this one story of *Shenandoah's* naval altercation to her eight-year-old self, her nine-year-old self, her ten-year-old self, and so on. He had spoken with pride that *Shenandoah* came through unscathed. The knots in her stomach untangled. With absolute confidence, her voice firm and bold, she replied, "Totally. This is a done deal. It's all going to work out, Captain. I promise."

The four men nodded, almost in unison. Tess searched Hawk's face and found the respect and admiration she'd waited over two years to see. She smiled at him, and he smiled back at her. A real smile, a smile that went below the surface and straight to her heart.

Tess knew the guys were strategizing, even though they weren't saying a word. She was grateful for the quiet, happier still to be standing so close and so near to Hawk. Even better, he wasn't making a move to run in the opposite direction. Time could freeze, as far as she was concerned.

The captain broke the silence. "With certainty, the men of Gloucester saw our ship and guessed our allegiance. In a port of patriots, one would not have missed our hurried retreat. The departure of the HMS *Greyhound* shortly after we sailed would likewise not have gone unnoticed. A vigilant patriot will have alerted the men in town of our impending danger. I have faith a Continental ship from Cape Ann will be underway as we speak, and we shall be restored before the sun sets."

Jonah glanced over his right shoulder in the direction of Gloucester. "Did anyone notice what sloops were at anchor? Tess noted that a sloop would come to our aid. As Commander Hopkins has ordered vessels furnished for a convoy from Newburyport to Philadelphia, mayhaps a Navy sloop took shelter in the harbor as we had done."

A loud crack startled every one. Tess nearly jumped out of her skin. Hawk put his right arm around her as the cannonball hit the surface and water splashed onto and over the starboard side of *Shenandoah*.

Ben looked out across the water. "A warning shot."

"Is it time, Captain?" Adam asked.

"Aye, Adam, it is." Ben clapped a hand on Hawk's left shoulder. "Hawk, please man the helm. I will return momentarily."

Hawk squeezed Tess's arm, his fingers gently reassuring her and awakening her senses at the same time. "You okay?"

His words were soft, tinged with a warmth Tess had longed for. She couldn't speak. Her emotions were too raw. She merely bobbed her head. For a second, she considered pretending she wasn't okay, pretending she was terrified and needed his arms around her. She knew it wasn't right, knew it wasn't the time or place for pretending, but it was what she wanted to do.

She felt his arm leave her body. Through the fabric of the pullover linen shirt she'd thrown on for her disguise, Tess's skin ached for his touch. She smiled as the four men studied her, gauging what they assumed was her response to the cannonball.

A quick thumbs-up and a casual chuckle shifted her focus. "No worries, guys. I was just caught off guard. Can't stand firecrackers, either. Get me every time." She stepped away from Hawk. "Do what you gotta do. I'm good."

Ben raised his left arm and signaled to Will before going below deck. Will instructed the men on deck to stand down. Tensions were high. A shot had been fired, though it had not been launched to strike the ship.

Four men stood beside each of *Shenandoah*'s cannons. A dozen men were in the hold, ready to carry and pass extra cannonballs if needed. Tess noticed a dozen or so of the crew on deck had pistols tied into their waistbands and belts. There were also numerous muskets resting against the bulwark.

The crew all knew Captain Reed was going to surrender. As a privateer posing as a merchant ship, Ben flew no colors on *Shenandoah*. They had no flag to strike, or lower, to show the British they weren't going to fight, so the white flag had to be raised. Still, the air sizzled with anticipation. Tess guessed that for almost every man on board, this was as close as they'd come to enemy fire.

Hawk squared his shoulders and walked over to the helm. He placed both hands on the wheel. Tess sucked in her breath, her lungs stretching to their capacity. She hadn't noticed Hawk had changed his clothes. He'd probably needed to after getting drenched last night, but her attention had been elsewhere all morning. Now, dressed in white slops, with a white shirt and navy blue waistcoat, standing behind the wheel of *Shenandoah*, Hawk could be Ben's first mate. She felt the air leave her lungs in one cleansing whoosh. The man before her was a colonial sailor. And he was magnificent.

He caught her staring, and he grinned. She blushed, not at all the response a young galley boy should have for a first mate. She'd been around ships and sailors her whole life. Her father's crew dressed in casual clothing for the kids' cruises. The guys on the *Lady Katherine* dressed in khakis and company-embroidered navy polo shirts. Uniforms, sailors or otherwise, were not something Tess had ever given much thought too. Until now.

Hawk looked hotter than any man had a right to. And it wouldn't do to have an eighteenth-century galley boy going gaga over a first mate. She would have to steer clear of Hawk when the British boarded *Shenandoah*. Until then, she wanted to drink in the site of the man she loved in uniform.

He must have read her mind. He stood taller, prouder, and stronger. As the crew prepared to surrender, as Ben went below deck to retrieve the white flag, as danger loomed in the very near distance, something changed between Tess and Hawk. She didn't know what was happening, not really. He hadn't said anything to her, hadn't kissed her, but suddenly they were different.

The wall he'd built between them two summers ago had disintegrated, almost as if it had cracked as he crossed the time barrier. The attraction they'd first experienced the warm, sunny afternoon she met him—those feelings were swirling in and around them, magnified over time and years of wanting.

The wind filling the sails couldn't cool Tess. Her heart was pumping a rush of heat throughout her body. She didn't want to move, didn't want to leave, didn't want to change anything. She wasn't the captain's daughter on Ben's ship. She was the woman Hawk put his arm around.

She heard the crew moving on deck behind her, getting into position, ready to fight in case the British attacked. She had no interest. Her hands resting on her slops, her thumbs tucked over and behind her makeshift rope belt, Tess was content to lean against the captain's rooftop and watch Hawk as the action unfolded around her.

Soon enough the real world would invade her fantasy life. For the moment, for as long as time allowed, Tess was going to stay where she was, in Hawk's sight, in his heart.

26

BEN RETURNED CARRYING THE WHITE FLAG. Will joined him at the helm. Tess stood and moved closer to Hawk at the wheel. Adam and Jonah, who had been talking by the cleat for the rigging of the captain's gig, walked over to stand beside Will.

"Captain, the men are ready. Should I call them to attention?" Ben's first mate asked.

"Yes, thank you, William." Ben's voice was flat. Tess couldn't imagine what it would feel like to surrender your crew, your life, and your ship into enemy hands. Her promise that everything was going to be okay probably didn't change Ben's feelings of loss and concern.

"Roberts," Hawk shouted as Tess stepped closer to Ben, William, Adam, and Jonah, hoping to hear their strategizing. Hawk's tone was terse and insistent. "Stay with me at the helm. I don't want you out of my sight."

His words hit her ears like fingernails on a chalkboard. She couldn't believe how quickly he was back to giving her orders. Shortest fantasy ever!

Tess was about to snap a snippy retort when Hawk motioned with his right hand for her to come behind the wheel and stand beside him.

"Please," he said, imploring her, "I want you next to me. I'll worry if I can't see you."

She hadn't needed to look. His words alone had sealed her fate for eternity. But she did. She raised her eyes to stare into his depths of blue. In an instant, she was drowning in an endless azure ocean of love. She could almost feel the warm water caressing her skin, inviting her to stay there forever. Her breath caught, a lump lodged in her throat, her heart swelled, and Tess Roberts fell head over heels in love.

Without releasing Hawk's gaze, Tess nearly swam toward him, her feet floating over the deck. She stopped about a yard from the wheelbase. He took one step to the left, reached for her arm, and lovingly pulled her next to him. Tess lost any hold she had on reality. All she could see or feel was Hawk's presence surrounding her, lifting her, carrying her as though she were sailing in tropical waters with her face toward the sun, the wind in the sails, and her hands on the wheel.

Less than an inch of air space separated them. Hawk was smiling at her, beaming even. His feelings for her were visible to the world. And to Tess.

She was about to burst, her happiness beyond anything she'd ever known. How long had she waited for this moment? How many times had she seen Hawk on the ship, in town, or driving by and wished he'd notice her? Felt like thousands, probably was. Now, finally, he wanted her next to him. She was the happiest girl on earth. Cinderella had nothing on Tess Roberts!

Adam was the first to notice the status update in their relationship.

"Roberts!" Adam exclaimed. "As relieved as I am that our galley boy has reconciled *his* differences with Master Hawk, your proximity to the man is…unnatural."

Tess doubled over laughing. Their "proximity" to each other didn't look natural? Ha! It wasn't. Everyone at home would agree. She would have too— at home.

Well, she wouldn't have agreed that she shouldn't be next to Hawk, but she would have agreed that Hawk and her father and probably the entire Island had been against her being in close proximity to Hawk. But not here, not now. In 1776, she could be, and was, as close to Hawk as she could get. Best part—he'd asked her, even begged a little.

Her laughter faded as she thought about where she was. Her location wasn't on *Shenandoah* or in 1776. She was located next to Hawk, beside Hawk, with Hawk. And that was exactly where she wanted to be. It was the greatest feeling in the world. She sighed with contentment.

"Sorry, Adam. I forgot who I was for a minute." Tess slid about six feet to her left, away from Hawk. "I'll just move my *boy* butt over here and pretend I'm waiting for orders."

Adam coughed. Jonah blushed. Hawk laughed.

For a brief moment, Captain Benjamin Reed smiled. Tess wondered if he was remembering when he fell in love with Rebecca and how crazy and different her words and actions must have appeared and sounded to a man from the eighteenth century.

Before Tess could think of something else witty to say, Ben's smile disappeared behind the worry and contemplation his face once again reflected. She was glad Rebecca wasn't onboard and that they didn't have cell phones to text one another or Facebook for status updates. She wouldn't want Becca stressing out about Ben, her, or anyone else onboard.

Tess twirled and untwirled her ponytail around her index finger. She was fairly certain Rebecca didn't know about the *Shenandoah* being captured by the British. The subject wasn't taught in Island schools because there was no written record of it. Her father didn't even know! For all Rebecca knew, Ben and the *Shenandoah* sailed through the Revolutionary War without a single care in the world, at least not one that resulted in a battle or capture or damage to the ship or an injury to any person on board. Being without technology definitely had its advantages.

A soft breeze carried the odor of gunpowder from the cannonball. Tess shuddered. She couldn't help but compare the shocking acts of violence in the twenty-first century to the mildness of a warning shot. Rebecca was better off without technology. No school shootings in Colonial America. No bombs killing little boys waiting for their dad to cross the finish line at the Boston Marathon.

Bombs. They didn't exist in 1776. Terrorists didn't exist in 1776. Chemical warfare and automatic weapons didn't exist in 1776. War was somewhat civilized. One could surrender without blood and guts flying all over the place. Strike your colors, ask for quarter, or raise the white flag, and men universally agreed to stop maiming everything in sight. Goosebumps rose on Tess's arms. She released her hair and rubbed her arms. Life may be "easier" back home, but it was a lot kinder in 1776.

Jonah nudged Tess. "Roberts, I have not seen a lad toy with his hair in the manner ye were a moment past."

"Oh. Right. Boy again." Tess ran her hands down over the fading goose bumps and tucked her thumbs into the waistband of her slops. She was going to blow her cover in sixty seconds flat if she didn't start to focus on Ben and the ship instead of Hawk and home. "I make a lousy boy, don't I?"

"I am certain you have talents better suited for your natural state. Are you good with a needle and thread?" Jonah asked, no jest in his voice.

"Um, not really. Can't cook, hate to clean, wouldn't be caught dead sewing a dress or doilies. I'm not your average wife material, not even close. Just put me on a boat and leave me there."

Tess saw that Jonah wasn't paying attention. She followed his gaze to see Ben, Will, and Adam striding toward the main mast, the white flag neatly folded in Ben's left hand.

"Are you okay, Jonah? This really is going to work out," Tess said.

"I do not doubt your word, Miss Roberts…Roberts. I trust you have information much the same as Rebecca and Aunt Missy. Alas, I regret a surrender to the British on principle."

"I get that. Totally. But don't worry. The shoe will be on the other foot faster than a car running through a yellow light. I don't know what sloop is coming, but the HMS *Greyhound* is about to get their butt kicked. Trust me." Tess swung her right leg, stopping her foot inches from Jonah's backside. "A good old Yankee butt whooping."

"Watch yourself, Jonah. Tess, er, Roberts, has been praised and cursed for the accuracy of her foot," Hawk joked.

They all laughed. Jonah's back relaxed, his stance less rigid.

"Hey," Tess said, looking back at Hawk, "think we can leave the helm and scoot over to hear what Ben's gonna say to the crew?"

"The sails are down. We're not going anywhere, at least not quickly. What do you say, Jonah?" Out of respect, Hawk waited for the younger man's reply.

The captain's brother lowered his gaze to the deck. Tess could feel his reluctance. Hesitantly he said, "Aye, we should gather with the others."

Jonah led the trio up the port side of the deck and around to the main mast. The crew standing closer to the captain parted to allow Jonah and his guests a front-row spot.

Captain Benjamin Reed squared his shoulders and adjusted his waistcoat, then addressed his men. "I have reason to believe a sloop from Gloucester is under sail at present to aid our endeavors."

Ben slowly scanned the deck, making eye contact with each crewmember. "We are outnumbered and outgunned. I lost my brother Magnus at Bunker Hill. I shall not risk your lives here today. I shall raise the white flag in faith and belief that assistance is drawing near and none shall perish. As I surrender, take heed, men. We submit not to the British rule, but to the Lord's will and safekeeping."

Cheers sounded. The men clapped. Tess stared, mouth open.

Hawk leaned over and whispered, "Close your mouth, Tess. They'll take you for an agnostic, or worse."

"Huh? They'll think I'm weird? Their captain is surrendering, and they're clapping, and I've got a problem?"

Hawk shook his head and grinned. He looked as if he wanted to kiss her. Tess could see the desire in his eyes. Sure, he was amused by her, but he also had the passionate fire of a man who liked what he saw. "It's about faith, Tess. What Ben said about giving it to God—these guys believe it. And it's cause for joy, in any situation."

She didn't get it. As much as her parents believed, Tess had never jumped on the bandwagon. "You believe it too, don't you?" She wasn't sure she wanted an answer. This new side of Hawk was a little much to take in.

He nodded. "Yeah, I do, Tess."

"Okay." She spoke the words, but her heart was heavy. It wasn't okay.

He bumped into her playfully. "Hey, we'll talk later. It's all good."

She didn't say anything. What could she say? That it wasn't good. That later he would realize she wasn't so big on God. That later he would realize her faith could fit into a thimble. That later he would realize he needed a different kind of girlfriend, and she would be right back where she'd been, only worse. Now that she'd had a few minutes of being the woman Hawk looked at with love, she couldn't go back. But she couldn't lie either. If God was so great, why did she hurt so much?

As the men stood at attention while Ben raised the white flag, Tess's heart sank for an altogether different reason. She wanted to go back in time—again. Not way back, not even a few years, just back to an hour ago when she still had a chance with Hawk.

27

A SOMBER ATMOSPHERE FELL OVER THE SHIP. Tess was so wrapped up in her thoughts on God and Hawk, and Hawk and God, she hadn't noticed the enemy approaching until the man she couldn't get out of her head spoke directly into her ear.

"Earth to Galley Boy Roberts," he teased, then pointed in the direction of a small boat advancing off their starboard side.

The HMS *Greyhound's* captain's gig was nearing *Shenandoah*. There were six men in the boat. The one dressed to the nines had to be the captain. His white breeches, white vest, and navy blue jacket with gold piping and accoutrements looked rather regal. Tess couldn't make out what the coxswain was saying but knew he was calling commands to the four oarsmen who alternated rowing two to a side. The whole situation was surreal to Tess and rather cool. She pushed aside her worries about Hawk and her lack of faith and zeroed in on the history that was playing out in front of her.

She was aboard *Shenandoah*, the real *Shenandoah*, her father's dream vessel. And she was about to witness the only confrontation *Shenny* had during the American Revolution—the unpublished, unconfirmed, undocumented surrender, however short-lived it would be. Oh, and Hawk was with her, as in *with her*. She would remember this day for the rest of her life.

When Rebecca described meeting George Washington, Tess had been a little jealous. Now, she was riding a high probably akin to what her best friend had felt. Living out history was soooo much better than any book or class she'd been forced to participate in. Too bad her father couldn't transport all the Island school kids back in time for a real-life history lesson.

She tipped slightly to her left. "This is amazing. Could you imagine taking all the middle-schoolers back in time on a real history cruise? They would love it," she whispered to Hawk, holding back a high-five for her rather brilliant idea.

He leaned down. "Why don't you propose that idea to your father? But do it when I'm in the room. I want to see his reaction."

Tess refrained from giving Hawk a good-natured punch. Captain Reed glanced over at them, his jaw set, the rigidness returned. "Hawk, please step back with Jonah and Roberts. Be watchful of the galley boy."

Standing taller, Tess's first mate replied, "Aye, aye, Captain."

The oarsmen rowed the gig up alongside *Shenandoah*. Captain Reed stood at attention. His navy jacket, though lacking any military insignia or gold trim, looked almost as impressive as the British captain's. Tess offered a silent "Thank you" to her father for sharing this portion of history with her. His many re-enactments and embellishments of what he thought might be *Shenandoah's* big moment in the Revolutionary War allowed her to be fully present. She felt no fear, just awe. She moved with Hawk and Jonah to the third row of men, peering through the space between the crew in front of her as they all waited for the enemy to board.

The rope ladder went taut as the British began their ascent. Tess refrained from smiling. She didn't dare glance up at Hawk. They were the only two who could enjoy the moment. They knew the outcome. And they could leave any night they wanted to. The crew may have put their trust in God and Ben, but Tess was confident of the facts her father had recounted during his evening stories.

Ben and William were tall and handsome standing by the bulwark ladder. If Ben was nervous, there was no sign of it. When the British captain stood on deck, Ben extended his right hand. "Good day to you, Captain. Captain Benjamin Reed. My first mate, William Barton. The *Shenandoah* and her crew call for quarter."

"Captain Archibald Dickson." The two captains shook hands. "On behalf of King George, I accept your surrender. The *Greyhound* sails posthaste for New York. My supply officer will inventory your ship when we arrive and drop anchor. Time is of the essence. To seal your surrender, I require half a dozen men for servitude on the *Greyhound*."

Tess sucked in her breath. This wasn't part of her father's story. Make believe or not, he'd never created prisoners. Her spine went rigid as she clenched her fists.

Hawk must have felt her stiffen. Though he didn't move or so much as glance in her direction, she heard him whisper. "Take it easy, Tess. Just because you didn't read it, doesn't mean it didn't happen. Prisoners of war were standard then just as they are now."

Keeping her eyes on Ben, Tess expressed her concern. "But what if our being here changed things?"

"Not likely. Just stay calm. You said yourself Washington's journal entry was short. If he didn't mention the ships involved, why would he write down the names of a few prisoners?"

What Hawk said made total sense. Tess relaxed. Her shoulders softened. Everything would be fine. The sky was blue, and the sun was shining. How could anything go wrong?

The crew in front of Hawk and Tess stepped closer together as Captain Dickson scanned the rows of men and stepped through the gap three men down from Jonah on her right.

"Captain Dickson," Ben said with a calm Tess thought he might not be feeling, "with all due respect, my crew is light. If you oblige an expedient journey to New York, each hand is needed on deck."

The British officer didn't respond to Ben. Tess wondered if he rolled his eyes in annoyance, but she couldn't risk looking at him. He was too close. The calm she felt moments ago was gone.

Five seconds later, he stopped in front of her. Tess held her breath. She focused on his black, well-polished boots. *Keep moving*, she thought, *keep moving*. He didn't.

"Ye name, lad." An order, not a question.

Without lifting her head, Tess knew he was addressing her. Fear gripped her throat as her mouth went dry and closed over her tongue. She honestly couldn't make a sound.

"Boy!" he demanded.

At his sharp reprimand, Tess snapped her head up and looked into the face of her worst nightmare. The British soldier could force her to leave Hawk, to leave *Shenandoah*, to leave Cabin 8 and her only way home to her family. He was worse than any mystical sea serpent that had slithered into her childhood dreams. He was real.

Tess opened her mouth and croaked out an inaudible, "Rawww…bbb…erts."

In a flash, Tess saw herself stuck in 1776 just like Melissa when she had been taken ashore years ago and then stayed in 1770. But Melissa had Isaiah. She had found love and happiness, according to Rebecca. Tess would be without Hawk, without Rebecca, and without her family. Her body began to tremble.

"Excuse me, Captain," Ben said. "The lad, my wife's nephew, has been forced into service as a galley boy. He stowed away to be with his cousin. He is neither sailor nor seaworthy. The youngest of six, he has been coddled and pampered. My wife would not forgive me if Master Roberts was not returned home."

"I'll go."

She heard the words, felt a second of relief, then realized who had spoken them. Tess turned her head slightly to the left and confirmed that Hawk had volunteered as a prisoner in her place.

"No!" She screamed the word in her mind, but it came out strangled.

Hawk gazed down at Tess, and though he said nothing, his look all but told her not to argue with him. "Yes," he insisted.

Anger rose and pushed fear back into the recesses of Tess's mind. Hawk was not, absolutely not, going to leave *Shenandoah*. Someone had to do something to stop him. Maybe if she revealed to this captain that she was a girl, he would believe they were simply a merchant ship, and he'd leave them alone. Rebecca had posed as Ben's wife to convince another British captain that they were sailing home from the Vineyard after a visit with her family. If it worked then, maybe it could work again.

Tess reached up toward her ponytail with her right hand.

"Roberts!" Hawk growled.

The sailors in the immediate vicinity turned toward Tess and Hawk. Captain Dickson saw her hand in the air. "You have a question, lad?"

"No, he does not," Hawk answered. He spoke to the captain, but his focus was on Tess. She stared back at him, mad and hurt. How could he even think of leaving her? Swiveling away from his relentless gaze, she pretended to be fascinated by the folds of the lowered topsails.

Ben walked a few paces over to Hawk. He extended his hand. "All will be well. Matters will be tended to. Be of courage and faith."

Hawk shook his hand, then headed for the bulwark ladder.

Captain Dickson followed Hawk. Tess heard them moving and fought every urge to scream and rage. She clenched her fists and pounded them against her thighs. Life was so impossibly unfair. Tears threatened, but she would not give in, nor would she watch Hawk leave her.

"Roberts," she heard Hawk call. She ignored him.

"Roberts!"

Tess flinched. She wanted to curse him, but she pivoted on her heel to face the man who had volunteered to leave her. Hawk had paused on the rope. He was standing on the top rung, his hands holding onto the iron stanchions on either side of the gangway.

He smiled at her, an expression that on any other day might have been her undoing. At that moment she was too hurt to cave in. "Will you do me a favor?" he asked.

"No." Tess crossed her arms over her chest. If he was going to walk away from her, she wasn't about to do a darn thing for him.

"Please. It's important to me, more important than my life, than the air I breathe."

It wasn't the please that tugged at Tess's heart. It was the urgency in his voice. "What?" she snapped back, not wanting him to think for one second that she cared what the favor was or why it was so important.

He smiled again. This time the smile reached his eyes, and the depth of blue drew Tess in, calling her to dive in and surrender.

"Roberts." He spoke softly, not as one speaks to a galley boy but as a man to his lover. "In case my return is impossible, tell Tess that I love her. Tell her that I've loved her since that first day I held her hand."

The world stopped moving. Tess saw only Hawk, his words enveloping her and filling her. She wanted to run into his arms. She wanted to melt into him and stay there forever.

Jonah grabbed her right arm. Tess looked down at his hand and up into her friend's eyes. She nodded, understanding that a rash move on her part could change history and cost them all their lives.

She couldn't go to Hawk. She couldn't respond. She was trapped between her world and Rebecca's world. Her voice held only four words, and unable to say "I love you, too," she had no other words.

Jonah, who at five inches taller than Tess appeared older than his twenty-one years, spoke for her. "Be at ease, Hawk. Roberts shall not fail to deliver your message. You may be certain Tess shares your feelings."

Hawk smiled but didn't move. Tess was beyond grateful that Jonah had said what she couldn't, but there was no way she could stand another second of torture. They were taking the man she loved, the man who loved her, and there was nothing she could do. Nothing. And he was staring into her eyes with an intensity that scared her.

"Roberts," he said, his gaze unwavering, "go to the infirmary tonight."

The impact of his words nearly knocked Tess over. He was telling her to go home without him, to leave him on the British ship, to return to the twenty-first century alone. There was no way on earth or sea she was going anywhere. "No!"

"Yes. You have to." His tone changed from bossy to begging.

"No. Save your breath." Tess's voice broke. Ben stepped forward. Tess watched him bend over and say something to Hawk before shaking his hand. Tess gritted her teeth. If Ben thought he could force her to leave Hawk, he had another thing coming.

The air left her lungs when Hawk moved down one rung on the ladder. She locked her eyes with his and hoped he could read everything she couldn't say. In the next second he was gone, his blond hair and blue eyes below her line of sight as he climbed down to the enemy's waiting gig.

Jonah tightened his grip. Tess remained motionless, nowhere to go, no way to help. She hadn't realized she was trembling until Adam hurried over and was in front of her, steadying her with his two hands on her upper arms. Jonah gave her right arm a gentle squeeze before he headed over to Ben.

Tess spotted the gig rowing away from *Shenandoah*. She took a gulp of air and stifled a sob. Adam kept a firm but tender hold of her. His voice was compassionate when he tried to console Tess. "Hawk is in the Lord's care, Miss Roberts. Do not fret. Cast your cares unto Him who hears all."

Tess jerked her arms free, took a step back, and then brought her hand up sharply, stabbing her right index finger at Adam. "Don't speak to me of God! He hasn't heard or answered one of my prayers. And now He's allowed Hawk to be taken prisoner. Your God is not my God!"

Tess whirled around and all but ran to the companionway. She didn't notice the stunned expressions on the face of every man within earshot. She was so over God, she didn't care if the Being himself heard her. She slid down the ladder, hit the floor hard as she landed, marched down the hall, and then slammed the storage room door behind her.

28

ANDY WAS THRILLED TO BE HEADING DOWNSTAIRS and back outside for a shower. The day had dragged on endlessly. He'd gone for a run in the morning but then sat at the kitchen table, unable to think of anything else he wanted to do with his Saturday...other than be with Allyson. Which wasn't an option until dinner. At nine in the morning, his date felt decades away.

When he saw his mom heading out to the tool shed, he'd offered to help with whatever she needed done. Anything to keep him occupied until seven, which a fifth glance at the clock revealed was another nine hours and thirty-seven minutes away. He'd all but begged her for chores to do.

Before lunch, they had cut back the summer-blooming flowers, weeded the annual bed, and cleared out the spent squash plants, cucumbers, and a couple of tomatoes that no longer bore fruit.

They ate lunch on the patio. Three cheese-and-tomato sandwiches, plus a side salad for Andy. His mom had dug into a salad of every vegetable in the garden.

When Andy mowed the lawn and trimmed the hedges during the afternoon, he considered how little his mom had quizzed him about his personal life. Oh, she'd asked about Allyson, but mostly about her work and if she was going to continue to teach Sunday school throughout the winter months.

Andy had been relieved at the time. Later, he had to wonder why she'd been so tame in her questions. When he'd mentioned that he was having dinner with Allyson, Mom had remarked about what nice girl she was. "I'm pleased you're seeing her again. Such a bright woman," she'd said. And then she'd dropped the topic.

Shaking his head as he walked across the paver stones to the outdoor shower, Andy wondered why his mother, who almost never backed off, had dropped the subject. What did that mean? He guessed it meant she approved. Or maybe she'd already figured out he was falling for Allyson and didn't need a push.

Either way, his mom was right. The woman he was so eagerly waiting to see tonight was a nice girl. A very nice girl. And he was one lucky guy. Who smelled of sweat and dirt and needed a shower.

Clean, shaven, and dressed in dark denim jeans and a white and maroon striped collared shirt, Andy sauntered out to his truck, carrying a baggie with yesterday's striper filets in one hand, a bottle of Chablis in the other, and humming one of the songs that played on Allyson's station.

His cell phone rang as he pulled out of the driveway. Wilson Construction came up in the display screen. "Hey, Tom, how's it going?"

"Did you hear who got arrested last night?" Tom Wilson asked.

"No. Been working all day."

"Good old Jim Hensley. His ex, Tara, came home to find him in her house going through drawers."

"No way!" Andy laughed, though he felt bad for Tara. Hensley was a creep any way you viewed him.

"Yup. Tara called the cops and Hensley's spending the weekend in a cell, waiting for a court hearing on Monday. Probably put a damper on the whole honeymoon phase of that Facebook marriage." Tom snorted. "Be sure to pass on the news to Tess. She looked pretty upset Wednesday in the grocery store."

"Will do. Have a good one." Andy hung up and grimaced. The mention of Tess dampened his great mood. His mom hadn't said much about her all day. He'd caught her staring up at Tess's window a few times. The first time he'd walked over and given his mom a one-armed hug.

The second time he'd looked at the woodpile and joked, "At least she got the wood chopped and stacked before she took off."

His mom had chuckled, but only half-heartedly. "She's safe. I know she is. I simply miss her." His mom hadn't said anything else. Andy didn't voice his thoughts either. He did mutter a few phrases under his breath each time he saw his mom glance at the window. He couldn't wait for Tess to get back and give her a piece of his mind for upsetting their parents, then scream at her for disrupting his pre-date fantasy time.

Headlights from an oncoming car snapped him out of his internal monologue yelling at Tess. He switched on the radio, heard the band daring him to move, and laughed. He pushed aside thoughts of Tess and focused on the captivating woman he was about to have dinner with. He was ready to move, all right. Forward. With Allyson.

Dating didn't sound strong enough for what he was feeling, but it was a good place to start. Fourth date in four days, and he was wondering what they could do tomorrow. And the next day. And the day after that.

He turned down the dirt driveway and glanced at the clock: 6:58. Punctual was good. He didn't want to appear too eager and scare her off. Not that she'd given him any vibes to suggest she wasn't interested. He sensed she was, but he wanted to keep it light, just in case.

A charcoal grill was set up to the left of the walkway near the front steps. Andy knocked once on the door and was greeted by the most beautiful smile.

"Hi, Drew," Allyson said, then leaned over and gave him a quick hug. When she stepped back, Andy sensed she was nervous. Her hello hadn't lingered like her good-bye had the day before, after their morning fishing.

"Hello, yourself," he said. "I've brought some white wine and your fish. Fileted, of course. Wouldn't want you to have to deal with the slimy stuff."

She laughed and opened the door wider, inviting him in. Andy realized, as he looked around the living room of her small cottage, that having him over for dinner was pretty major. It was just the two of them in the house. Alone. Not even a dog. She had every right to be a little nervous, and he was going to do everything he could to put her at ease.

"Would you like me to get the grill going?" he asked, passing her the bottle and fish.

"That would be great. I'll pour us a glass of wine and get the fish ready."

When Andy came back inside, she was adding olive oil into a small bowl that held finely chopped herbs. She looked stunning in her black jeans and clingy royal blue sweater. They were in trouble if he didn't shift his focus to something more mundane.

"If you share your dressing recipe, I might be able to finagle the brownie recipe from my mom." He took a sip of his wine and watched her eyes light up.

"I'm pretty sure your mom already makes her own dressing, but if divulging my hidden ingredient will get me the secret to her brownies, you're on." She winked.

Andy watched as she whisked the herbs and olive oil, adding half a teaspoon of coarse Dijon mustard, sea salt, freshly ground pepper, and a splash of orange juice.

"Now," she said, glancing about the kitchen as though looking for spies before reaching into the cupboard, "the *piéce de resistànce*. Summer peach white balsamic vinegar."

"Is that some exotic ingredient you mail away for? I know for a fact that all the brownie supplies can be purchased on Island. I think that should be a prerequisite for sharing recipes," Andy said, raising his glass in a mock victory toast.

Allyson nodded, smirked, and whisked the vinegar into the dressing. "No worries, Drew. You can buy your mom a bottle of the summer peach at the kitchen store downtown. They stock it. Every day." She stuck her tongue out at him and giggled. "I'll be expecting that brownie recipe tomorrow. Would you like my e-mail address?"

Andy held up both hands. "You win. I'll probably have to steal it from my mother and betray my family. I hope you're happy." He was happy. Joking around with her had eased the tension he'd felt when he first got there. The smiling, teasing woman before him was the Allyson he knew and liked. Liked a lot.

"Just don't get caught and then try to renege on our deal," she quipped.

"Don't you worry, I'll make good. You might have to provide me with housing once my mom kicks me out, but I'm sure baking the best brownies on Island will be worth my being homeless."

They both laughed, and Andy's heart beat a little faster. She was so easy to be around, to talk with, to flirt with. She was almost too good to be true.

With the salad dressing done, Allyson brushed the bass with olive oil and lemon and sprinkled some herbs on top. She held the platter out to Andy. "Would you do the honors?"

"Love to. Do you have a spatula? And a rag I can use to oil the grill?"

"What? You're going to oil my grill?"

"Keeps the fish from sticking. Better than those chemical sprays. You mind?" Andy asked.

"Not at all. Learned something new. Thanks, Drew."

While Andy poured some olive oil onto an old yellow and blue checkered towel, Allyson brought a handful of red peppers and a bowl of chopped tomatoes over to the counter. "Are you good with a little spice?" She asked. "I waited to add the serranos to the relish until you arrived."

"Spice is good. I can take it."

The striper filets grilled quickly. When Andy carried in their entrée, candles were lit and the place settings were out. A basket of warm rolls and the salad were already on the table. Andy brought the fish into the kitchen. Allyson scooped the tomato-pepper relish on top of the bass. "Shall we?" she asked, gesturing toward the table.

"Please. I'm starving and this smells incredible."

They sat across from each other, the candlelight casting a warm glow. Allyson reached for Andy's hand. "Do you want to say grace?"

Andy felt honored. Grace was said every day in his home, but this was different. He felt as though her request confirmed his place as the man in her life. He bowed his head, hoping he could pray as eloquently as his father did. "Lord, we thank You for the food and the company tonight. Please nourish our souls as this food feeds our bodies. Amen."

"Amen," Allyson said, and squeezed his hand before letting go.

For two hours, they sat and ate and talked and laughed and shared stories of their lives. Andy was enchanted. Didn't hurt that she'd popped a homemade berry tart into the oven and whipped some fresh cream. After his second slice of dessert, Andy offered to wash the dishes.

"It's the least I can do."

"I can live with that," Allyson said. "You wash and I'll dry."

Andy had never had so much fun washing dishes. Unfortunately, the job was done all too soon. He rolled down his sleeves and watched Allyson wipe the counter clean. He wanted to shout, "You're just like my mother," but he didn't think she'd take it in the positive way he meant it.

And he definitely meant it in a good way. Not only that, he didn't want to disrupt her cleaning. He enjoyed watching her move, especially when she didn't know he was checking her out.

When she finished and had hung the towel over the oven bar to dry, there was an awkward moment of silence. Andy didn't want the evening to end, but he wasn't going to pressure her and suggest they go sit down and talk some more.

The invitation had to come from Allyson. He wanted her to feel special and respected and cherished. He wanted to be a man worthy of her affections.

She crossed the kitchen to stand in front of him. "I've had a great time."

"Me, too," Andy said, his heart sinking at the thought of saying good-bye. He stood perfectly still, wanting to reach out and take her hand but knowing he had to wait on her.

"I can make some coffee…or tea if you want."

"That would be great," he blurted out.

Allyson chuckled. "What would be great, coffee or tea?"

Andy laughed, too. "Either. Whatever's easier for you."

"I could go for some tea and honey. Go have a seat in the living room, and I'll be right back."

Andy walked across the floor to the seating area. There were two chairs and a sofa placed around a rectangular table. If he sat in a chair, Allyson wouldn't be able to sit next to him. If he sat on the sofa, she could choose. He opted for the sofa, hoping she'd sit beside him, close beside him. While he waited, he picked up the book on the coffee table.

As she walked over, Andy held up *Middlemarch*. "A little bedtime reading?"

"I'm struggling to get through it, so don't be impressed." Allyson said as she handed him a steaming mug.

"I'm impressed you're halfway through. Been ages since I read anything that wasn't work related."

Allyson sat beside him. Andy's heart soared.

"I force myself to read at least one serious book a year. Trust me, I'd rather be buried in a good romance," she confessed.

Andy leaned forward. "Romance, huh? So what makes for a great romance book?"

She looked up and met his gaze.

Andy gave her a lopsided grin. "I'm curious. Honest. You women seem to love them. What is it that has you reading more than one?"

Allyson smiled but didn't look away. "A great guy who's smart, funny, sexy, would die trying to save our heroine, and he's a bit of bad boy. There's got to be an amazing attraction between the two leads, even if one or both of them doesn't want to feel anything at first. Then the story takes over and sucks you in and you're turning the pages hoping and..."

Andy stifled a chuckle watching how animated she became. Her hands were moving, and her eyes got a dreamy, faraway look. There were not words to describe how much Andy wanted to kiss her.

He watched her mouth move but lost track of the words. She began describing some of her favorite characters and books. When she slapped his leg to accentuate her "can you imagine," Andy came out of his daze and put his mug down on a coaster.

"Well, that explains it," he said, not at all sure he understood the genre, but he'd definitely learned that Allyson was a sold-out fan of a great romance story.

"Oh, geez, guess I got carried away. Serves you right for asking." She drained the rest of her tea and noted his half-full cup. "Do you want me to nuke that for you?"

"No thanks. I'm good." Tea was not what he wanted, but she hadn't offered anything else.

Allyson stood quickly, fussing with the cups. "Okay, well, let me put these in the sink, and I'll walk you out."

Andy got up and resisted the urge to grin. She was fidgety, in a good way. Maybe she was thinking about a good night kiss too.

29

ANDY STOOD AT THE DOOR, his hand on the knob, his heart with Allyson. He didn't want to leave. Most of all, he didn't want to leave without kissing her good night. She stood about six feet away. Much too far.

"I want..." He twisted the doorknob back and forth with his left hand. "Would it be okay if..." The door opened as he fumbled with the brass. The cool night air was a welcome relief on his skin, but he hurried to close it.

He felt like an idiot. Or worse, as if he was thirteen again, in the movie theatre with Natalie DiComo, clumsily trying to get to first base while she sat enthralled with Sean Penn in *Fast Times at Ridgemont High*. He'd kissed quite a few girls since then, but no kiss seemed to matter as much as this one with this woman.

He shoved his left hand in his jeans pocket and searched Allyson's eyes. She was grinning at him—a highly amused twinkle in her baby blues. His heartbeat accelerated. She was gorgeous, smart, compassionate, giving, funny, and had amazing legs. He wasn't sure what she saw in him, since his reputation as a swinging single normally attracted a different kind of girl. His luck seemed to have changed. He'd be even luckier if he could kiss her.

He offered her his right hand, never shifting his focus from her eyes. A warm glow welcomed him as she slipped her hand into his. He closed his fingers around hers and drew her gently to him.

Andy eased his left hand out of his pocket and laid his palm against Allyson's cheek. She nestled into his hand and closed her eyes. With a feather-light touch, Andy ran his fingertips down the side of her face. Her skin was soft and smooth. He slipped his hand behind her head, cradling her neck, and leaned over, whispering into her ear, "May I kiss you?"

She brushed her cheek against his and whispered back, "I thought you'd never ask."

Allyson leaned back into Andy's palm while he lowered his lips to hers, tenderly brushing a kiss on the corner of one side of her mouth, then the other, tasting and teasing. She moaned and Andy lost himself in the sound.

His lips claimed hers. She laced her fingers into his hair and kissed him with an intensity and passion Andy had never experienced. His mind exploded, his heart opened, and love moved in. He explored the wonders of her mouth until they were both in need of oxygen. As they drew back to catch their breath, Allyson gifted him with a dazzling smile.

He gazed into her eyes, stroking her face with his right hand, needing to touch her. "I've wanted to do that since the beach picnic on Squibby a few weeks ago."

Allyson sighed. "I think I've waited a lifetime."

In the second it took for her words to reach his brain, Andy knew he felt the same way. "Me, too."

Andy pulled her back into his embrace, eager to devour her lips. Allyson rested her hands firmly on his chest. "As much as I want this, Drew, I think you'd better go."

Desire and temptation coursed through his veins. He reeled back and tried to imagine a plunge into the Sound in the freezing February waters. Andy released her slowly and stepped back, running a hand through his hair. "I know. You're right." He shoved his left hand back into his pocket and reached for the doorknob.

Allyson ran her fingers down his right arm. "Thanks for coming to dinner. And bringing the wine."

"Thanks for having me...I mean, inviting me."

Allyson chuckled. "See you tomorrow?"

"Tomorrow?" He racked his brain, trying to recall when he'd asked her out and where they were going. He'd gotten so wrapped up in their conversations, he didn't think he'd remembered to say anything about Sunday.

"Church. Are you coming with your parents?"

"Absolutely!" Andy exclaimed with more enthusiasm than he'd felt for church in the last six or seven years. "Wouldn't miss it for anything."

"I'll bite my tongue and refrain from commenting on the last time I saw you there." She was ribbing him, and he loved it.

"Easter. I was there on Easter. You wore a blue dress with pink flowers."

He watched her eyes register surprise and delight. "Wow, Drew." She stood quiet for a moment, reflective, then a teasing glint appeared in her eyes. "What did your mom wear?"

He was bagged, and he didn't care. He covered his face with his left hand, feigning embarrassment. "A dress."

"I'm flattered." Allyson closed the distance between them and pressed her lips to his. The heat of her coursed through his body. When she stepped back, he shivered. The loss of her warmth affected him to his core. He might not survive this relationship, not if she wasn't by his side every day, and he meant every day.

He glanced up and found her reading his expression. He sensed she saw him, understood him. She reached for his right hand and gave it a quick squeeze. "Drive safely. I'll see you in the morning."

Andy opened the door and stepped into the September night. If he were a little girl, he would have skipped joyfully to his truck. He finally knew what the fuss was about. He was in love, and he felt as though he could fly to the moon, catch a few stars on the way back, and hang them outside Allyson's window.

The roads were empty as Andy drove home. He'd turned off the radio, not wanting any distractions from his thoughts and the images of the gorgeous blonde who'd talked and laughed with him all evening and then had kissed him with a passion and depth he'd never experienced.

Maybe he'd talk to his mom in the morning before church. Then again, she'd be grilling him as soon as he announced he was going to church. He chuckled and pulled into their driveway.

As corny as it sounded, he couldn't wait to go to sleep. He knew his dreams would be filled with Allyson, and he wanted to be wherever she was.

30

TESS PACED THE DECK, up the starboard side, down the port side. She'd been in a bad mood since waking up. Adam had the good sense to give her a wide berth. When she walked past, most of the guys in the crew pretended to be busier than they were. A few would tip their heads and nod. Not one spoke to her, which was fine with Tess.

Two hours ago, she'd asked Ben what was going to happen next, and his answer had done nothing to ease her mind.

"Sail, wait, and watch, Miss Roberts," had been his short, unsweetened reply. Then he'd added, "And pray."

"I'll leave that up to you," she'd replied, as politely as possible, and then began her walk about the ship. She hadn't intended to circle the ship for hours, but then again she had hoped the darn sloop that was supposed to be rescuing them would have shown up before ten. Didn't anyone, including Ben's God, realize that the man she loved was about a hundred feet away on an enemy ship?

Tess stomped by the galley and didn't see Adam wave. She wondered where Jonah had escaped to. He had attempted to make small talk until she'd chewed his head off. It wasn't completely her fault. Not really.

Jonah had foolishly spouted some stupid saying about a watched pot never boiling. Of all the things to say! Of course she was watching the *Greyhound*. If Hawk was anywhere to be seen, she needed to see him. Plus, she had to stay on lookout for the sloop. Jonah should have known that.

Now, a couple hours later, Tess would be the first to admit she could have reacted differently. Threatening to throw the captain's younger brother into the ocean if he didn't shut up and leave her alone wasn't the nicest thing she'd said since coming up on deck.

The sky was clear and sunny. Moderate breezes kept the sails full and the ship gliding over calm seas. On any other day, she'd be thrilled to be out on the water, listening to the wind rustle the sails and feeling the sea air sliding across her skin.

Tess leaned on the windlass. She'd love to climb out on the bowsprit, but then she wouldn't be able to see anything behind her, and she was pretty sure the sloop would be coming from behind.

She sighed and started walking again. Ben was preoccupied with navigating the ship and staying close to the *Greyhound*. Tess wanted to climb the rigging and ride lookout, but she knew he wouldn't let her. Though she wasn't certain, they had to be close to the Vineyard. Later, she'd have to ask Ben their coordinates. Nantucket should be on the horizon soon.

Ben nodded as she strode past the helm over to the starboard rail. "Is the walk improving your disposition, Miss Roberts?"

Tess heard the jest in his voice. She guessed her constant movement was driving him up a wall, but she couldn't sit still either. Without stopping, she called over her shoulder, "Not much. A little, though."

Lucky for all of them Ben had told Captain Archibald Dickson yesterday that she was a stowaway and had been forced into service though she wasn't really crew material. If anyone on the *Greyhound* had the looking glass trained on the *Shenandoah* and witnessed the supposed galley boy pacing about for hours on end, they would probably be glad she hadn't gone on their ship.

On the other hand, Hawk was there and that sent her head reeling. Frustrated beyond belief, she smacked her right hand on the cap rail every other stride. Oh, how she wished she could climb to the fore topsail yard and scream to—or at—the heavens.

What was Hawk thinking? Why in blue blazes had he offered to go with Captain Dickson? Someone else could have gone. Not Jonah, or Ben, or Adam, or William, but there had to have been one other guy on board who could have gone instead. Why Hawk? That was one major question she had for that mule-headed man. And, come to think of it, for Adam's God. Not that she expected an answer from Him.

Tess stopped in her tracks and cringed. He, whatever He was, wasn't just Adam's God. He was Hawk's God too. And her parents'. She shook her head, not needing faith confusion on top of worrying about Hawk and why he'd volunteered to leave her and what was going to happen to him aboard the *Greyhound*. And there was the sloop to worry about too. Where was it? When would they arrive to free *Shenandoah*? Would they arrive? Did she remember the story exactly as her father had told her?

She grabbed the cap rail with both hands and started pounding on the polished wood. Ignoring the two dozen men working the lines and rigging, she yelled, "Enough! Enough! Enough! I've had enough."

God knew she was ranting at Him. Tess knew it too. She did believe in God. She just didn't like Him, didn't trust Him, and didn't think He was all her parents, Adam, and probably Hawk made Him out to be. Tess didn't trust

142

anyone who played favorites, and God certainly had His favorites.

Since she was fourteen, Tess had known she was cursed to be a girl in a home where boys got to work on the ships. God loved her parents and her brothers, but she doubted she was on His radar. She bet she wasn't even on His Top Ten list, as in ten million.

Tess stopped banging her sore palms and gently rubbed them together to relieve the sting. The more she thought about God, the more frustrated she became. She had a better chance of making David Letterman's Top Ten list than she did of being in God's top ten million people pool. She looked across the water over to where Hawk was. God had kept Hawk out of her reach for years, and now He'd taken him away again! Definitely not one of God's favorites.

"I've brought ye a light repast, Miss Roberts. Seeing as how ye skipped breakfast, ye need to eat something with all ye'r walking." Adam passed her a plate of biscuits and ham with a hardboiled egg.

Tess shook her head. "I'm not hungry, Adam, but thank you."

"When Hawk returns, he shall not be pleased to have ye fainting. The food might help to calm your nerves as well as replenish ye'r spirit," Adam said, genuinely concerned.

Tess accepted the plate and took a bite. Her stomach growled. They both laughed.

"There, now. Food, wind, and sun. The day holds promise, does it not?" Adam smiled at Tess.

Swallowing the last of the ham and biscuits, Tess set the pewter plate on the deck and picked up the egg. She rolled it firmly under her throbbing palm and began to peel away the shell. "Adam, why can't we see Hawk? I've looked for him all morning."

"I know you have, Miss Roberts. I suspect they have him below deck, shifting ballast or moving supplies. He is well, though. Rest assured he is well."

"How do you know?" Tess asked as she dropped the eggshell overboard. "And why did Hawk volunteer to go in the first place? He knew we couldn't leave *Shenandoah* and get back home."

"Ye know why he left, lass."

"No. No, I don't. It makes no sense to me. If he loved me, he should have stayed here with me, and we both could have gone home last night. I've waited over two years for him to give me the slightest sign that he noticed my existence, and then he ups and leaves. Voluntarily!" She lightened her grip on the egg before she squished it to an inedible mess.

"He left to protect you, lass, because he loves you. Captain Dickson might have taken you, Miss Roberts. I have no doubt Hawk believed he had no choice. His affection for you would not have allowed him to stay."

Tess's eyes widened, her heartbeat accelerated. "Do you really believe that, Adam? You're not just saying it to make me feel better? 'Cause I have to tell you that I just figured Hawk was bolting like he normally does whenever I'm around. Hawk running away from me is a familiar sight."

Adam shook his head. "Does he normally tell you he loves you before he departs?"

Tess hung her head. "Um, no. That was a first."

"I suspected as much," Adam said with a nod. "Waiting is ever so difficult. Try to have faith. The sloop shall arrive, you said so yourself, and Hawk shall return today."

Adam bent over and picked up the empty plate. "I shall leave you to some pleasant thoughts."

"Thanks, Adam. For the food and the pep talk." Tess grinned. Thinking about Hawk loving her made everything better.

"You are most welcome, Miss Roberts."

Tess finished her hardboiled egg and looked out across the water. Hawk was on the ship sailing a hundred feet or so away. Soon, she hoped, he would return and she could tell him she loved him too.

With a light heart, Tess walked back to the helm. Ben looked like a captain, his eyes on the horizon, standing tall in his white breeches and blue waistcoat, one hand resting on the wheel as *Shenny* gracefully skimmed across the massive blue-green Atlantic. Her dad would have so appreciated this day on his ship.

"Your spirits have lifted, Miss Roberts."

Tess giggled, still feeling giddy over Adam's interpretation of Hawk's actions. "Hawk loves me," she practically sang.

Ben laughed. "That he does, Miss Roberts. That he does."

"He's over there," she said, pointing to the *Greyhound*, "because he was ready to risk his life for me."

"To be willing to lay down one's life for another is the greatest act of love." Ben sounded stuffy, preachy almost, but Tess still couldn't wrap her mind around the fact that Hawk loved her.

Tears rolled gently down her cheeks. "I'd given up. That's why I came here. I didn't want to worry anyone or hurt anybody. I'd lost hope and wanted to see Rebecca. She's always known what to say."

Ben passed Tess his handkerchief. "In this time, you have found hope. The Lord's plan is always best. I cannot fathom a life without Rebecca, yet I could not have imagined her in a thousand lifetimes. The circumstances could not have occurred without the Lord's intervention."

Tess nodded and dried her eyes. Ben had a point. Rebecca had never said, "Gee, I hope one day I wake up in 1775 and meet Prince Charming."

Who would have thought time travel was possible? Never mind moving to another century and living happily ever after. With a captain and a boat, no less!

She held out Ben's now-soggy linen with an apologetic expression. He declined to take it. "Examine what you hold in ye'r hand," he said.

The white cloth was handmade. A blue monogram, R.R., was stitched in the bottom right corner. Tess sucked in her breath. Her throat tightened. "Becca made this?"

"Aye, she did. My wife would wish for you to have her fine work, a reminder that the Lord's plan far exceeds that which we mortals dream."

Tess ran her finger over the stitching. Fresh tears welled in her eyes. She hugged her friend's creation tightly to her chest. "Thank you."

They stood together, quiet, both lost in thought. The crew was at ease. The sails needing little tending. Tess wondered what Hawk could be doing below deck. She decided not to give in to worry. She would believe he was coming back. In one piece. Today. To her.

Ben ran a hand through his black hair then turned slightly to face Tess. "I know ye have doubted our Lord's divine plan and goodness. May I suggest ye spend some time in reflection while we wait for Hawk's return? I trust ye will find His hand of love and protection throughout your life. A treacherous storm you sailed through safely. Illness overcome. A family reunited. A friendship healed. Love found when you had given up."

Ben walked two strides to stand next to Tess. "His mercies and blessings are bountiful. I share with you now what I believe Rebecca would wish for you to know."

A prickle of fear pierced her heart. Was Rebecca okay? Had she been sick? The fear started to move through her until she looked at Ben's face. His eyes were shining with joy, and his smile was broader than any she'd seen.

"God has given us a great blessing. Rebecca is going to give me a child. She carries our firstborn. She will be a mother in early October."

"No way!" Tess let out an enthusiastic whoop. "Oh, my gosh. Pregnant? That's great. The best."

Ben squirmed a bit at her response, clearly not quite prepared for her twenty-first century exuberance. Tess wanted to dance and clap and call Rebecca and shout into the phone. She began walking in circles around Ben.

"How is she feeling? Is she taking her vitamins? Those prenatal ones you hear about on…ah, skip that. I bet she hasn't gained any weight, has she? A baby. Becca's going to have a baby."

"Oh." Tess stopped moving. She looked into Ben's eyes. "A baby. I'll never get to see her or him. I won't…"

Loss bruised Tess's heart, deflating much of her excitement. She turned away from Ben, staring out over the water, trying to control the sudden sadness that overwhelmed her. She didn't want to be selfish, didn't want to ruin Ben's news or his happiness, but she'd never share a moment of her best friend being pregnant or being a mom.

"Rebecca wept over your absence. Your sentiment is understandable. Were there another way…" Ben moved back to the helm.

Tess mentally kicked herself and concentrated on the joy her friend must be feeling, the excitement and wonder. Her smile returned as she thought of the perfect gift. She faced Ben. "You have to find a rabbit, a stuffed bunny. Becca had one when she was little. Kept Peter Rabbit for years. It would be the perfect gift. Please, will you buy one for me and give it to Rebecca?"

Ben returned her smile. "I shall endeavor to locate a stuffed rabbit. I have not previously seen a child's toy as you described. If none can be found, I shall hire a neighbor to sew one. Will that do, Miss Roberts?"

"Perfect. Thank you. The bunny would be wearing a blue coat, in case someone is going to make it for you. Tell Becca—"

A piercing whistle cut Tess off.

"Captain, sloop on the starboard side."

146

31

AS WILLIAM BARTON CALLED OUT the approaching sloop, Ben transformed from expectant dad to Captain Reed in a split second. He returned to the wheel, picked up the spyglass resting on a shelf built into the base, and located their rescuers. "*Liberty*. Do you recognize the vessel? Perhaps relatives of yours, Miss Roberts? Did your ancestors sail for the Colonies?"

"Why? Where are we?" Tess walked over to stand beside Ben, stopping at the compass behind the wheel.

"Our coordinates place us off the south shoal of Nantucket." Captain Reed kept his eyes on the approaching vessel.

"No way! It can't be! THE *Liberty?*" Excitement tingled up and down Tess's arms. "You have to have heard of the *Liberty*, Captain Reed. She's probably the most famous Vineyard sloop in the War."

"Aye, Miss Roberts. If this *Liberty* be the one and the same that captured the HMS *Harriot* on March 7, then I am acquainted with the vessel."

"And did you know that her captain is also a Ben? Captain Benjamin Smith from Edgartown." Tess grinned, then pointed toward the approaching sloop. "This is incredible. I'm going to see her live and in person. There's nothing left of her, not even a piece of the hull in the Martha's Vineyard Museum. The Museum does still have the original letter *Harriot's* captain, Weymes Orrock, sent to George Washington, pleading for release after his capture. A couple of books in the museum library mention the event, but nothing remains of the ship—no log books or record of sale."

"Your enthusiasm is contagious, Miss Roberts. Would you enjoy the use of my spyglass?" Ben held it out.

"No brainer there." Tess reached for the monocular. Ben shook his head. Tess cocked hers. "What?"

"Am I to presume your response is affirmative?"

With a quick laugh, Tess changed her reply. "Oh, yeah. Yes, please, Captain Reed." She mocked a curtsey.

Ben chuckled and passed her the spyglass.

Like a pro, Tess brought the old-fashioned telescope up to her right eye. She scanned the sea until zoning in on *Liberty*. "She's moving, practically skimming across the water."

"That she is. A beautiful ship. Sleek and fast."

The small sloop, about half the size of *Shenandoah*, had been sailed by brave Vineyard men in March. Tess wondered if Captain Smith was at the helm as they came to retake *Shenandoah*.

She voiced her pondering. "Captain Smith does not own *Liberty*. Reports said he commissioned her when he heard the *Harriot* was anchored off Nantucket, waiting for fair winds. He may not be onboard today."

"You do know your history, Miss Roberts."

"Between school and my father, I managed to learn naval history. The rest bored me to tears." Tess turned toward the *Greyhound*. "May I?"

Ben extended his right hand, palm up. "Of course."

Although they were still a hundred feet away, Tess searched the deck of the *Greyhound*, hoping to see the man she loved. Two minutes of tedious scanning left Tess more restless than before she looked. "Still no Hawk."

She handed the telescope to Ben. "Do not despair, Miss Roberts. Victory is in sight."

"I know. I just wish I could see him." Tess left Ben at the helm and walked over to the starboard bulwark. She gazed past the sloop toward the Vineyard, toward home. The Island was nowhere in sight, but she hugged herself tight, closed her eyes, and whispered, "I love you, Mom."

A loud, hard voice startled Tess. "Captain, the men are inquiring as to our strategy." William Barton, waiting for Ben's reply, nodded curtly at Tess, whose heart banged in her chest.

Ben must have noticed her frightened expression. He held her gaze and shook his head. "William, please tell the men that we shall stay the course. No need to alert the *Greyhound* to our potential rescue. We have a man held captive, and I shall not risk his life. There shall be no weapons fired on this day."

"Aye, aye, Captain." Will turned to leave.

"William." Ben spoke before the sailor was out of earshot. "Prepare the colors to be raised. If friend, the sloop will show their colors first. If foe, the white flag is flying."

Will saluted Ben. Tess thought the first mate looked annoyed, frustrated at least. "Is he mad at you?" she asked.

"No man likes to surrender. Yesterday I chose the course of action I felt best in our situation. I am quite certain there are men onboard who would have preferred a fight. William is one."

Tess's heart beat harder. "Does he want to fight today?"

Ben nodded. "Though we are a privateer ship in the business of acquiring and transporting valuable cargo, the crew all believe in our colonies' united cause. Each demands freedom from British rule. The *Greyhound* represents King George and his monarchy. Some would consider it noble to die in battle for their beliefs."

"But…" Tess's breath was coming in shallow gasps.

"Please, Miss Roberts, rest easy. I shall not fire unless fired upon. We have every reason to believe the *Liberty* is the sloop you spoke of. Therefore, I do not expect the *Greyhound* to engage in combat. I would wager Captain Dickson is no fool. The odds are against him this day."

One thought, one question resounded inside Tess. "What about Hawk?"

"Within the hour he shall be aboard ship with you." Ben pointed to the *Liberty*, now about sixty yards from their stern and heading toward the *Greyhound*. "Look hence. They are raised, and she is flying her colors. The time has come to strike our colors as well."

Her lungs filled, and Tess released her pent-up tension and fear in a long exhale. "I've never been so happy to see a sloop in my life."

"Aye, Miss Roberts, the Lord has blessed us this day. Now I believe William is ready with the flag."

"What flag will you raise?" Tess's heart now beat at its normal rhythm once again.

"We carry the Rebel stripes. I fly…"

"No way!" Tess cut Ben off. "I've seen pictures. Saw what was left of a Rebel flag in a museum in Boston. This is going to be totally cool. Why don't you sail under the stripes?"

Keeping one hand on the wheel and glancing starboard and port to ascertain where both ships were and what they were doing, Ben continued. "I fly no colors in the hopes that our missions raise no alarm. Should the need arise, as is the case now, we have our colors ready to bear."

"Wow." Tess was grinning like a winning contestant on a game show. Her fears and concerns for Hawk's safety dispelled, she was back in the moment. In thirty or so minutes, when the ships drew closer, she'd watch *Shenandoah's* first mate unfurl the red and white horizontal strips of the Rebel flag. "My father would have loved this. I wish he was with me now."

"I believe you, Miss Roberts, yet I also believe your father has chosen to remain where he resides."

Tess cocked her head to the left. "Huh?"

"Forgive me if I presume too much, but your father is captain of *Shenandoah* and in full knowledge of her capabilities to transport him to another place and time in her history. Yet he remains on Martha's Vineyard beside his wife, with his family. I trust he knows what is of value to him and where his heart lies." Ben shifted his focus to Tess and held her gaze for a moment. "He is a fortunate man."

His words caught Tess off guard, left her speechless. She had never considered that her father could have stood where she was. In her mind, he couldn't go because he was her dad and her mom's husband and he had to stay home. But Ben was right. If her dad had wanted to, he could have slept in Cabin 8 and traveled back in time to see the original *Shenandoah*, just as she had. Tess sat on the roof of Ben's quarters, her head lowered, her hands in her lap. While *Shenandoah* eased through the Atlantic at about eight knots, her thoughts raced.

She couldn't count the number of times her dad said he wished he could have seen *Shenny* in all her glory, and she'd believed him. She realized now that his words were dreams he'd never choose over his life on the Island— over her, over her brothers, and never over her mom. Her dad loved his life.

"Miss Roberts." Captain Reed broke into her reverie. "Your flag."

Tess looked up and saw Ben pointing toward the sloop. Their conversation and her subsequent thoughts had passed the time quicker than most sailing outings. The *Liberty* was alongside at last. Their Rebel flag waved proud and high. It was an amazing, beautiful sight. Tess stood and scanned the deck, spotting William midship between the gangway and the longboat. He was holding *Shenandoah's* Rebel flag, waiting for Ben's signal.

Adam and Jonah were standing next to the galley hatch. Jonah waved at her. Tess hoped that meant he'd forgiven her for snapping at him earlier. She gave him an enthusiastic response.

Captain Benjamin Reed lifted his right hand slowly until his arm was straight overhead. William nodded in reply, then Ben lowered his hand, signaling the unfurling of their flag.

Goosebumps rose on Tess's arms as the first mate and an unfamiliar shipman began to lower their Patriot colors over the starboard side of the ship. If the British were watching from the port side, which they probably were, they would not be able to see Ben joining forces with the sloop.

Sailors on the *Liberty* gave a shout. The sloop tacked slightly right to come behind *Shenandoah* and sail to the port side of the HMS *Greyhound*. With a patriot ship on each side of her, Tess hoped Ben's prediction of Captain Archibald Dickson's capitulation would unfold before the hour was up.

Then Hawk would be set free, to come back to her. Tears pooled in her eyes. She wiped them dry and focused on the flurry of activity that signaled Hawk's imminent release.

The crew was in motion with more hands on deck. Others lifted cannonballs up through the companionways. They were preparing for battle. Just in case, or maybe to scare the *Greyhound* into surrender. The white flag was lowered as *Liberty* closed the gap on the *Greyhound.*

Tess's pulse quickened. He would be safe. He had to be safe. She couldn't stop herself. "Captain Reed, how long?"

The vessel was tacking port, drawing closer to *Greyhound* to aid *Liberty* in her attack. He kept his eyes on the action while answering Tess. "Soon, Miss Roberts, soon. Now would be a time for prayer."

The words hung in the air. Tess let them approach slowly, thinking about what Adam and Ben had said a short time ago. Maybe everything did happen for a reason. Hawk had said he loved her, and Becca was happy with Ben. She couldn't see the future, or even tomorrow, but maybe God could. And maybe He knew what He was doing. She was willing to give Him a shot. "I can do that," she said.

Tess sat back on top of the captain's roof and bowed her head. *God, it's me, Tess. You might not remember me; it's been a few years. Like a dozen or so.* Tess grimaced, finding it difficult to form the words she thought she should say. *Sorry for all the comments about You not being so great and all. This might be totally selfish, probably is, but we need some help here. Your kind of help. I would be really grateful, like going-to-church grateful, if You would bring Hawk back safely and keep everyone on the* Shenandoah *safe and then get me and Hawk back home in one piece.*

She took a deep breath and exhaled in one rush of air. *And if I could ask for one more thing, I'd really…could you…would you*—Tess paused before racing through her request—*Can Hawk still love me when we get back home? Please?*

There, she'd prayed. It wasn't so hard after all. She remembered it being easier when she was little, but her mom or dad had always been beside her on the bed then. *Oh, I almost forgot…in Jesus' name, amen.*

Phew. Tess opened her eyes. The ships were still sailing, the crew was still manning the lines and working the deck, the war was still being fought, yet she felt different. Lighter? Relaxed? Something Tess couldn't quite name.

Peaceful, that's what she felt. Maybe prayer was a good thing. Maybe her mother knew something she didn't. Maybe Tess would pray more often—not every night, but a couple of times a week wouldn't be so bad. She'd talk with her mom about it when she got home.

The stinging gone, Tess rubbed her now-sweaty palms on her slops and laughed. She really had been nervous about praying. She felt better, though.

She stood and walked port side to join Jonah and Adam.

The *Liberty* was almost in position, cutting through the water faster than *Greyhound* or *Shenandoah*.

"'Tis a beautiful sight, is it not, Miss Roberts?"

"Fantastic, Adam," Tess replied. "I hope Captain Dickson will surrender in a few minutes. Without guns or cannons going off."

Adam gave Tess a firm nod. "Ye'r words shall come to pass, lass. Do not worry."

"I'm not." Tess winked at Adam. "I prayed."

Jonah slapped a hand to his thigh. "Ye have seen the light then, Miss Roberts. A blessing for you and for Hawk."

Her palms grew sweaty again. She was all for being the center of attention when she was doing backflips off the rigging, but she'd rather not be the focus of anyone's discussion on prayer.

"How close would you say she is now?" Tess asked. She could easily gage the distance between *Liberty* and the *Greyhound*, but she wanted to divert their attention.

Tess could see the twinkle in Adam's eyes. He was proud of her, as her dad would be, and his approval made her feel good. At the same time, he didn't bring it up again. She really liked the old man. Too bad he couldn't come back with her, though she doubted he'd enjoy life in the twenty-first century. Everything about his demeanor told Tess that he was a happy man, just like her dad. He pulled a wooden telescope out of his back pocket.

"Did you make that, Adam?"

"That I did. A bit of carving and then I polished the wood with the hide of a sand shark. It is neither as fancy nor as functional as the captain's, yet it serves me well enough." Adam rolled the foot-long wooden piece in his hand before peering into the smaller end. "*Liberty* is not more than fifty feet from the *Greyhound*. The moment has arrived. Her captain will surely call for Captain Dickson to surrender and relinquish any prisoners."

Ben called out orders, and the ship tacked port as the crew rushed past her. She kept her sights on the *Greyhound*, wanting only to see Hawk get off the ship alive.

Adam held out his monocular. "Would you appreciate the use of my scope while I aid the men, Miss Roberts?"

"Oh, yes, Adam. That would be wonderful. Thank you."

"Jonah, we can be of better service at the bow." Adam and Jonah walked away, leaving Tess to focus solely on Hawk. She looked through the telescope and waited.

Sails were trimmed and rigging changed, then the *Liberty* drew close on *Greyhound*'s port side. Ben guided *Shenandoah* skillfully along the starboard side until the two Patriot ships made a boat sandwich of the *Greyhound*.

As members of *Greyhound's* crew milled about, Tess spotted Hawk. She waved furiously, hoping he would see her. Whether he sensed her or saw the movement, he finally raised his hand and saluted her. Tess's heart leapt. He was safe. She could see him. And Captain Dickson had ordered the raising of his white flag.

Before Tess could call out to Hawk, he hopped onto the cap rail and dove into the water.

"Ben!" Tess screamed. "Hawk's in the water."

"Port tack," Ben ordered. "Man overboard forward of the port beam."

Tess ran to the bow. Life preservers were tossed overboard. Jonah hurried to stand with Tess. They backed up a few steps to the let the crew work on bringing Hawk in. "He shall be fine, Miss Roberts. He is swimming well."

No shots were fired at Hawk, which Tess expected when he first dove in. Too many action movies had put her brain in overdrive. Relieved, she watched him swim toward *Shenandoah.* "Oh, he's got this now, Jonah. I'm not worried. I know he can swim."

By the time Hawk had reached the first life ring, Tess was breathless with excitement. As the crew pulled him up, though, her confidence flew off on the breeze, and she wondered if he would still love her now that he was safe. What if he'd said the words only because he thought he was about to die? What if he'd said them only to make her feel better since it was her fault he was being taken hostage? What if he didn't mean them?

Tess felt as though her heart had plunged through her chest and had nailed her feet to the wooden deck. She was stuck. Adam motioned for her to join him as the men hauled Hawk into the boat. She shook her head. He searched her face, compassion reflecting in his eyes. He nodded before bending over the rail to help Hawk onto the ship.

Tess chewed her bottom lip, her voice ready to scream, "I love you," while her mind slammed on the brakes and waved caution flags. Her stomach twisted into knots. She should have been happy. She should have been running into his arms, but she felt as if she was about to throw up.

Hawk got to his feet, thanked the crew, then asked Adam, "Where's Tess?"

The cook and not-so-subtle matchmaker pointed in Tess's direction. "She waits for you, a bit uncertain, I suspect, as to the truth of your parting words. Sentiment spoken from the heart or in a moment of fear? Ye left her wondering and hoping."

Tess wanted to hug Adam. He said what she didn't have the courage to express. Hawk ran a hand through his wet hair and met her gaze. He smiled that melt-an-iceberg smile and walked toward her. Tess couldn't breathe. With his every step, her heart beat faster and harder. Still, her feet were glued.

Hawk stopped an arm's length in front of her. "Nice day for a swim, don't you think?"

He didn't wait for her to respond. He wrapped his right arm around her, slipped the fingers of his left hand under her ponytail, and lowered his mouth to hers. Two years of buried passion and longing exploded inside her the second his lips met hers.

She was hungry for everything he offered. She gave everything she had, and still she wanted more. The sound of cheering and clapping brought her back to reality. She'd forgotten where she was, and when. She stepped back, flushed and warm.

Hawk looked around at the applauding crew. "The rest will have to wait until we're home. We can go home now, right?"

Tess nodded, took a long, comforting breath of summer salt air, and let her heart sing. "Home would be nice."

The skirmish was over. Hawk was safe. They all were safe. *Greyhound* continued on her southwest course, soon to be nothing more than a speck on the horizon. *Liberty* sliced through the water behind the British ship and appeared to be heading back to the Vineyard. To their home. Where Tess and Hawk would soon go. Ben called out orders for a starboard tack, turning *Shenandoah* around and heading north.

Hawk hugged her close. Tess leaned into him, oblivious to his wet clothes. She wished she could stay there, her head on his chest, their arms around each other, for the rest of her life.

Adam tapped Hawk on the shoulder. "Though I gather ye'r warm enough, I suggest you go below and find a change of clothes. Miss Roberts shall await your return."

Tess flushed from head to toe. Hawk grinned at her. "Don't go anywhere, Tess. I crossed time lines and swam the Atlantic for you. Do me a favor and sit still for a few minutes."

"Just hurry up." Tess gave him a gentle shove. She wasn't going anywhere, not without Hawk, not ever again.

32

TESS LEANED AGAINST THE MIDSHIP HATCH, waiting for Hawk to return. She grinned. It seemed she was always waiting on Hawk. Only now that he wanted to see her, too, waiting took on a whole new meaning. And Tess liked it.

She knew they wouldn't have much private time. Ignoring the dozens of men slogging it out on deck to get into homeport before nightfall, Adam had asked Hawk to talk with Ben after he'd changed. Tess hoped she was allowed to be there. Though she knew the rudimentary schoolbook facts, Tess was as curious as Ben about what had happened on the *Greyhound* and what Hawk might know of the British plans.

She heard Hawk yakking with some guys below deck and knew he was on his way up. Her heart raced and her stomach fluttered. She felt giddy and silly and joyously happy.

His hands, strong and tanned, grabbed the top rung of the ladder, followed by a wavy mop of sun-bleached hair, then all six feet of well-muscled hunk. He had changed back into his blue jeans and Irish-knit sweater. Tess held her breath, waiting for him to turn and for those blue eyes to focus on her. He was gorgeous. And he loved her. Life was good with a capital G.

Hawk stepped onto the deck and turned to find her staring at him. "Never thought I'd live to see the day," he quipped, shaking his head. "Tess Roberts, are you sitting still and waiting for me as I asked you to?"

If anyone in the fastidious crew had left a rag or brush lying around, she would have tossed it at him. Instead, she stuck out her tongue. "Funny, very funny. Actually, I was soaking in the rays, waiting for Adam to call us for lunch. You flatter yourself."

He walked over and reached for her left hand, pulling her to her feet. Tess refrained from jumping into his arms. She wanted to. Desperately. But she knew Ben wouldn't appreciate her public display of affection. No PDAs in 1776. Not to mention the fact that she rather liked Hawk pursuing her for a change. She'd leave the jumping to him for a while.

Hawk placed a sweet kiss on her forehead. "I'm sure you've instructed Ben on which course to take. Did you also tell Adam what to serve for lunch? There's no way you've been sitting here alone with nothing to do or say."

He was teasing her, and she loved it. And she was more than happy to dish it back. "As a matter of fact, Ben is sailing to the Vineyard right now. I thought it would be a shorter trip for us tonight if we were nearer to the Island, so to speak. Haven't you noticed the course change?" Tess pointed toward the east.

"As for your lunch," she said, while crossing her arms over her chest, "I ordered Adam to make lobster rolls that will put Grace Church to shame, though he has no idea what Grace Church is or how popular their Friday night lobster fest is. Are you satisfied?"

His laughter caressed her ears as though his hands were gently stroking her arms. "There's my Tess. I knew you wouldn't let me down. I'm starving, and three or four piled-high lobster rolls should do the trick."

"Glad you're hungry, 'cause I think it's pickled beets and ham. You can have my pickled slime. I'm not hungry enough to cram beets down my throat." Tess scrunched up her face at the word *beets.*

She watched the laughter fade from his eyes and an unfamiliar, serious expression stared back at her. He squeezed her hand. "I like beets, but there's something else far more appealing. We have a lot to talk about when we get home tomorrow, but I want you to think about something, Tess."

He reached for her hands, holding both of hers in his left, and then placed his right index finger under her chin and brought her gaze to his. One second passed. Then two. Tess held her breath.

He whispered, "Can I have you?"

She opened her mouth to shout, "Yes!" but he placed two fingers over her lips. "Think about it, Tess. Don't answer me now. We'll talk tomorrow, okay?"

Was he nuts? Tomorrow? Tess wanted to talk immediately. Tomorrow was too far away. Tomorrow was who-knew-when in their time. Tomorrow was not what she had in mind.

Mulling over her annoyance and her joy, Tess opted to focus on the happiness. If Hawk wanted to talk tomorrow, she could wait until then to tell him that he could have her for the rest of her life.

"Tomorrow is good. Maybe around lunch time? Assuming we get home in time for breakfast, I want to go see my family and tell them I'm back. Then I'm all yours." She meant every word she'd said, especially "all yours." She hoped Hawk had the good sense to read into what she was saying.

He lifted a strand of her hair and toyed with it between his fingers before tucking her brown tresses behind her left ear. "Deal."

Peter Murdock, now back on full galley-boy duties, rang the lunch bell. Hawk helped himself to Tess's serving of beets and finished off two servings of ham. As they sat on the galley rooftop relaxing in the sun, Ben asked to speak with them privately.

"We have matters of importance to discuss." Ben led them toward the stern. "Hawk," he said, extending his right hand, "well done."

The two men shook hands. Tess felt a shiver of apprehension. She didn't know where it was coming from or why she felt it then, but the feeling was undeniable.

"Miss Roberts." Ben motioned for her to step closer. That was it. Tess realized they were the only ones around the helm. No one worked the rigging. No one stood or leaned against the cap rail. No Adam or Jonah. Just them.

Captain Reed considered each of them, his eyes shrouded. "Miss Roberts, I fear I shall disappoint you, yet I have a request you cannot deny me."

Tess knew what was coming. She and Hawk had already talked about it. She was ready.

"Rebecca will be saddened she was unable to visit with you. Nevertheless, I must ask you and Hawk to return to your home tonight. The stakes have been raised. A greater battle is on the horizon." Ben met Hawk's eyes. "I suspect Hawk will impart information both grim and stark. I cannot risk my crew or ship protecting you. Do you understand?"

Tess traced a finger over the compass. "It's okay, Ben. I'm ready to go home. I have a date tomorrow that I wouldn't miss for anything in the world." She could feel Hawk's gaze upon her.

Then she thought about what else tomorrow would bring. The cabin, Cabin 8, would be changed. Her dad would probably begin work an hour after he knew she was home.

No Cabin 8 meant no Rebecca. Ever again.

"Oh, crud." Tears formed and pooled on her eyelashes. Tess left them there. Her heart hurt. She glanced out over the water. They were heading north toward Rebecca. "Is there any chance, any at all, that Becca will be waiting for you at the dock?"

Ben shook his head. "Slim at best, Miss Roberts. I am sorry. In her condition, I asked her to reside with my parents until my return."

Hawk held up a hand. "Wait. What condition? Is Rebecca sick?"

The tears rolled down Tess's cheeks. She waited for Ben to share his good news.

"My wife is with child."

Hawk brightened instantly. "Aw, man, congratulations. That's great."

Tess's shoulders began to shake. She tried to muffle her cries.

Hawk stepped next to her and wrapped a protective arm around her.

157

"What's wrong, Tess?"

"I'll never see her again. My best friend. I won't meet her children or get to watch them grow up. No trips to the beach or days with Auntie Tess." She wiped her cheeks on Hawk's sweater, then eased back enough to see both men. "I knew this last month, but now it's real. Dad will change the boards tomorrow. And there's nothing I can do about it."

Tess leaned back into Hawk's embrace. She welcomed the comfort of his arms and the sound of his heartbeat. He kissed the top of her head, and an ounce of pain healed. She needed more kisses. She needed a best friend.

He must have sensed her longing. He rested his lips on her forehead and squeezed her, hard.

Ben cleared his throat, reminding them they were not in the twenty-first century. Hawk ran his hands down her arms and took a short step back.

"Miss Roberts, if there was a way, if I had but known, I would have sent for Rebecca. Though I imagine my gesture shall offer little consolation, I shall find a stuffed rabbit and present Rebecca with a precious gift from her dear friend."

His words should have made her feel better, but she wanted to buy the bunny. She wanted to give it to Rebecca. She wanted to tell her best friend that she loved her and couldn't wait for the baby to come. Fresh tears fell.

"I've got to go below," she mumbled before running down the port side to the companionway.

*

Both men watched Tess descend the ladder. Hawk wanted to go after her but knew that Captain Benjamin Reed expected him to share whatever information he had heard or seen on the *Greyhound.*

"She'll be okay," Hawk said to Ben, who looked plagued by guilt. "You're absolutely right. We have to go back tonight. Yesterday was too close for comfort. There can't be a next time."

Ben put both hands on the wheel. Hawk knew from watching Captain Roberts that the man often grabbed the wheel to help him center his thoughts or calm down when one or two school kids on the cruise got out of control.

Captain Reed appeared to have the same habit. After a few seconds, his frown was gone, and his mood had visibly lifted. "I regret the necessary demand, yet I would be negligent in my duties if I allowed Miss Roberts to remain onboard. The danger is too near. Rebecca would not forgive me if any harm came to her friend, nor would I forgive myself."

Ben grew reflective, the next subject no better than the first. "I reckon your report is not good?" Ben asked the question with no trace of fear at the coming battles.

Hawk admired him and envied him a little too. He wondered what it would be like to sail *Shenandoah* on privateering quests and help America win a war. A lot different than kids' cruises.

Two seamen, probably hoping for a hint of news, meandered down to the stern. Ben asked them to move midship before Hawk divulged what he'd heard and seen on the HMS *Greyhound*. When the sailors had walked past the galley, Ben nodded for Hawk to continue.

"The British have an armada sailing toward New York City. Talk was that they would have around one hundred ships converging in the harbor. They are fully armed and under the direction of General Howe. And I can't say this for sure, I've never so much as seen a picture of the man, but I think Howe was on the *Greyhound*."

Ben raised an eyebrow. "What gave you that impression?"

"Last night they assigned me floor space in the crew's quarters. I overhead a few of the men talking. They spoke of Howe as if he was onboard. I wish I had Tess's memory for history. I can't recall when Howe was in New York or how he got there." Hawk shrugged.

Ben filled in the blanks. "General Howe was in Halifax. After his resounding defeat at Dorchester Heights in March, the Loyalists evacuated Boston. Most thought he would sail to New York. For ten days the Lobster Backs sat at anchor until at last they sailed for Halifax on March 27. Shouts of return and revenge could be heard from British Loyalists as they departed. It is inevitable that Howe would confront His Excellency in New York. I would not be surprised if the general was aboard."

Hawk rested a hand next to the compass. "I can't say for certain, but I'd bet on it. The men on the frigate acted as though there was more going on than face value."

"Did you assess their manpower and weaponry?" Ben gestured westward.

"Captain Dickson kept me midship. I never got a chance to get down to the hold. There were dozens of guns, rifles mostly, as well as swords. Cannonballs were stacked on deck, and no doubt hundreds more were below. They easily have three or four times as many men onboard as you do. The frigate is armed and dangerous, as we say back home."

Ben put both hands back on the wheel. Hawk knew the information he'd given painted a grim future for the colonists. He also knew the Patriots won the war, and that Ben and the *Shenandoah* never saw battle. Whatever contemplation Ben was giving to the months ahead, the outcome wouldn't change.

Hawk walked over to the rail and sat down, facing Ben. "Mind if I ask you a question?"

"By all means."

"How much has Rebecca told you? Do you know what happened? Do you want to know?"

Ben gave a short laugh. "Though many would not agree, it is a challenge to live with a woman who knows the future. I am aware that we win the war. I have asked Rebecca to withhold details, and she has respected my request. On occasion, she has spoken naturally of a past event in her life and disclosed what is to me a future fact. At a time such as this, one might wish to know what tomorrow brings or what new device shall be invented, such as the camera or cell phone. And yet, if I were to live asking about the morrow, I would neglect today."

Hawk thought about Ben's answer. Would he want to know the future? Maybe. But maybe not. "I hear you. Knowing would take some of the mystery and adventure out of life."

"Precisely."

"So, what can you do about the armada and General Howe and the *Greyhound?*"

The clear blue sky contrasted with the dark talk of war and the horrors to come. Hawk was not about to tell Ben about the shoeless soldiers marching in the dead of winter, the outbreaks of smallpox and dysentery, the years of hardship the Colonists experienced, or how long the battles would continue. He watched Ben think through his question and admired his calm in the midst of turmoil.

"I shall send a rider to New York with news of our capture and release. My message shall inform His Excellency, General Washington, of what you overheard. The timing shall be close, though. The British fleet may arrive before or within hours of the rider. If His Excellency is unaware of the Loyalist ships descending on New York, he shall have no time to prepare."

Hawk refrained from telling Ben that the Declaration of Independence would soon be signed in Philadelphia on July 4. Nor did he want to relay to Ben that the British slaughtered the Patriots in New York, and Washington was forced to flee. "What is *Shenandoah's* next mission?"

"We shall reach Quincy Harbor tonight. The men will unload the cargo on the morrow. We shall spend five days in port. Then, weather permitting, we sail north once again to retrieve supplies. And you, Hawk, what shall your days bring upon your return?"

Hawk stood and looked out over the whitecaps. The wind was strong, and the sea was perfect for sailing. How he wished he could travel as Ben did, raising anchor and riding the waters of the Atlantic and, with any luck, the Caribbean.

"I don't know. It's fall back home. *Shenandoah* is done for the year. We'll have some work to do, breaking her down for winter. Cabin 8 will be remodeled immediately. After that, I haven't a clue. A lot will depend on what happens when Tess and I get back. Speaking of Tess, I'd better go check on her."

Ben glanced toward the companionway. "Our destiny is not our own, no matter the course we chart. The Good Lord shall provide the path and the way and the light for our steps."

"I know. And I'm counting on it. Dating Tess was never in my plans. I've got to have faith that everything will fall into place once we get back."

33

TESS WALKED NUMBLY DOWN THE PASSAGEWAY to Cabin 8. She entered the room and sat on the cot. She didn't want to be sad. She wanted to focus on Hawk and the future, but it hurt to come face to face with the reality that she'd never see Rebecca again.

She dropped her head into her hands and rocked back and forth. Though her tears had dried, Tess didn't want to go back up on deck and listen to Ben and Hawk talk strategy. Truth be told, she didn't want to watch the miles sail by. With every ounce of her being, she wanted to start a life with Hawk. She also wanted Rebecca to be a part of it. She was happy for Becca, thrilled she'd found a great guy with a loving family and they were about to start their own family.

"Argh! I'm so tired of wanting more!" Tess flopped back onto the cot and curled into a ball. In the back of her mind, she heard her mom saying, "Count your blessings." Tess closed her eyes and pictured Hawk walking toward her, telling her he loved her, kissing her. Within minutes she drifted off to sleep....

She twitched at his first snicker. "Marriage? Are you kidding me? I'm not going to marry her. I brought her home only to have some bargaining room with the captain. You'd have to be crazy to think I'd marry Tess Roberts." When the snicker became a cackle, Tess lurched upright.

She looked around the infirmary, but no one was there. The door was still open, and she couldn't hear anyone in the passageway. She must have been dreaming. Bad dreams. Nightmare material.

Hawk loved her. He'd said he did. Yesterday.

Her stomach twisted. Yesterday. He hadn't said it again, though.

Tess shook her head. "No. I was napping. It was just a bad dream. A nightmare. No one was in the room when I woke or in the passageway. Hawk never said those malicious words. I've waited too long for him to notice me. His love has to be real. He couldn't have said them."

She stood and walked over to the table, hoping there might be some water in the pitcher. No luck.

Tess strummed her fingers on the wood. Was she sad about losing Rebecca and that was why she was doubting Hawk's love? Or was her dream something more?

Her fingers strummed faster. What did the dream mean?

Wait…a…minute!

What had really happened between them since he'd gotten back? One rather nice kiss, a few touches here and there during lunch, and he'd held her like a friend while she'd cried about Becca.

Oh, and the talk. Or she should say the talk before the talk. The talk he wanted to have at lunch in Vineyard Haven. Tomorrow.

Her fingers froze mid-tap. Hawk hadn't actually said he wanted to date her or marry her. His declaration of love as he was taken prisoner aboard the HMS *Greyhound* had been music to her ears. His kiss when he returned had felt like he loved her. But.

But, in the last three or four hours since he'd been back onboard, he hadn't exactly spoken the words to her. Sure, he'd asked if he could have her. Typical guy wanting a one-night stand. She'd been foolish to think he meant marriage.

What he'd said was that they had a lot to talk about. Tomorrow. Tomorrow, when they got home. Tomorrow, when she was back with her parents and he was back on her dad's *Shenandoah.* Tess turned and leaned against the table.

Doubt pierced her heart. Tears formed, but she promptly swiped them away. She'd cried enough in one day to last her the rest of the year. She needed to think rationally. She needed to determine if Hawk's declaration of love was real or…or…or something she hadn't figured out yet.

Tess clenched the edge of the table with both hands. Hawk had uttered the one vow of love when he was taken captive and then told her to sleep in the infirmary, which really meant go home without him. They'd kissed when he'd swum back, but when she thought about it, Adam had pretty much read him the riot act and all but forced Hawk to show her some affection.

So, maybe getting her all doe-eyed was his plan all along. Maybe he really was a jerk, and he'd played on her emotions, knowing she would fall hard for him. Then he'd be able to bring her back to her father and play the hero. Maybe she was just a way for him to get to sail *Shenandoah* down to the Caribbean in the off-season.

Two years of rejection overrode twenty-four hours of love. Tess smacked her hand on the table. "That's it! He's faking it to get me to go home. He doesn't love me. He wants me to believe he loves me so I'll go back without a fight."

The table wobbled. Tess had braced her legs and was pushing off the floorboards. The four legs couldn't hold her anger. She stood and paced the room. She paid no notice to the cot, to the jars of medical supplies on the shelf, or to the chest of bandages and rags. She marched and fumed, fumed and marched. Hawk had another thing coming if he thought she was stupid. She may have played the lovesick fool over him for two years, but she was done. Over it. Good-bye, Hawk!

How dare he try to trick her, to play with her emotions? Well, he had met his match. She wasn't going anywhere with him. She wasn't even going home. She'd show him. If Ben wanted her off the ship, she'd get off. Rebecca and Missy were happy there. She could be too. Maybe she'd date Jonah. He was nice to her. Then she and Becca could be neighbors and friends for life.

"Hmph!" Tess crossed her arms over her chest and gave a sharp nod to herself. She'd find Hawk and tell him to go home by himself, and to drown in the Sound when he got there.

It was a good plan. She merely wished the hollow feeling in her chest would go away. Staring blankly at the walls of the infirmary, she zeroed in on a dark spot about three feet up from the base. "Becca's board!"

Tess walked over and placed her hand on the wooden knot. She felt connected to Becca, and to home. Rebecca had mentioned that this board and its large knot was how she'd figured out that the cabin was the time machine portal. She'd recognized the marking in her cabin in both centuries.

The wood warmed under Tess's hand. If she stayed there, in Cabin 8, she'd be home tomorrow. Home with Hawk rejecting her once again.

Tess drew back her hand and clenched her fist. "Not this time." She strode out of the cabin in search of Hawk.

The moment her feet hit the deck, she spotted him at the helm. She was so intent on telling him off, she didn't notice they were pulling into port. Nor did she notice the sun was much lower in the sky.

He spotted her immediately and began walking toward her. "Hey, Sleeping Beauty, I went down to check on you an hour ago and found you napping. Do you feel better?"

Tess winced. He sounded all soft and sweet. She wanted to scream. He could stop faking it. She was totally onto his game.

He continued on as though everything was peachy between them. "Can you believe this? Look at the harbor."

Tess put all her sarcastic comments on hold as she took in their surroundings. "We're dropping anchor? Why didn't you wake me up?"

The question was rhetorical. Hawk walked over to stand beside her, and they moved as one toward the gangway.

"Where are we?"

"Quincy." Hawk lifted his left arm to drape it over her shoulders.

She slid out from under his touch. "I'm going to look for Rebecca."

Hawk gave her a puzzled look, but Tess wasn't getting sucked in again. No matter what, she was keeping her distance for the next few hours. If Rebecca was there, Tess would just leave the boat and go be with someone who really cared about her.

Shortly after the lone bell signaled 6:30 p.m., Tess began walking every inch of the ship, scanning the shoreline and docks. She stepped sideways to avoid the shipman kneeling on the deck, coiling the lines of the foresail. "Sorry, didn't see you." He glanced up, smiled, and went back to work.

The crew was in a hurry. Many were home, or close to it. If they could get the ship secured, dozens of them would probably go ashore for the night and return in the early hours of morning to unload the cargo.

After about forty minutes, the sun was beginning to set, and Rebecca wasn't anywhere to be seen. Another lap of the boat would be a waste of time. A pain stabbed Tess's heart. Where would she be come morning? Home in Vineyard Haven and rejected by Hawk again? Or on her way to see Rebecca?

"Are ye eager to depart, Miss Roberts? A dish of apple pie shall be served to me on the morrow." Jonah oozed exuberance.

Tess would have sworn he never had a bad day. She hadn't seen him so much as frown. He was much nicer than Hawk.

"I'm thinking of staying," Tess stated flatly.

Jonah laughed. "I know ye jest. Ye'r family awaits your arrival and, I gather, banns shall be posted shortly."

"Bands?" Tess asked, giving him a quizzical look. "You're crazy, Jonah, if you think my father or brothers would play music to welcome me home. I'll be lucky if the neighbors don't call the cops when the shouting starts."

This time it was Jonah's turn to puzzle over her words. "I had no thoughts of music, Miss Roberts. I spoke of your wedding banns."

At the mention of the word *wedding,* Tess's anger boiled again. She glanced around deck to find Hawk. He was talking with Adam by the galley hatch. She had a few words to say to him.

"There will be no wedding banns either," Tess spit out, immediately regretting the vehemence with which she'd spoken.

Jonah's eyes popped open. He'd probably never heard a girl blowing off marriage before.

"Sorry, Jonah. Nerves, I guess."

His head bobbed in recognition. "I'm familiar with bridal jitters. My sisters fretted before their engagements, guessing when or if the moment would occur. Then, once betrothed, they fretted over details too minute to matter. Alas, the day arrived and the house returned to normalcy when the bride and groom departed."

Tess couldn't contain her laughter. Jonah did honestly look annoyed while he shared his impression of his sisters' weddings. "You should cut them some slack, Jonah. I think it's pretty common for a woman to be nervous and a little obsessive-compulsive when she's planning her big day. It happens only once, and every girl wants it to be magical."

Jonah chortled. "I do not know about magic. I take great comfort, though, knowing Lucy and Abigail each found a suitable husband and there shall not be another sister planning a wedding."

Tess gave him a playful jab to the ribs. He did lighten her mood. Though four years younger, Jonah was great company. He was more mature than twenty-one-year-old guys at home, and his lighthearted nature was easy to be around.

Hawk, on the other hand, was not easy to be around. But she'd recognized while chatting with Jonah that she had better play it up to Hawk just as he was doing to her. While the full crew was on board, Tess needed Hawk, Adam, Jonah, and Ben to believe she was going to time-travel tonight.

Once everyone went to sleep, especially Hawk, she'd sneak out of the cabin, let Hawk go back without her, and then she'd go visit Rebecca. And, the more she thought about it, the better the plan became. Her father would leave the boards intact, and when she was ready to return, probably after the baby was born, she'd sleep on *Shenandoah* and go home.

"What is that gorgeous smile all about?"

Tess cringed inwardly as she heard Hawk's voice, but she managed to keep a cheerful expression. Jonah offered his opinion, which worked for Tess.

"We have been discussing weddings and the posting of banns," Jonah offered. He turned to face Tess. "I shall take my leave before you raise the topic of flowers, fabric, or counting linens. I shan't survive another word about napkins and how they shall be folded."

Jonah ambled away, singing a shanty Tess hadn't heard before. She wanted to walk away with him, but she had a clever ruse to act out. Performing her part, Tess reached for Hawk's hand and gave it a squeeze.

"What have you been up to? What's the plan for what's left of the day?" She nearly gagged on the sugary sweetness of her words.

He pulled her closer. "Sorry about Rebecca. Although I enjoyed watching you walk the deck and bend over the bulwark to get a closer look at the shoreline, I'm sorry she's not here."

166

Gosh, he was good. Tess almost believed he'd been looking her over. Almost. She put her guard up a little higher. He was going to be hard to resist for another two to three hours. She hoped he was exhausted and would fall asleep quickly. In the meantime, she wanted to know what was going to happen on the ship now that they'd anchored and at least half the crew had gone ashore.

"Is Adam still onboard? I haven't seen him."

"He just got back. He went ashore with the first group to pick up some dinner. He promised hot beef and potatoes," Hawk said.

"You'll be happy then. Don't think I've ever seen you skip a meal." Tess was doing her best to flirt and tease.

"Hopefully you never do."

"Now that you mention it, I'm kinda hungry. It's got to be close to eight." Tess started moving toward the galley.

Hawk stepped in behind her. "Those slops don't do you justice, Tess."

She didn't give him the satisfaction of a thank-you. "Just keep up, or I'll eat your dinner."

Peter Murdock climbed out of the galley as Tess approached the hatch. "Oh, Miss Roberts, Adam has asked me to notify you that supper is ready. Please go below."

"Thanks, Peter. We'll be right there." Tess gazed down at the stern area. "I wonder where Ben is."

"He's probably already at the table. Let's go before the food's gone."

Hawk stepped aside and let Tess descend the companionway first. Once below, they sat side by side, the last to arrive. Ben folded his hands and bowed his head. Memories, fond ones, flooded Tess's mind. Her father said grace before dinner on every kids' cruise. She loved that Ben was doing the same thing.

"Lord, we thank ye for the bounty before us. And we thank ye for safe harbor. Our praise we give unto you. Amen."

Cutlery clanged as a dozen people consumed the beef and gravy. Hawk kept brushing his knee up against hers. She wanted to stab him with her fork. Every time he touched her, she wished it was real. And every time she wished it was real, she reminded herself that he needed to be tortured, preferably by her.

When the food was gone, Tess decided the time had come to finalize her plans. "How many men are onboard tonight, Captain Reed?"

"A dozen, including myself, Jonah, and Adam. Nathaniel and Jacob are on first watch. The rest are before you. Two men shall keep watch throughout the night. I trust your sleep will be peaceful."

Tess knew Ben's words held greater meaning. Hawk ran his toes across the top of her foot. She felt shivers going down her spine. She cursed her traitorous body and conjured images of stomping on Hawk's bare foot with a pair of cleats.

"I am looking forward to a good night's sleep," Hawk said, moving his foot back and forth over hers.

Tess couldn't resist much longer. She had to get up from the table. With all the love and caring she could muster, Tess managed not to choke on her words. "Hawk, you must be exhausted after all that adventure. Maybe you should go lie down."

Ben rose from the head of the table, and the crew followed suit. Peter Murdock cleared the remaining dishes and took them to the galley. The large room felt particularly empty with only herself, Ben, Jonah, Adam, and Hawk standing there. Jonah wouldn't meet her eyes. She wanted to tell him she would see him in the morning, but she kept her mouth shut.

"The day has been long for all. Turning in early would be a welcome reprieve," Ben said. "We had best say our good-byes now without the eyes of others watching."

Adam shook Hawk's hand. "Good luck, young man. You have a fine woman. She shall keep you on your toes and love you well. Be good to her."

"I will, sir."

The matchmaking cook held out his right hand to Tess. "I believe the journey has been good for you, Miss Roberts. And I trust the Lord will keep you safe as you travel home. I shall remember you fondly and shall keep you in my prayers."

Tess pushed Adam's outstretched hand aside and hugged him tight. "You're the best, Adam. Thanks for talking with me and for being patient. I'll miss you."

Adam patted her back and released her.

Tess stepped over to Jonah. "Rebecca was right—you are sweet. And sweet is good where I come from. There would be women all over you back home. I'm glad I met you. I've got three older brothers, and now I feel like I have a younger brother too."

"You're not calling me a brother purely to terrorize me with another wedding, are you?"

They both laughed. She lifted her arms to hug him, and Jonah scooped her up. "I shall be forever glad you came to visit." Jonah put her down and extended a hand to Hawk. "Safe voyage to you, Hawk. Commendable bravery.

Glad to have met you. Take good care of Miss Roberts."

"Thanks, Jonah. I'll try to be sweet." The two men clapped each other on the arm.

Adam and Jonah left them alone with Ben. He approached Hawk first. They were the same size and about the same age. One dark-haired, one blond. Their lives were the same, yet very different. Ben shouldered responsibility she couldn't imagine. But looking at them facing each other, Tess knew, begrudgingly, that Hawk could step into that role and excel.

Ben held out his right hand. "It was an honor to serve with you, Hawk. If the circumstances were different, I would be pleased to call you my first mate." Ben shook Hawk's hand.

Tess tried not to get choked up. She reminded herself that she was mad at one of them.

"The honor was mine, Captain Reed. Thank you for allowing me passage. And thanks for looking after Tess while I was gone."

Ben glanced at Tess and smiled. "The pleasure was mine." He walked two steps to stand before Tess. "I promise to have a seamstress sew a rabbit with a blue jacket."

Tears sprang in Tess's eyes. She hugged Ben quickly, then stepped back before she lost all control. "Thank you. And please tell Becca that I love her and I'm happy for her. Don't let on how much I miss her, okay? Tell her—" Tess paused. "Tell her my life is great, and everything is working out just like we always talked about. Okay?"

Ben nodded. "I shall relay your message."

"Thanks."

"Rest well. I trust the cabin will carry ye both where ye need to go. Godspeed." Ben lifted his hand in a brief good-bye, then headed for the companionway.

As soon as he was out of sight, Hawk reached for Tess's hand. "Hey, what did you mean, 'Tell her my life is great?' Your life is great, and everything is working out."

"Ha!" Tess yanked her hand free of his and stomped toward the supply room.

34

"WHAT NOW, TESS?" Hawk called after her.

She didn't stop. Running into the storage room, she shut the door loudly behind her. She leaned against Hawk's only access route and braced herself. He would not be easily put off. She was surprised when he knocked a couple of times.

"Tess, open the door, okay? I know you're upset about Rebecca. Let me talk to you."

Tess smacked her palm against the door. "Go away, Hawk. Your game is up. You can stop pretending to care about me. I figured out your self-serving, egotistical plan, and I'm not going anywhere with you!"

She heard the door handle move and then felt his gentle push against the boards. She leaned all her weight against the door and kept it closed.

"Tess, what are you doing? What are you talking about? Let me in there. Let's talk this through so we can go home."

"I guess you're deaf as well as arrogant. Like I said, I'm not going anywhere with you. But you are free to leave, and the sooner the better."

"For Pete's sake, Tess! What is going on?" She heard the frustration in his voice and felt a moment of happiness. He was going to be really ticked off when he couldn't trick her into going home with him so he could turn her over to her father.

When she refused to answer him, Hawk pushed harder against the door. "Just open the door, Tess. I don't know what's gotten into you, but we need to go home tonight, and this is not the time for one of your drama scenes."

Tess crouched lower so her knees were almost at a 120-degree angle and her back was fully against the door. She didn't respond.

"Fine, Tess, have it your way. I'll wait for you in Cabin 8."

Footsteps followed his words, but Tess didn't relax. She didn't trust him. She held the position for a few minutes until her legs started to cramp. She listened for a sound, any sound. When she didn't hear anything, she straightened and stretched her legs.

The room was nearly dark. Very little moonlight came in through the port hole. Tess noticed that Jonah, or someone in the crew, had removed the makeshift cot and some of the supplies from the room. She'd have to sleep on the floor, without a blanket or pillow. *Just my luck they're so efficient, getting ready for tomorrow.*

A few of the crates looked as if they might hold something useful, but all Tess found was dried beans and more dried beans. As she was lowering the lid on the third crate, Hawk opened the door.

Tess dashed across the room and threw herself at the opposite side, struggling to keep him out. His strength far outmatched hers, and Hawk was in the room in a matter of seconds. "What's going on, Tess? Why are you blowing me off? Why don't you want to go home all of a sudden?"

"Don't play dumb with me! I figured out your plan. You're just trying to get me to go back with you so you'll look like a hero and my father will let you have *Shenny* in the off season. Get away from me! I'm not going anywhere with you!" Tess held it together externally, but she was breaking on the inside. She wasn't going to last much longer. She shoved hard and was surprised when she felt no resistance.

The door crashed into Hawk at the exact moment Adam walked down the passageway. "Miss Roberts, is there a problem with the supply room's entry?" Adam asked.

Tess looked from Hawk to Adam and back to Hawk. "He was pushing on the door." Tess turned to Hawk. His eyes looked dazed, though his head hadn't been hit. "Why did you let go? What's wrong with you? Stop staring at me like I have three heads."

Hawk seemed to slouch before her eyes. There was no spark in him, though she saw hurt and anger cloud his baby blues.

Adam adopted an annoying grin. "Ah, a lover's quarrel. All is well then. I shall leave you two to work out the problem. I only ask that you reduce the volume of your...ah...communication."

"There won't be any more yelling. My apologies," Hawk said to Adam, who smiled at Tess before he walked away. With their friend and matchmaker out of the room, Hawk turned toward Tess. "I can't believe you said what you did. Get over yourself and meet me in Cabin 8."

Tess shook her head. "I'm not going back with you, so get over yourself."

"That's where you're mistaken, Tess. I'm not leaving here without you." Hawk lunged across the small eight-by-six-foot room and grabbed Tess around her waist, picked her up, and threw her across his right shoulder.

She started flailing, whacking his back with her fist. He held her legs against him so she couldn't kick him in the stomach. "Put me down, you Neanderthal."

"Don't worry—I plan to. As soon as we're in Cabin 8."

Tess continued to pound on his back. "You can't keep me there, so just put me down."

Hawk stormed into the infirmary, but Tess held out her arms as they went through the door. His grip on her legs gave for only a second. Tess thought she'd surprise him, but he pulled hard, and her arms couldn't hold up. She ground her teeth and muttered curses under her breath as he yanked her through the threshold.

She was so infuriated by his manhandling of her that at first she didn't notice Hawk had grabbed some bandages and tied her legs together. She seethed with fury.

He tossed her down on the cot and, with a murderous glint in his eyes, reached for her hands.

Tess threw a hard right at him but missed, and he snatched her wrist.

"Cool it!" Within seconds, he had wrapped a length of cloth around her right arm and captured her left one too. He stood and looked down at her.

If looks could kill, Tess would be dead. She thrashed herself into a sitting position and stared him down. "Untie me now, or so help me I'll scream 'til the whole crew hears me."

Hawk walked back to the chest, snatched a bandage off the top of the pile, then strode toward Tess. "Have it your way." He frowned and tied the gag around her mouth.

For a second, Tess was stunned. She couldn't believe Hawk had actually bound and gagged her. She'd never have pictured her blond dreamboat forcing a woman to do anything.

Then it hit her. He must really want to impress her father.

With renewed anger, Tess twisted and squirmed until she was on her feet. Hawk watched with mild amusement while she managed to hop a few times toward the door. Then he scooped her up and dropped her back onto the cot.

"So help me, Tess, just stay put. I'm done fighting you. We're going home tonight. Both of us." No sooner were the words out of his mouth than Hawk laid down half on top of her and half beside her.

The contact, the nearness of him, the presence of him in a bed with her, pushed Tess over the limit. She screamed into the gag and brought both knees up hard, hoping to injure him where he would remember the day for the rest of his life.

He dodged her attack, bringing both his legs down on hers and pinning her to the cot. Then, ever so calmly, he whispered into her ear, "Stop, Tess. Nothing is going to happen tonight. I don't know what you take me for, but

I'm in this cot with you for one reason and one reason only—so we both go home tonight."

Tess raised her bound hands and tried to scratch his face. He grabbed them before she could draw blood. She wanted to kill him or, at the very least, inflict enough bodily harm that he never walked again. She hated him, absolutely hated him. She jerked at her hands and twisted to her left. He pinned her wrists over her head and wrapped his legs around hers in what felt like a vice grip. "Let me go, you jerk," she screamed into the cloth.

"Stop fighting me, Tess. Believe me, I don't want to be in bed with you before we're married. I will have to explain this to your father and assure him that I had every intention of asking for your hand in marriage before your behavior made this sleeping arrangement a necessity. I know your father will understand, and I will promise him that we will not share another bed until our wedding night. Still, I can't believe that you think…"

His words stopped her heart. *Did he say wedding night?*

Alarmed by her sudden stillness, Hawk looked down at Tess. She must have looked like a zombie mummy. Her eyes felt as if they were going to pop.

"Tess? Can you breathe?" He rolled her onto her side and frantically untied the cloth over her mouth.

She took a deep breath, finding her voice. "What did you just say?"

"Are you okay? Can you breathe?"

Tess captured his face in her hands, oblivious to the bandage still wrapped around them. "I can breathe just fine. Now tell me again what you just said."

She was met with a blank stare. Lucky for him, her hands were still tied together. She couldn't decide whether to smack him upside the head or shake him. "Hawk! My father. You mentioned speaking to my father. Hello? That ring any bells?"

Tess hadn't intended the pun, and it went right over Hawk's head, but she kind of chuckled.

"Of course it does," he said, sounding exasperated. "I'll talk to him tomorrow afternoon."

"You will? Talk to him about marrying me?"

"Of course." Hawk spoke the words as fact, then his eyes grew wide. "Tess, please tell me that you did not for one second think I would sleep with you and not have married you first."

"Ah, duh. It happens every day."

Hawk smoothed a strand of hair off her face. Tess melted under his gentle touch. "Okay, yeah, it does. But not between us. I love you, Tess. I want to honor you. I've stayed away from you for two years so I wouldn't disgrace you or your family."

She felt the grin on her face widen into a jubilant smile. "You did?"

"What, you think I didn't feel anything that first day? When I took your hand in mine, I thought lightning was going to strike any second. Then Andy introduced you as his sister. I had to get away from you as quickly as possible. There was no way I could date the captain's daughter, and there was no way I could be around you and not be in love with you."

Tess held up her wrists. "Will you please untie my hands?"

Hawk grinned. "Can I trust you?"

"Untie my hands," she demanded, offering him an impish smile that both teased and insisted. Tess knew he saw the need and urgency sparkling in the gold flecks in her brown eyes.

He leaned up on his right elbow and tugged the knot. Tess worked her hands free as the cloth loosened, and then she sunk her fingers into his wavy blond hair. "Why didn't you say so earlier?" She gazed into the depth of blue she wanted to swim in for the rest of her life.

"I couldn't, and you know it." He traced a finger along her hairline and down below her jaw.

She trembled under his touch. "I thought you couldn't stand to be around me."

"I couldn't." He tilted her chin up slightly and hovered inches from her mouth. "Being anywhere near you was torture."

"Good," she managed to mumble between breaths. Her heart pounded stronger then hurricane-force winds. "'Cause seeing you was killing me, too."

"I love you, Tess."

She ran her fingers through his hair and wrapped her arms around his neck. "I love you, too."

He lowered his mouth to hers, his full lips pressing against hers, giving and taking. Tess's toes curled as her heart soared. Nothing, absolutely nothing, had ever felt as sweet or as warm as Hawk's kiss. She pressed herself along the length of him, into him, wanting to get closer. He pulled her tight against him, his hands caressing up and down her back.

Breathless, they broke away and gulped in oxygen. Hawk kissed her forehead, her cheeks, the corners of her mouth, and the tip of her nose. "I knew you would taste this good."

"Really? You thought about kissing me? Seemed like you were always thinking about how to get away from me." Tess wanted to hear every word of love she'd been yearning for over the last two years.

174

"Yes, really. And we'd better not try that again tonight." Hawk shifted his weight so they were both on their sides, facing each other but with a fraction of distance between them. "This cot is too small, and you are too close."

Tess couldn't contain the mischievous grin or thoughts that rose as he spoke. "So, I'm a little too close, am I?" She ran the fingers of her right hand down his arm and back up again. As she began walking her fingertips along his neck, he seized her wrist within his right hand and held her palm against his shoulder.

"Behave, Tess. You are too tempting. I have enough to explain to your father already. I'm not going to add another apology to the list." He planted a soft kiss on her lips. He scanned the infirmary. "Trust me, if I knew for sure that we'd both leave tonight if one of us slept in the cot and the other on the floor, I'd opt for the floor. But I don't know, and I'm not willing to take a chance of being separated from you."

Tess wiggled her hand free. She laid her palm on his heart and rested her head on his chest. "Oh, we should definitely stay together," she purred. "This is perfect."

Hawk kissed the top of her head and drew her close. "Yes, it is."

"Maybe we could snuggle like this tomorrow night."

"No way, Tess."

She leaned back and pouted. "Why do I never get any choice in anything?"

Hawk burst out laughing. "You have no choice because your actions are always dictating the precarious predicaments we've found ourselves in. Now go to sleep before we get into trouble." He kissed her gently on the lips.

"Hey, what did Ben say to you before you left?"

"Huh?" Hawk kissed her forehead, then her right eyelid, then her left.

Tess struggled to stay focused. "Remember...yesterday...right after your declaration of undying love for me...Ben went over and said something to you. What was it?" She pushed gently against his chest, creating a bit of breathing room between them.

Hawk grinned. "You talk too much."

He was rewarded with a playful smack on his shoulder. "Quit stalling. Tell me, or I'll be forced to torture you, and you know how creative my mind is." Tess narrowed her eyes and smirked. "Up to you."

"That devilish grin doesn't scare me. But I'll tell you so you don't nag me for the rest of my life." Hawk reached for her hand and kissed her fingers one at time. "Ben told me that he would guard you with his life, and, if I did not return within twenty-fours, he would send you home, one way or another."

Tess pulled her hand back. "How dare he threaten to send me home! As if he could make…"

"Earth to Tess." Hawk kissed the tip of her nose. "Let's not ruin a perfect moment getting angry over something that didn't happen. Okay?"

His puppy-dog expression gave her a chuckle. And he was right. Again. She was getting worked up over nothing. As if her mother hadn't pointed out that habit a million times over the years. Maybe it was time to work on her short fuse. Just a little, some minor tweaking, stretching it out a bit.

"Ah, yeah, we'll let that one go. Now, where were we?" She slid up and pressed her lips to his.

He kissed her tenderly. She felt him holding back, and she silently thanked him for caring that much about her. Another guy might take advantage of the situation. He really was one in a million.

Tess sighed. "You better marry me soon, because I'm not waiting another two years to lie down beside you again."

"How's next Saturday for you, assuming your father accepts my resignation and gives his permission?"

Tess bolted up. "What?"

Hawk tried to pull her back down beside him. "Next Saturday. I'm free if you are."

She brushed away his hand. "Not that part, but I'll be there, count on it. What did you mean—your resignation?"

He sat up, awkwardly balancing them in the narrow cot. "You know how your father feels about favoritism and nepotism. There is no way he is going to allow his first mate to marry his daughter. But if you'll have me, and you did just say you'd be there next Saturday, I'd rather have you than the job."

Tess couldn't take in everything that had been said in the last half hour. Hawk loved her. Hawk was going to ask her father for her hand in marriage. Hawk was going to quit his job, because he would rather have her. Because he loved her more than sailing. And, oh, by the way, they were getting married next Saturday.

"Don't worry, Tess. I have faith. Everything is going to work out. God has a plan for us, and it is good. He's given us enough light to see this far, and He'll provide the direction we need for the next step."

As he drew her down and wrapped his arms around her, she breathed in the scent of him—the sun and wind and sea and salt. He didn't feel like a man with any worries. He felt relaxed and happy and…perfect.

Maybe he was right. Again. She was willing to turn this one over to God. She wasn't about to start a Jesus revival, but she wanted to open her heart to trust God and see where they, she and God, went from there. She liked the idea of God lighting their path, especially if she was walking that path with the man she loved.

She snuggled into Hawk, resting her cheek over his heart and listening to the rhythm of his life beating with hers. Her heart was too small to contain the depths of her feelings. Love overflowed within her. She would need this century and a dozen more to give Hawk all the love inside her.

"Thanks for coming to bring me home."

"I didn't have a choice. I couldn't stay there without you, and who knew when you'd get around to coming back." He joked, but Tess knew there was a weight of emotion behind those words.

"I'm glad you came." She hugged him tightly, never wanting to let go.

"Me, too, Tess. Now close your eyes and go to sleep. It's time to take you home so we can begin our life together." He kissed her forehead and drew her close.

"I think I can get used to you telling me what to do."

With his eyes half closed, Hawk rubbed her back. "I'm going to remember you said that."

"As long as your idea is good and I agree with you, we'll be fine." Tess patted his chest and closed her eyes.

Hawk ran a hand over her hair. "Now there's the Tess I know and love. Sweet dreams, Beautiful. I'll see you at home."

35

TESS STOOD IN CABIN 8 and gazed into the full-length mirror her father had delivered at her mother's insistence. She couldn't believe everything that had happened in the last week. Not even a week, six hectic, ferry-riding, meeting-intense perfect days.

She walked about the newly refurbished bunk. The scent of fresh-cut pine and oak filled the air. While she was gone, her father had drafted plans to turn Cabin 8 into an official chaperone space. The top and bottom bunks had been removed, and two twin beds were fixed on opposite walls, each with a built-in dresser drawer on the bottom. A small desk had been constructed and nailed securely between the new bunks.

Tess ran her hand over the top of the desk. The pine had been sanded smooth. Stain and sealer would be applied next week, after today's sail, so the fumes wouldn't gag Tess or anyone else.

Behind the new bedrail, Tess noticed Becca's board was gone, the one with the knot about three feet up from the base. Additional sections of timber had been changed out, and all had been burned, but that one missing piece held the most significance for Tess. With its removal, she knew for certain there would be no further time travel to or from the *Shenandoah*. Cabin 8, as she, Rebecca, and Melissa had experienced it, was gone.

A twinge of sadness gripped Tess's heart. She hadn't participated in the reconstruction, her mother insisting the women had more than enough to do. In truth, she was glad she hadn't helped. She wouldn't have had the strength to cut off all passage to and from her childhood friend.

She leaned down and placed her hand on the wall and pressed softly against the new oak. *I love you, Becca. I wish you were here today, but I'm so happy for you. You'll be a great mom.*

A few tears pooled in Tess's eyes. She reached for a tissue on top of the desk and blotted, careful not to smudge her mascara. She didn't want a single tear of sadness to roll down her cheeks. Not today. Not on her wedding day.

The morning had dawned to a sunny blue sky and Hawk calling on her cell phone. "Tonight, Tess. Tonight you'll be mine forever."

"I know. I still can't believe it. I feel like I'm dreaming," she'd said.

"You're not dreaming. We're real, and I'll see you at the helm tonight."

Hawk's words wrapped around her as if his arms were holding her.

"Wait, aren't you coming to breakfast? I thought everyone was meeting at the Black Dog Tavern at 9."

He snorted. "I wish. The guys all gave me a hard time last night and said I couldn't see you until the wedding. My family will be there, though. And I'll take them and Reverend Gillespie out to *Shenny* at five. Then I've been ordered to lock myself in the captain's quarters."

She couldn't help but giggle. "Guess that bachelor party didn't have any naked, dancing women."

"Ha. Your father and my father and your brothers and all we talked about was you, marriage, and how Drew was the only lonely soul in the group."

"Aww. I love you," Tess said.

"I love you, too. See you later."

Now it was later. Hawk was sequestered in the captain's quarters, and they would soon be husband and wife. Discarding the tissue in the small plastic bag beside the desk, Tess knew that Becca would have loved sharing in the craziness of the last week. Rebecca might even appreciate the make-up, Q-tips, hair spray, and other "essentials" her mother claimed were vital to a bride's preparations. Tess was beyond grateful for the efforts everyone had gone to in order to make her wedding perfect.

The Roberts family and friends had scrubbed, planted, clipped, trimmed, and called in a few favors to coordinate a wedding in six days. Her mom's favorite pastry chef, Liz Kane, was delivering a magnificent wedding cake with a miniature Shenandoah carved in white and dark chocolate for the top. Chesca's crab cakes, Anjou pear salad, filet mignon with demi-glace, roasted fingerling potatoes, and Island fall vegetables would be served under the tent, surrounded by twinkling lights, to the hundred and twenty guests who would arrive at the Roberts' home at seven.

But that was over an hour away. Tess had a wedding to attend before the reception. They were anchored off Menemsha, thanks to her dad and eight crewmembers. Just in time for a beautiful sunset ceremony.

Two weeks ago, Tess wouldn't have thought she'd ever be standing in a wedding dress. But here she was—marrying Hawk. Despite her frustration, despite her giving up all hope, despite her trying to take things into her own hands, God had come through. Big time!

She walked back over to the mirror and gazed at her reflection. The ivory satin extenuated what remained of her summer tan. The elegance and simplicity of the high-low off-the-shoulder gown reminded Tess and her mom of Audrey Hepburn. Tess loved the beaded neckline. Just enough, but not too much. Her twenty-five-year-old tomboy self had felt beautiful and classy and womanly the moment she'd put it on.

"Oh, honey, you are stunning."

Tess glanced over to the doorway and saw her mom, hand over her mouth, tears in her eyes. "Jacqueline Kennedy wouldn't hold a candle to you."

Tess couldn't help but smile. Her mother had admired Jackie O's style for as long as Tess could remember, and now she was comparing her less-than-feminine daughter to one of the most sophisticated women who'd ever lived. Tess did feel gorgeous, but her mother was the stunning one. Slim and fit in her sixties, Katherine Roberts wore a vintage Coco Chanel navy skirt suit, her grace and carriage like that of a prima ballerina.

"I must have inherited something from you after all." Tess wrapped an arm around her mother's shoulder and drew her into the reflection. "Can you believe you're standing next to me...and I'm in a wedding gown?"

"I knew this day would come, though the years passed too quickly. Your father, however, is not ready. He's putting on a good show. He admires Hawk, and we both believe Hawk is ideal for you, but your dad had the misplaced hope that you'd continue to be his somewhat challenging, but always little, girl."

Tess lowered her arm and took her mom's hand in hers. She gazed into her mother's eyes in the mirror. "I'm sorry I wasn't more of a daughter for you, more of a girly girl."

"Nonsense, Tess. You were, and are, exactly the daughter I want. I never expected you to play with dolls or ply your time at cross-stitching. Mind you, I would have loved more enthusiastic help in the gardens, but your life course is different than mine, and I wouldn't have it any other way." Her mom smiled at her in the mirror.

"You are, over and above any of your brothers, your father's image. The two of you are more at home at sea than on land. I would not change a thing about your father, nor would I wish for you to be any different. Hawk is a lucky man." Her mom squeezed her hand.

Tess couldn't speak. Her heart overflowed with happiness.

Gazing at each other in the mirror, mother and daughter lapsed into a companionable silence. Tess got lost in thought and guessed her mom was also reminiscing about her childhood.

A knock on the door broke the silence. "May I come in?" her father asked. He stepped into the room as her mom opened the door. "You ladies put the flowers to shame. I don't believe I've seen two more beautiful women."

Her mom walked over and reached for his hand. "You look so handsome,

John. Are you ready, dear?"

Tess saw it then. Her father's lips were trembling. "No, love, it's too soon. Just yesterday she was chasing her brothers down to the dock, begging to sail with us."

"Aww, Daddy." Tess ran the few steps into his arms. "I'll always be your little girl. Always."

Her dad gathered the two women he loved in a bear hug, a few tears rolling down his sun-weathered face.

Her mom once again became the tower of strength. "Okay, you two. We don't want to have a blubber fest and keep Hawk waiting." Katherine passed them both tissues and tucked one into the sleeve of her suit jacket.

"One moment," her dad said after he crumpled the used tissue and tossed it into the plastic bag beside the desk.

He clasped Tess's manicured, polished hands in his rough, burly ones. Tess smiled at the familiar feeling. She'd held onto his calloused papa paws many times as a child. He had never steered her wrong. She knew, whatever he needed to say now, would be well-chosen words.

"Your mother is the love of my life. She is the backbone of our family and the beacon that guides me and leads me home. I pray you will know, nurture, and yield a love like ours with Hawk. He is a godly man, the perfect mate for you, Tess." Her dad cleared his throat. His lips were trembling again. "In a few minutes, when I place your hand in his, know that I trust him to love and care for you exactly as I would wish for you to be loved."

"Oh, Dad, that means everything to me." Tears misted Tess's eyes at her father's love and blessing. "You're my hero, Dad. I think I fell in love with Hawk because he reminds me of you." Tess took a deep breath.

Her mom passed her and her dad another tissue. "John, do you have something for Tess?" Her mom's tone was light and secretive.

Her father grinned. "I do. Should we give it to her now?"

"Probably a good idea, before we run out of tissues."

Her dad reached inside his tux and withdrew a thin, square package. He handed the wrapped gift to Tess.

"What's this?" she asked, bouncing the light object between her hands.

"Something that arrived special delivery for you," he said in a conspiratorial tone.

Tess glanced toward the door. "Should I wait until after the ceremony to open it with Hawk?"

"He knows we're giving it to you now," her mom said.

Tess arched an eyebrow and pulled the ribbon loose. She tore into the paper, then let out a squeal. "Oh, my gosh! It can't be. It's from Rebecca. It's just like the one I borrowed from Ben." Tess held up a white linen handkerchief sewn and embroidered by her best friend. "Mom, look at this." Tess traced her index finger over the blue stitching: *T.P.*, for *Theresa Prescott.* "Hey, how did she know Hawk's last name? I only found out his real name is Daniel this week."

"Hawk told us that Ben asked him what his given name was before he was taken to the HMS *Greyhound.* Just in case." Her dad reached out and squeezed her hand. "We found this on Tuesday behind the board with the knot. Ben must have tacked it there. There's a note too."

Tess passed the handkerchief to her mom and opened the folded sheets of yellowed paper. The black ink was somewhat faded, but Tess could read every word.

October 11, 1781
Dear Tess,

My previous letters have not been found. I'm wondering what day it is there and when Captain Roberts will change out the cabin. I can only hope this note will reach you, that the cabin wasn't changed before I wrote the first letter in October 1776.

Felicity turns five today. She is the apple of Ben's eye, though don't let that fool you into thinking she isn't incredibly precocious. You two would enjoy each other's company. LOL.

I've enclosed a sketch of the four of us an artist drew last month on Nathaniel's third birthday.

Tess stopped reading and lifted the page. She gasped when she saw the drawing.

"What's wrong, Tess?" her mom asked.

"Felicity." A lump formed in Tess's throat. "Look. She's holding a rabbit with a blue jacket. Peter Rabbit. The bunny Ben promised to have made as a gift from me," Tess explained, hugging the sketch to her chest.

The ship's bell rang once. Six o'clock.

"It's time, Tess," her father said.

The letters, as precious as they were, would keep. Tess folded them and handed Rebecca's notes back to her dad. "Hold onto these for me, will you?"

"Of course," he said and placed them back in the interior pocket of his tux. Her mom passed her the handkerchief with the blue stitching.

"Something blue?" she asked.

Tess nodded and walked over to the mirror. Gone was the little girl with pigtails and a desire to be just like her brothers. The reflection before her was one of a woman, her long brown hair half up in a bun laced with four pink beach roses and half down in cascading curls, courtesy of her sister-in-law and Emily's trusty curling iron.

Tess smoothed the front of her dress, reveling in the feel of the satin and the reason she had it on. She tucked Rebecca's handkerchief inside her bra, close to her heart. "Becca's here after all," she said, taking her mom by the hand and walking toward the companionway. "Let's go."

Her father ascended the ladder first. As he stepped onto the deck, he signaled to Andy to bring Hawk out of his quarters. Tess watched her mom, in skirt and pumps, climb the ladder as glamorously as Jackie Kennedy herself would have.

When Tess put her right foot on the first rung, she was immensely grateful for the high front of her dress. There was no way she'd be tripping over yards of fabric. When she reached the top, her dad bent down and lifted her out of the hatch.

Her eyes immediately found Hawk standing at the wheel. He had never looked so handsome, and it was more than the tux. He looked like a groom— earnest, eager, and everything she'd dreamed of. Her heart fluttered in anticipation of their vows, of the night ahead, and of the future they would have.

As soon as he locked his gaze on her, serenity settled over her. He was the love of her life, and this was their destiny. She didn't doubt it for a second. When her mom, her matron-of-honor, approached the freshly rolled-out white carpet runner, jubilation crackled in the air, as though every being on earth and in heaven was cheering for them.

Her mom glided gracefully toward the helm. Her dad passed Tess a bouquet of blue hydrangeas and pink beach roses wrapped in lime green satin ribbon, then offered her his arm. Tess inhaled the sea air and glanced around the ship and over to shore. The sky was a blaze of pinks and oranges against the darkening blue. The water was calm and clear. The sunset seekers on the beach were in for a great display.

"She's beautiful," her dad whispered, captivated by his wife.

Tess squeezed his arm and smiled. Her parents were one of the all-time great couples, whether the world knew it or not. Watching her mom and observing the guests, Tess noticed that Andy hadn't so much as glanced at his mom. Since the ceremony started, he hadn't taken his eyes off of Allyson.

"Dad, get a load of Andy. I'm gone four days, and he's infatuated with

Allyson? And she's here as his date?" Katherine arrived at the helm. Andy was still oblivious. Tess leaned in and whispered to her dad, "I think Andy's in love."

Her father patted her hand and spoke softly. "Your mother is convinced they'll be engaged by Christmas, though she's hoping Andy will propose before Thanksgiving."

Few words could have made Tess happier, and those words she was about to hear from Hawk and the minister.

The first notes of the wedding march brought goose bumps to Tess's arms. She zeroed in on Hawk and found him smiling that smile she'd fallen for two years ago. She sighed at the memories of the moment her heart became his. *Thank You*, she offered after a swift glance up.

With the crew at attention, she and her dad walked down the starboard side. Jack and Emily, Todd and Jennifer, and Allyson lined up on the port side. Hawk's parents and sister, who'd flown in on Wednesday, stood nearest him and Andy at the helm.

Reverend Gillespie, ten years the captain's senior and a long-time friend, looked at her dad. He nodded with a father's understanding and smiled before asking Captain Roberts, "Who gives this woman?"

Captain Roberts placed Tess's hand in Hawk's. "I give you my most precious gift."

Hawk straightened, his expression one of gratitude and respect. "Thank you, Captain. I will treasure her."

Warmth permeated every molecule of Tess's body. Her dad had surprised them on Monday when he refused Hawk's resignation.

Sitting around their kitchen table, holding his wife's hand, Captain Roberts had listened as Hawk spoke.

"...and sir, I hope you know how much I've appreciated and enjoyed working for you. Sailing on *Shenny* was my dream job. But now my dream has changed." Hawk had wrapped an arm around Tess and slid his formal resignation across the table.

Captain Roberts, smile on his face, had simply shaken his head. "You risked your life to bring our daughter home to us. Your actions have defined your love greater than any words could. I welcome you as my son-in-law, and I'm grateful to have an honorable man to hand the wheel over to."

"What?" Tess had exclaimed.

Her mom had nodded. "The timing is perfect. We've been talking about your dad's retirement for years, but we knew neither Andy nor Todd truly wanted to captain *Shenandoah*. With Hawk a member of the family, he's your

184

dad's first choice."

Five days later, she lost herself in Hawk's eyes the moment her dad kissed her cheek and went to stand with her mom. She heard Reverend Gillespie's words, yet couldn't tear her gaze away from Hawk.

When she felt Hawk reach for her hand, Tess looked down in wonder as he slid the gold band over her finger. She was his—forever. Her mom passed her Hawk's wedding band, and her heart quickened as she placed her promise of all her tomorrows on his hand.

Hawk mouthed, "I love you," as Reverend Gillespie placed their left hands between his two.

"As you chart your course and depart on this new adventure, anchor your hearts to God and secure a line of three cords—one for you, Tess, one for you, Hawk, and one for God. Whatever the weather brings, a three-part cord will offer the greatest strength. In days of clear sailing, give praise, and in the midst of storms, trust God to provide the light for the path you're on."

Reverend Gillespie nodded at Hawk. "You may now kiss the bride."

Tess melted into the warmth of the kiss. Cheers erupted on the deck. Andy popped open the champagne, and her brothers poured drinks for all, while Jennifer snapped dozens of pictures.

For thirty minutes, they toasted and celebrated and watched as the sun dropped below the horizon, leaving the sky aglow in pink hues.

Tess's dad called Hawk over. "Captain Prescott, would you do us the honor of navigating *Shenandoah* home?"

For the second time in less than an hour, cheers erupted on deck. Her father had, for the first time, handed over the helm to another.

Her new husband shook her dad's hand, then opened his right arm, inviting Tess in. With her head on his chest, and her arms wrapped around his waist, Hawk ordered the crew to weigh anchor.

A favorable wind carried them home…to their reception, to their future, to their beginning.

* * *

"Your word is a lamp for my feet,
a light on my path."

PSALM 119:105

Author's Notes

The *Shenandoah* is a real and magical ship, though her magic lies in her ability to transport you back in time through your imagination, not in actuality. Captain Robert S. Douglas dreamed of, designed, and commissioned the 108-foot square topsail schooner in the early sixties. She was launched on February 15, 1964, from the Harvey Gamage Shipyard in South Bristol, Maine. I took the liberty of dating the fictional ship's origins to a 1770s cargo vessel. In reality, the *Shenandoah* was created to resemble the fast U.S. revenue cutter, *Joe Lane*, from the nineteenth century, "America's Golden Age of Sail."

Moored in the Vineyard Haven Harbor and sailing from Martha's Vineyard, the *Shenandoah* is truly one-of-a-kind. She is the only non-auxiliary square topsail schooner in the world, and she boasts the longest-standing captain and schooner tandem in the nation. The kids' cruises depicted in the book are the *Shenandoah's* primary function.

Captain Douglas offers a reduced-rate charter to the students from the five Vineyard elementary schools. Island fifth graders raise money all year long and then enjoy a special week on the water between the summer of their fifth- and sixth-grade years. The kids learn how to raise and lower sails, a variety of essential ship knots, the art of coiling tight lines, what it means to flake, the importance of wind direction, the indications if there is enough wind to sail, the strength and teamwork needed to raise and lower the anchor, and the effort involved in keeping a beautiful boat ship shape. With no electricity or modern conveniences to distract them, the students work hard and play hard, spending hours in the water swimming, diving, jumping, and even catching the occasional baby sand shark. As my youngest daughter can tell you, sailing on the *Shenandoah* is an unforgettable experience.

To learn more about the *Shenandoah,* please visit her websites: **www.theblackdogtallships.com** or **www.shenandoahfoundation.org.**

All the characters in *Shenandoah Crossings* are fictional, although some of the names used are those of family and friends. I attempted to be as accurate as possible with the historical references and the time frame of the setting. Any errors are mine. The story, however, is a work of fiction, and I took great liberty creating characters both American and British, embellishing the actions of General William Howe, Captain Archibald Dickson, and General George Washington, as well as transporting *Shenandoah* into the Revolutionary War. Many of the events portrayed in the book happened during America's fight for independence. Anything relating to the *Shenandoah* in the eighteenth century is merely a product of my imagination.

SHENANDOAH
NIGHTS

L I S A   B E L C A S T R O

Could this all be a bad dream?
How was she to know?
Rebecca had far more questions than answers.

Tisbury, Massachusetts, Martha's Vineyard

The last thing sixth-grade teacher Rebecca O'Neill wants to do during the final week of her summer break is chaperone twenty-five kids on a six-night, seven-day trip aboard the schooner *Shenandoah*. But after a desperate phone call from the school principal, she doesn't have a choice. Worse, the ship is rumored to be "haunted." Five years ago, during the Holmes Hole student cruise, teacher Melissa Smith complained about hearing voices and seeing visions, then disappeared without a trace—from the very same cabin where Rebecca will be staying.

Everything seems normal on Sunday as Rebecca boards the impressive *Shenandoah*. But as she sits in Cabin 8, she hears hushed voices that don't sound like they're from this century. Mike, a crewmember, insists he believes the crazy Island story that Melissa time-traveled to Colonial Boston. His eerie interest in constantly tracking Rebecca's whereabouts rattles her nerves.

Her first night onboard, Rebecca drifts off to sleep…and wakes the following morning with memories of a secretive conversation about a battle with Britain. Monday night Rebecca crawls into her bunk after an adventurous day of sailing, swimming, and overseeing students. She's startled awake when a man grabs her and yells, "Stowaway!" Dragged in front of Captain Benjamin Reed, she looks up into the most gorgeous brown eyes she's ever seen….

A Vineyard Romance
Romance, history, adventure.
Get swept into the exciting Winds of Change series.

www.lisabelcastro.com
www.oaktara.com

Acknowledgments

Shenandoah Crossings and the *Winds of Change* trilogy would not have been written if Captain Robert Douglas had not designed the schooner *Shenandoah* and then graciously extended a discounted charter rate to all the elementary schools on Martha's Vineyard. My chaperone experience on the *Shenandoah* was unforgettable. Thank you to Captain Douglas and his son, Morgan, for allowing me to use your beautiful ship in my story, for answering my questions, and for sharing in my enthusiasm.

A warm thank you to my publisher, Ramona Tucker, for her enthusiasm for *Shenandoah Crossings* and for encouraging and believing in the *Winds of Change* trilogy. I am also grateful to Christina Miller for her superb editing skills, as well as her support and friendship.

Hugs and many, many thanks to Alison Shaw. Your photographs take my breath away. Long before I asked you for cover photos, I had a dozen (or so, but who's counting!) of your gorgeous pictures decorating my home. The images you shot for all three books have captured the story beyond what I'd hoped for. Thank you, Alison, for sharing your gift with me and allowing your work to grace the cover of my books!

Ursula Kreskey and Captain Karen Kukolich were generous with their time and fishing expertise. Thank you, ladies, for your guidance with the fishing lingo. Any mistake or misrepresentation is mine.

A huge THANK YOU to my Wednesday night writers' group led by mystery writer Cynthia Riggs. Erin Block, Emily Cavanagh, Catherine Finch, Scott Goldin, Mary Lou Piland, Amy Reece, Valerie Sonnenthal, Linda Wilson, Nancy Wood, and Cynthia encouraged, critiqued, tweaked, and applauded throughout the writing of *Shenandoah Crossings*. Wednesday night remains my favorite night of the week!

An extra big hug to Erin Block, Catherine Finch, Cynthia Riggs, Valerie Sonnethal, and Nancy Wood for the days and nights you spent proofing the chapters I couldn't read in group. Your edits, suggestions, kindness, and enthusiasm are greatly appreciated.

If I didn't run, I probably wouldn't be able to function the other hours in the day. Hugs to my friend and running partner, Allyson Metell Cook. You are a fantastic mom, a terrific friend, and an awesome marathoner. The talks we have while running lift me and encourage me. You inspire me in so many ways. And I'll be forever grateful that you are the world's best masseuse. Congrats on being voted Best of the Vineyard once again.

My family is my greatest blessing and deepest joy. My mom and stepdad, Betty Belcastro and Jack Kobelenz, are generous, kind, loving, supportive and, to top it off, amazing grandparents. We spend a lot of time together, and it still isn't enough. I keep hoping you'll move next door. Thank you for always encouraging me!

My brother filled my growing years with friendship (and the occasional, or not so occasional, sibling conflict) and he continues to be a godly man I can trust, confide in, and laugh with, especially when I need to laugh at myself. I'm grateful for the days I spend with him and his family.

The children in my life are my true treasures, though they are more young women than children now. Kayla, my baby girl, is halfway through high school. Where has the time gone? I remember a few years ago when you looked so young standing on the podium in New Orleans talking about our week spent rebuilding homes after Katrina. Though you were the youngest speaker, you brought tears to my eyes when you said, "This week I was the change I want to see in the world. We rock!" Thank you, Kayla, for being a terrific daughter! Over the last year you set high academic goals, tried new sports, and now you're helping me understand what social media is. Where would I be without you? I love you, Pumpkin, and I'm proud of you.

Starr Starr, you are as precious to me as life itself. Your dad was my best friend, my partner, my better half, and the biggest goofball. I miss him every day, yet he left me a piece of himself—he gave me you. For twelve years you have been like a daughter to me. Thank you for allowing me to love you, for sharing your life with us, for singing to us in the Starr and Kayla Talent Shows, for all the drawings and artwork you have given me, and simply for being the sweet, vivacious, enthusiastic, Disney-loving young woman that you are. I love you and will always be here for you.

Hugs and love to Ashleen—so far from home yet never far from my heart. You entered our lives in 2006, bringing joy, laughter, and beautiful music. Now you're about to graduate, start your career, and begin a new and exciting phase in your life. Thank you for choosing us as we chose you. And thank you for your enthusiasm for my books. I hope you enjoy Tess and Hawk's story as much as I enjoy listening to you sing. Love you lots.

Above all, I am grateful for God's unending, unchanging love. His love story for us is the greatest love story ever told. He is our safe harbor, our beacon in good times and bad. It is with a humble heart that I try to serve Him and create characters and situations that will reflect God's love and promises. I hope this story will touch your heart and God's light will shine on you.

About the Author

LISA BELCASTRO lives with her family on Martha's Vineyard. She was inspired to write *Shenandoah Nights,* the first book in the Winds of Change trilogy, while chaperoning two Tisbury School summer sails with her daughter, Kayla, aboard the schooner *Shenandoah.* The weeklong adventure, sans electricity, Game Boys, iPods, and modern conveniences, kindled her imagination to dream of an altogether different voyage.

In addition to writing *Shenandoah Nights* and *Shenandoah Crossings,* Lisa currently pens the cuisine column for *Vineyard Style* magazine. She has worked as a staff and freelance reporter and photographer for *The Chronicle of the Horse* and as assistant editor at *The Blue Ridge Leader.* She has written articles for *USA Today, Dressage (London), USA WEEKEND Magazine, The Blue Ridge Leader,* and *Sidelines.*

When she's not at her desk working on *Shenandoah Dreams,* the third book in the trilogy, Lisa is living in paradise, volunteering at her daughter's school, serving in her church community, planting and weeding her numerous gardens, trying to run a marathon a month, or walking the beach with her husband, looking for sea glass.

www.lisabelcastro.com ▪ www.oaktara.com